TALES
FROM THE
PLUM GROVE HILLS

Illustrations by
WOODI ISHMAEL

TALES
FROM THE
PLUM GROVE HILLS

by

JESSE STUART

Edited and with an Introduction by
CHARLES H. DAUGHADAY

The Jesse Stuart Foundation
Ashland, Kentucky
1997

TALES
FROM THE
PLUM GROVE HILLS

Library of Congress Cataloging-in-Publication Data

Stuart, Jesse, 1907-
    Tales from the Plum Grove Hills / by Jesse Stuart ; edited by
Charles H. Daughaday.
        p.   cm.
    ISBN 0-945084-62-5
    1. Appalachian Region, Southern—Social life and customs—Fiction.
2. Kentucky—Social life and customs—Fiction.   I. Title
PS3537 . T92516T28   1997
813' .52—dc21

Published by:
The Jesse Stuart Foundation
P. O. Box 391 Ashland, KY   41114
1997

CONTENTS

DEDICATION

To our parents and to our teachers who taught and prepared us for life; and to those who follow in their footsteps and teach.

Carl and Mabelle Leming

PREFACE

Jesse Stuart's life and literature are guides to the solid values of America's past. With good humor and brilliant storytelling, Stuart implicitly praises the Appalachian people, whose quiet lives he captured forever in his novels and stories. In these works, readers will find people who value hard work, who love their families, their land, and their country—people who play by the rules.

Today, we are so caught up in teaching Americans to read that the process has often obscured the higher purpose of producing an informed and responsible citizenry. This clearly requires more than mere literacy. We need to learn, from reading, the unalterable principles of right and wrong, the basis of good citizenship.

That is why Jesse Stuart's books are so important. They make reading fun and they teach solid values in the process. The Jesse Stuart Foundation, a non-profit educational publishing house, is editing and republishing Stuart's out-of-print books, along with other books which focus on Kentucky and Southern Appalachia. As part of that effort, we proudly present this new edition of Stuart's great short story collection, *Tales From The Plum Grove Hills*.

Many people contributed to the beautiful book in your

hands. Charles Daughaday, an English Professor at Murray State University, edited the original text, with assistance from the Jesse Stuart Foundation office staff. Jim Marsh designed the dust jacket and Pamela Wise and Associates, Inc. produced the camera ready pages.

Finally, all of us associated with this project offer special thanks to Carl and Mabelle Leming, who sponsored the republication of this important book. In 1992 Carl suffered a heart attack and his wife had breast cancer. To cheer and encourage him, Carl's sister Joann gave him a copy of *The Year Of My Rebirth*. Carl and Mabelle were so inspired by the book that they have since collected and read all of Stuart's books. The Lemings, who recently celebrated more than fifty years of marriage together, are life members of the Jesse Stuart Foundation. They hope to encourage others to follow their example of promoting literature that encourages reading and character development and promotes an interest in Kentucky history and literature.

Jesse Stuart believed that teaching was the "greatest profession on earth" and that teachers "should strive to create good citizenship." It is that same noble spirit that prompted the Lemings to dedicate this book to their parents, to their teachers and "to those who follow in their footsteps and teach."

James M. Gifford

INTRODUCTION

As the twentieth century closes, educational experts and theorists argue that in order for children to be successful in the next century, computers are essential; indeed, these experts and theorists want to break down the walls of the classrooms so that floods of information can enter. This new valuing of information for its own sake, devoid of any concern for either wisdom or knowledge, erases much educational concern for the moral character of our children. Both state and federal governments seem ready to spend millions of dollars for such technology to ensure our children can compete in the world marketplace. Unfortunately, this growing emphasis requires technicians rather than teachers, coaches rather than mentors, and it also means additional bureaucracies and bureaucrats. Such developments only further remove our children from the influence of a moral impact that has been an important component of traditional teaching concerns and techniques.

This new emphasis in education means that economic concerns replace moral concerns and our children are equated to the model of the machine rather than a human being. Of course, if the human being is a machine, then there is no human will, no passion, no character, no genuine life. And if this is the case, there is certainly no need or concern for "character." Perhaps our current lack of concern for character can be ascribed to America's obsession with transforming human qualities and values into numbers. But character cannot be measured in numbers.

This is exactly the awareness registered by Jesse Stuart when he said, while speaking as a teacher, that,"I had rather have a student with an A character and a C grade than a student with a C character and an A grade." And of course, that depiction of character lies at the very heart of Jesse Stuart's literary art, and no better examples are to be found than in the stories that comprise *Tales from the Plum Grove Hills*.

Tales from the Plum Grove Hills transports today's readers to late nineteenth and early twentieth century Appalachia. The author, Jesse Stuart, takes us back in time to a people who lived more like our pioneer forebears than the residents of today's fast moving, technological world.

Originally published in 1946, the twenty stories that comprise this volume are headed by the highly acclaimed and often anthologized, "Another April," which Donald Davidson praised as "unbeatable." Davidson had earlier bemoaned that many authors of the time "have been buying literary vitamins to try to make up for their lack of either knowledge or beliefs." He concluded that all Jesse Stuart needed to do was to "let his bucket down into the old Kentucky well, the well never runs dry, and up comes the stuff of life again; plenty of it."

Indeed, the characters who populate *Tales from the Plum Grove Hills* are as substantial as life itself. Time and again Stuart reveals that the true history of our land lies in the lives of the people who abide on it, work it, love it, and die into it. Memorable character after character arises from these stories, like Uncle Uglybird. In the third story of the collection, entitled "Whose Land Is This?," when the youthful Mick suggests, "Nothin' ever happened here," Uncle Uglybird responds, "Young man, you're too young to know," and he then proceeds to make the surrounding seemingly empty and dead land come alive with remembrances of his long life, until the reader nods in agreement when Uncle Uglybird, who is ready to depart, says, "Just want to see a little more of the old place that I have a deed fer in my heart!" How could the reality of the human spirit be more simply and beautifully expressed?

Then, there is the youthful narrator of "My Father Is an Educated Man," who thinks of the "members of the human family" he has known, "of my father's people, beardy-faced, tall, figures of the earth, tillers of earth, men who have cut the timber, cleared the fields and helped to build America." Why should they "strive to learn to read secondhand life in books when they had firsthand life before them to live?"

These stories of the Plum Grove folk are rich and varied, yet the author makes subtle links between or among them. This is accomplished by Stuart's treatment of the point-of-view, as his narrators run the gamut from being very conscious of to relatively unaware of their actions. Two such stories appear almost as "bookend" pieces; they are "Weep No More My Lady" and "Another Hanging." Both stories are told in the first person, but there is a great difference in the tones of the stories because of the differences in narrator awareness. In the former story we meet a young boy, Eif, whose father has been dead for seven years and whose mother has recently remarried, to a good man named Jason. On the morrow Jason must undergo an annual funeralizin' celebrated by the Mountain Baptists of the area, a day long ordeal of singing, praying, preaching, and extolling the virtues of the narrator's dead father. The narrator has a keen sensitivity to how well Jason will endure the coming day, not only because it will be a continuous and intense reminder of the man Jason has "replaced," but also because Jason is a "Free-Will Baptist," and is therefore considered by the Mountain Baptists to be "a son of Satan."

On the next day people come from far and near. The preacher begins by giving all the brothers and sisters the opportunity to reveal "sins," such as attending a frivolous worldly spectacle, like a circus or picture show; then each has the opportunity to say publicly if any person has been wronged by another. Next, they sing. Long before they reach the noon meal break, Eif slips out and is "revived" by some home brew.

With the aid of this liquid spirit, which blends well with the spirit of the funeralizin', Jason perseveres and Eif's mother is revived after a "sinking spell." After an orgy of noontime eating, strong young men break a path up the mountain to where Eif's Pa is buried. Brother Cyrus preaches so hard he breaks out in a sweat amid the frigid temperature, and he preaches a four hour sermon. Finally the funeralizin' is concluded with the singing of "Amazing Grace," which produces a lot of weeping. As the brothers and sisters break up to return to their homes, "everybody was happy in fellowship and human love," as they form "a chain of fellowship, holding each other's hand to get back safe down the steep mountain." Eif's earlier apprehensions regarding the funeralizin' are now dissipated as he observes, "And two of the strongest links in this chain of fellowship were Ma and Jason."

The people who populate Stuart's stories are strong and enduring. Their devotion to keep alive the memory of one of their departed members testifies both to the importance of the past and to their belief in the life that is yet to come. Important also, are their rituals meant to worship, honor, and keep alive the memory of their ancestors.

If "Weep No More My Lady" is a vivid testimony to the serious side of these mountain folk, then "Another Hanging" vividly and somewhat satirically offers a view of the slack side of their lives, when they indulge in "entertainment." Once again, Eif is the narrator, but he holds none of the sympathy and sensitivity which is present in the previously discussed story. Perhaps this is because Eif is both certain the man to be hanged should be hanged and also because he simply wishes to have a good time and show himself off at this event. In this story Eif is recalling a hanging that took place in 1903. One Willard Bellstrase cuts the throat of Blaze Gullet. Eif's Pa is very sympathetic to Willard, even though Willard once threatened him with a knife.

But young Eif is unmoved: "Didn't care nary a bit when I heard old Willard was going to hang by the neck. It tickled me for I thought he was gettin' what was comin' to 'im." The hanging is a major public spectacle; people come for miles around. Schools let out and even the teachers attend. The crowded train going to Eight-Mile Station strains under its load. Eif uses this event as an excuse to buy new clothes, so all may see he is "somebody." On the train ride many of the people are drunk, gambling, fighting or otherwise carousing. Eif is so excited he blurts out, "I'll tell you a night in May with a lively crowd on the train and a hangin' almost in sight is wonderful."

The crowd gathers around the jail in the darkness

preceding the coming dawn. Eif needs a girl on his arm to complete his happiness, and he finds one in Beadie Blevins. While Eif seems to remain oblivious to the underlying tragedy of the situation, Stuart provides ample details about Willard's family and the way he meets his death.

The hanging itself is over in an instant. The return train ride is even more wild with stray guns going off. Amid all this chaos, Beadie, with unrealized irony says, "It's so bad here you just can't have a decent hangin' any more," whereupon Eif agrees while bemoaning the missing buttons on his shoes. A man has lost his life and the young narrator has lost his shoe buttons. Stuart casts a cold eye upon the people in this story.

Simple events teach lessons about selfhood and identity in several of these stories. For example, in "Thanksgiving Hunter," the youthful narrator begins by trying to please his Uncle Wash who intends to teach him to hunt like a man. While the boy sits alone, determined to start shooting as soon as he heard the "flutter of dove wings," his thoughts nevertheless wander to "the way my people had hunted and how they had loved their guns." Slowly, the lad is moved by the vast autumn earth about him, and comes to perceive that it is a "sad world, a dying world." Finally, he hates to think of killing any part of this autumn world, so that when "I picked up my gun, I didn't feel life in it—I felt death."

In the moving tale "I Remember Mollie," Uncle Uglybird appears again and tells the story of Finnis poisoning his wife, Mollie Jason. Finnis does this because he has taken up with another woman. Uncle Uglybird is instrumental in bringing Finnis to justice, and later Finnis hangs for his crime. The youth listening to the story remarks, "I didn't know that happened here," and Uncle Uglybird responds poetically, "Grass, sprouts and briars will hide old scars....Lips of the hills and trees and wind can't speak their secrets. They hold them forever. They never get to the courtroom."

Other stories offer yet different versions of the indomitable spirit of these mountain folk. Works like "Grandpa Birdwell's Last Battle" and "Bury Your Dead" provide bigger than life tales of the individual and the clan respectively, while others like "Spring Victory" offer a moving image of the devotion, the discipline, the love, and the ingenuity which enables a family to survive a woesome winter of death and illness.

Rare indeed would it be to find more life, more joy, more sorrow, more loss, or more hope, than is contained between the covers of *Tales From the Plum Grove Hills.* Jesse traveled through England and Europe in 1938 and visited the beautiful, culturally-rich city of Salzburg. There he experienced the majesty of its musical heritage, especially music like Strauss' "Tales of Vienna Woods," which lifted his emotion "to the point of ecstasy," prompting Stuart to write in his notebook, the title of this work, *"Tales From the Plum Grove Hills."*

Jesse Stuart could plainly see even then that America had its own culture, its own music, its own beauty and its own character. Soon afterwards he caught and fixed forever a portion of this heritage for Kentucky and the world.

Charles H. Daughaday
Murray, Kentucky

"Does the terrapin know what Grandpa is sayin'?" I asked Mom.

ANOTHER APRIL

"Now, Pap, you won't get cold," Mom said as she put a heavy wool cap over his head.

"Huh, what did ye say?" Grandpa asked, holding his big hand cupped over his ear to catch the sound.

"Wait until I get your gloves," Mom said, hollering real loud in Grandpa's ear. Mom had forgotten about his gloves until he raised his big bare hand above his ear to catch the sound of Mom's voice.

"Don't get 'em," Grandpa said, "I won't ketch cold."

Mom didn't pay any attention to what Grandpa said. She went on to get the gloves anyway. Grandpa turned toward me. He saw that I was looking at him.

"Yer Ma's a-puttin' enough clothes on me to kill a man," Grandpa said, then he laughed a coarse laugh like March wind among the pine tops at his own words. I started laughing but not at Grandpa's words. He thought I was laughing at them and we both laughed together. It pleased Grandpa to think that I had laughed with him over something funny that he had said. But I was laughing at the way he was dressed. He looked like a picture of Santa Claus. But Grandpa's cheeks were not cherry-red like Santa Claus' cheeks. They were covered with white thin beard, and above his eyes were long white eyebrows almost as white as percoon petals and very much longer.

Grandpa was wearing a heavy wool suit that hung loosely about his big body but fitted him tightly 'round the waist where he was as big and as round as a flour barrel. His pant legs were as big 'round his pipestem legs as emptied meal sacks. And his big shoes, with his heavy wool socks dropping down over their tops, looked like sled runners. Grandpa wore a heavy wool shirt and over his wool shirt he wore a heavy wool sweater and then his coat over the top of all this. Over his coat he wore a heavy overcoat and about his neck he wore a wool scarf.

The way Mom had dressed Grandpa you'd think there was a heavy snow on the ground but there wasn't. April was here instead and the sun was shining on the green hills where the wild plums and the wild crab apples were in bloom enough to make you think there were big snowdrifts sprinkled over the green hills. When I looked at Grandpa and then looked out at the window at the sunshine and the green grass I laughed more. Grandpa laughed with me.

"I'm a-goin' to see my old friend," Grandpa said just as Mom came down the stairs with his gloves.

"Who is he, Grandpa?" I asked, but Grandpa just looked at my mouth working. He didn't know what I was saying. And he hated to ask me the second time.

Mom put the big wool gloves on Grandpa's hands. He stood there just like I had to do years ago, and let Mom put his gloves on. If Mom didn't get his fingers back in the glovefingers exactly right Grandpa quarreled at Mom. And when Mom fixed his fingers exactly right in his gloves the way he wanted them Grandpa was pleased.

"I'll be a-goin' to see 'im," Grandpa said to Mom. "I know he'll still be there."

Mom opened our front door for Grandpa and he stepped out slowly, supporting himself with his big cane in one hand. With the other hand he held to the door facing. Mom let him out of the house just like she used to let me out in the spring. And when Grandpa left the house I wanted to go with him, but Mom wouldn't let me go. I wondered if he would get away from the house–get out of Mom's sight–and pull off his shoes and go barefooted and wade the creeks like I used to do when Mom let me out. Since Mom wouldn't let me go with Grandpa, I watched him as he walked slowly down the path in front of our house. Mom stood there watching Grandpa too. I think she was afraid that he would fall. But Mom was fooled; Grandpa toddled along the path better than my baby brother could.

"He used to be a powerful man," Mom said more to herself than she did to me. "He was a timber cutter. No man could cut more timber than my father; no man in the timber woods could sink an ax deeper into a log than my father. And no man could lift the end of a bigger saw log than Pap could."

"Who is Grandpa goin' to see, Mom?" I asked.

"He's not goin' to see anybody," Mom said.

"I heard 'im say that he was goin' to see an old friend," I told her.

"Oh, he was just a-talkin'," Mom said.

I watched Grandpa stop under the pine tree in our front yard. He set his cane against the pine tree trunk, pulled off his gloves and put them in his pocket. Then Grandpa stooped

21

over slowly, as slowly as the wind bends down a sapling, and picked up a pine cone in his big soft fingers. Grandpa stood fondling the pine cone in his hand. Then, one by one, he pulled the little chips from the pine cone—tearing it to pieces like he was hunting for something in it—and after he had torn it to pieces he threw the pine-cone stem on the ground. Then he pulled pine needles from a low-hanging pine bough and he felt of each pine needle between his fingers. He played with them a long time before he started down the path.

"What's Grandpa doin'?" I asked Mom.

But Mom didn't answer me.

"How long has Grandpa been with us?" I asked Mom.

"Before you's born," she said. "Pap has been with us eleven years. He was eighty when he quit cuttin' timber and farmin—now he's ninety-one."

I had heard her say that when she was a girl he'd walk out on the snow and ice barefooted and carry wood in the house and put it on the fire. He had shoes but he wouldn't bother to put them on. And I heard her say that he would cut timber on the coldest days without socks on his feet but with his feet stuck down in cold brogan shoes and he worked stripped above the waist so his arms would have freedom when he swung his double-bitted ax. I had heard her tell how he'd sweat and how the sweat in his beard would be icicles by the time he got home from work on the cold winter days. Now Mom wouldn't let him get out of the house for she wanted him to live a long time.

As I watched Grandpa go down the path toward the hog pen he stopped to examine every little thing along his path.

Once he waved his cane at a butterfly as it zigzagged over his head, its polka-dot wings fanning the blue April air. Grandpa would stand when a puff of wind came along, and hold his face against the wind and let the wind play with his white whiskers. I thought maybe his face was hot under his beard and he was letting the wind cool his face. When he reached the hog pen he called the hogs down to the fence. They came running and grunting to Grandpa like they were talking to him. I knew that Grandpa couldn't hear them trying to talk to him but he could see their mouths working and he knew they were trying to say something. He leaned his cane against the hog pen, reached over the fence, and patted the hogs' heads. Grandpa didn't miss patting one of our seven hogs.

As he toddled up the little path alongside the hog pen he stopped under a blooming dogwood. He pulled a white blossom from a bough that swayed over the path above his head, and he leaned his big bundled body against the dogwood while he tore each petal from the blossom and examined it carefully. There wasn't anything his dim blue eyes missed. He stopped under a redbud tree before he reached the garden to break a tiny spray of redbud blossoms. He took each blossom from the spray and examined it carefully.

"Gee, it's funny to watch Grandpa," I said to Mom, then I laughed.

"Poor Pap," Mom said, "he's seen a lot of Aprils come and go. He's seen more Aprils than he will ever see again."

I don't think Grandpa missed a thing on the little circle he took before he reached the house. He played with a bumblebee that was bending a windflower blossom that grew near our corncrib beside a big bluff. But Grandpa didn't try to catch the bumblebee in his big bare hand. I wondered if he would and if the bumblebee would sting him, and if he would holler. Grandpa even pulled a butterfly cocoon from a blackberry briar that grew beside his path. I saw him try to tear it into shreds but he couldn't. There wasn't any butterfly in it, for I'd seen it before. I wondered if the butterfly with the polka-dot wings, that Grandpa waved his cane at when he first left the house, had come from this cocoon. I laughed when Grandpa couldn't tear the cocoon apart.

"I'll bet I can tear that cocoon apart for Grandpa if you'd let me go help him," I said to Mom.

"You leave your Grandpa alone," Mom said. "Let 'im enjoy April."

Then I knew that this was the first time Mom had let Grandpa out of the house all winter. I knew that Grandpa loved the sunshine and the fresh April air that blew from the redbud and dogwood blossoms. He loved the bumblebees, the hogs, the pine cones, and pine needles. Grandpa didn't miss a thing along his walk. And every day from now on until just before frost Grandpa would take this little walk. He'd stop along and look at everything as he had done summers before. But each year he didn't take as long a walk as he had taken the year before. Now this spring he didn't go down to the lower end of the hog pen as he had done last year. And when I could first remember Grandpa going on his walks he used to go out of sight. He'd go all over the farm. And he'd come to the house and take me on his knee and tell me about all that he had seen. Now Grandpa wasn't getting out of sight. I could see him from the window along all of his walk.

Grandpa didn't come back into the house at the front door. He tottled around back of the house toward the smokehouse and I ran through the living room to the dining room so I could look out the window and watch him.

"Where's Grandpa goin'?" I asked Mom.

"Now never mind," Mom said. "Leave your Grandpa alone. Don't go out there and disturb him."

"I won't bother 'im, Mom," I said. "I just want to watch."

"All right," Mom said.

But Mom wanted to be sure that I didn't bother him so she followed me into the dining room. Maybe she wanted to see what Grandpa was going to do. She stood by the window and we watched Grandpa as he walked down beside our smokehouse where a tall sassafras tree's thin leaves fluttered in the blue April wind. Above the smokehouse and the tall sassafras was a blue April sky—, so high you couldn't see the sky-roof. It was blue space and little white clouds floated upon this blue.

When Grandpa reached the smokehouse he leaned his cane against the sassafras tree. He let himself down slowly to his knees as he looked carefully at the ground. Grandpa was looking at something and I wondered what it was. I didn't think or I would have known.

"There you are, my good old friend," Grandpa said.

"Who is his friend, Mom?" I asked.

Mom didn't say anything. Then I saw.

"He's playin' with that old terrapin, Mom," I said.

"I know he is," Mom said.

"The terrapin doesn't mind if Grandpa strokes his head

with his hand," I said.

"I know it," Mom said.

"But the old terrapin won't let me do it," I said. "Why does he let Grandpa?"

"The terrapin knows your Grandpa."

"He ought to know me," I said, "but when I try to stroke his head with my hand, he closes up in his shell."

Mom didn't say anything. She stood by the window watching Grandpa and listening to Grandpa talk to the terrapin.

"My old friend, how do you like the sunshine?" Grandpa asked the terrapin.

The terrapin turned his fleshless face to one side like a hen does when she looks at you in the sunlight. He was trying to talk to Grandpa; maybe the terrapin could understand what Grandpa was saying.

"Old fellow, it's been a hard winter," Grandpa said. "How have you fared under the smokehouse floor?"

"Does the terrapin know what Grandpa is sayin'?" I asked Mom.

"I don't know," she said.

"I'm awfully glad to see you, old fellow," Grandpa said.

He didn't offer to bite Grandpa's big soft hand as he stroked his head.

"Looks like the terrapin would bite Grandpa," I said.

"That terrapin has spent the winters under that smokehouse for fifteen years," Mom said. "Pap has been acquainted with him for eleven years. He's been talkin' to that terrapin every spring."

"How does Grandpa know the terrapin is old?" I asked Mom.

"It's got 1847 cut on its shell," Mom said. "We know he's ninety-five years old. He's older than that. We don't know how old he was when that date was cut on his back."

"Who cut 1847 on his back, Mom?"

"I don't know, child," she said, "but I'd say whoever cut that date on his back has long been under the ground."

Then I wondered how a terrapin could get that old and what kind of a looking person he was who cut the date on the terrapin's back. I wondered where it happened and if it happened near where our house stood. I wondered who lived here on this land then, what kind of a house they lived in, and if they had a sassafras with tiny thin April leaves on its top growing in their yard. I wondered if the person who cut the date on the terrapin's back was buried at Plum Grove, if he had farmed these hills where we lived today and cut timber like Grandpa had. I wondered if he had seen the Aprils pass like Grandpa had seen them and if he enjoyed them like Grandpa was enjoying this April. I wondered if he had looked at the dogwood blossoms and the redbud blossoms and talked to this same terrapin.

"Are you well, old fellow?" Grandpa asked the terrapin.

The terrapin looked at Grandpa.

"I'm well as common for a man of my age," Grandpa said.

"Did the terrapin ask Grandpa if he was well?" I asked Mom.

"I don't know," Mom said. "I can't talk to a terrapin."

"But Grandpa can."

"Yes."

"Wait until tomatoes get ripe and we'll go to the garden together," Grandpa said.

"Does a terrapin eat tomatoes?" I asked Mom.

"Yes, that terrapin has been eatin' tomatoes from our garden for fifteen years," Mom said. "When Mick was tossin' the terrapins out of the tomato patch, he picked up this one and found the date cut on his back. He put him back in the patch and told him to help himself. He lives from our garden every year. We don't bother him and don't allow anybody else to bother him. He spends his winters under our smokehouse floor buried in the dry ground."

"Gee, Grandpa looks like the terrapin," I said.

Mom didn't say anything; tears came to her eyes. She wiped them from her eyes with the corner of her apron.

"I'll be back to see you," Grandpa said. "I'm a-gettin' a little chilly; I'll be gettin' back to the house."

The terrapin twisted his wrinkled neck without moving his big body, poking his head deeper into the April wind as Grandpa pulled his bundled body up by holding to the sassafras tree trunk.

"Good-by, old friend!"

The terrapin poked his head deeper into the wind, holding one eye on Grandpa, for I could see his eye shining in the sinking sunlight.

Grandpa got his cane, which was leaning against the sassafras tree trunk, and hobbled slowly toward the house. The terrapin looked at him with first one eye and then the other.

THE SANCTUARY DESOLATED

After Grandpa died Grandma lived alone in her big house that stood upon a knoll surrounded by giant black oaks and hickories. If the house had been a person it would have been a cripple for it was much older than Grandma and she was crippled with the rheumatics until she could hardly get about. But Grandma stayed on in this big house that had a moss-covered sagging roof and the tops of the two big chimneys were crumbling in the summer wind and rain and the winter freezes. Rosebushes and shrubs grew around the house until you could hardly see the downstairs windows. And when I went to stay with Grandma at night, I always got there before darkness hovered around it. I was afraid of the house and the dense patches of shrub and vines that grew so thick the morning sunlight couldn't filter through them to dry the moss-covered damp walls that were gradually falling to decay.

"Your mother can't go on livin' in that house," Pa told Mom. "That house is old. It's ready to tumble in. It's a damp house inside with too many shrubs and vines around it. She must come here and live with us."

"But Ma will never leave that house," Mom said. "She was born in it. She was married in it. And her seven children were born in it. Grandpa planted the oaks and hickories around it when he was a young man and Ma and Dad planted the shrubs and rose-vines around it. I was a little girl when they planted part of them. She'll never leave the house, Mick."

"But you've never explained it the right way to her," Pa said.

"Now you go see her," Mom said. "If you can do anything with her, I'll be happy. I'd be happy if she'd come here and stay with us. I won't be afraid of the house catching on fire or the roof fallin' in. Just a spark from one of the chimneys or from the flue would set the moss-covered shingles afire. You know that. And the roof is liable to fall any time."

I listened to them talk. I liked to go stay with Grandma, for she let me run all over the house—except I was afraid to go into a few of the dark rooms upstairs. I was afraid of the attic. I was afraid of snakes and lizards in the attic. But Grandma let me do as I pleased in the big house. She let me run through it fast as I wanted to run and I couldn't do that in our house. And she let Uncle Jason's boy, Will, do the same thing. She let Uncle Jake's boy, Herbert, do as he pleased too. And she let my sister, Mary, do as she pleased; she let Uncle Jason's girl, Effie, do as she pleased and she let Uncle Jake's girl, Carrie, do as she pleased. We had a good time with Grandma and all of us longed for our turn to go and stay with her.

I didn't want Grandma to come and stay with us. I wanted her to stay in the big house so sister Mary and I could go and stay our two weeks out of every six weeks with her. But Pa and Mom didn't want us to stay with her. He'd talked to Uncle Jake, Uncle Jason, Aunt Mallie and Aunt Phoebe about it. They had agreed to get Grandma away from the house and to take her to one of their homes. Each wanted her to stay but they would let her choose just so they could get her out of the old house. Even our neighbors were talkin' about us for leaving Grandma in such a wreck of a house. People said it was a sin. I heard the boys and girls at school talking about it and they asked me why my Pa and my uncles hadn't fixed the roof. I didn't bother to tell them why but I knew that Grandma wouldn't let 'em take a board from the roof and put a new one on. And she wouldn't allow a shrub or a tree cut no matter how near ready it was to fall of old age and she wouldn't allow a rosebush dug up. It was Grandma's house and land and she owned it, every foot of dirt, every shingle on the roof and every root of the rosebushes and every leaf on the tree and not one of her sons or daughters could tell her what to do with it.

"I'll go up there now and see her," Pa said to Mom. "I'll explain to her."

"I'd like to go with you, Pa," I said.

"All right," he said.

When Pa put on his hat and stepped out at the door, I followed him. It was good to put my feet on the soft green April grass again after they had been confined in shoes all winter and I walked behind Pa and stepped on every green clump of grass along the path. We lived the closest to Grandma's. If it were not for our apple orchard and the tall green rye that Pa had sown in the orchard to turn under for a cover crop, we could have seen Grandma's house from our house. We just lived around the slope not a quarter of a mile. In a few minutes we had reached Grandma's house and when we reached the front gate, Pa stood and looked at it. The gate posts had rotted and the gate was ready to tumble over. But

Grandma had had Cousin Herbert to nail a wire to the gate post and then nail the wire to an oak tree.

"This gate's even ready to fall," Pa said as he opened it carefully to keep it from falling. Then he stood under a front yard oak and looked at the hulk of a tree that held an immense top. Only the outer rim of the tree was sound and the interior of it had rotted and sparrows built their nest up in its hollow. Then Pa looked at the roof—the moss-covered shingle roof and it was as uneven as the ridges on a washboard. It was gradually sinking.

"The weight of a snow ten inches deep would cave that roof in," Pa said. "Mother Shelton must move from this house."

I didn't say anything to Pa but I hoped that she would tell him that she wouldn't move, for I knew if Grandma came to stay with us she wouldn't be the same Grandma to bake us pies and cakes and to give us money and to let us have the freedom that we didn't get at home.

"Well, Mother," Pa said with a big smile as we entered the house, "thought I'd come up to see how you were feeling."

"I feel all right, Mick," she said. "How's everybody down your way?"

"All right," Pa told her.

"That's fine," Grandma told him.

Grandma sat in a big rocker and looked at Pa. She knew that Pa had come to see her about something—maybe moving—and she just sat there and waited for him to ask her and I thought he would.

"Your gate needs fixin', Mother," Pa said. "It's about ready to fall."

"That gate's all right," Grandma said. "Herbert fixed that

gate for me. He fixed it just the way I wanted it fixed."

"But what about that big front yard oak?" Pa asked her. "Any windstorm is liable to push it over on the house."

"I've got birds that have built in that oak for twenty-five years," Grandma said. "I don't aim to have it cut. Let it fall on the house if it doesn't find some other way to fall."

Pa didn't say anything.

"Shan, there's some candy in there on the dresser for you," Grandma said.

I ran into the front room to get the candy and while I ate candy, I heard Grandma and Pa talking, but I couldn't tell what they were saying. Soon as I had finished the candy, I went back where Pa and Grandma were talking.

"If you all are afraid that I am going to be found dead in this house some morning," Grandma said, "I don't mind going down to your house and try staying for a while. I'll still be in sight of my house, but I want you to know that I was born in this house and I've lived here all my life and I don't mind to die in this house. I have always expected to die here. I'll have to do it someplace and this house is the best place I know."

"But we'll make things comfortable for you, Mother," Pa said in a pleased tone of voice. "Our children love you and I think you'll be happy with us. Sal will fix you a room off to yourself. And when you want to lie down and rest, you won't be bothered."

"I've never stayed but three nights away from here in my life," Grandma said. "And I've never been a hundred miles away from here. It may work out all right. I'll try it."

When Grandma came to stay with us, Pa had to haul the

furniture from her room and put it in the room that Mom had set aside for her in our house. But that was all the furniture that was taken from Grandma's house. She had Pa to leave the house as she had always kept it. Grandma had never locked her doors and she left the doors unlocked, though Pa and Mom wanted her to lock the doors.

"I've not got anything anybody wants," Grandma said. "Jake would never sleep in a house with locked doors. Now that he's gone, I'll leave the house the way he always left it."

Sister Mary and I did anything for Grandma that she wanted done. And when one of us went to the store, she always gave us money to get candy. And she sent money to Uncle Jake's and Uncle Jason's boys and girls to get candy. I thought that she thought she'd soon be going back to her old home again and that we'd be a-coming to stay with her. And I hoped that this would happen for it was better to stay in the old house with Grandma than it was to live at home.

One morning when I took Grandma a fresh pitcher of water, she poured herself a glass, looked at it, smelled of it and then she made a face when she tasted it. She took a sip of it and then she gagged.

"What's wrong with the water, Grandma?" I asked.

"It's not good water," Grandma said. "This water will finish me if I keep on drinking it. Go to my well and draw me a bucket of fresh water and bring it here, Shan."

I told Mom and Pa that Grandma couldn't stand the water from our well and Pa said the water in our well was the same kind of sweet water that Grandma had in her well and that the wells were not three hundred yards apart. Then Pa and Mom went into Grandma's room to talk to her about the water.

"I've drunk water from the same well for eighty-five years," Grandma told Mom and Pa, "and it's hard for me to drink this new water from a well that's not twenty-five years old."

"Then we'll carry you water from your well," Mom said.

"That will be fine," Grandma said.

Then she asked Pa if he'd been around her house many times since she had left. And Pa told her he had been around it every day. I wondered if she would ask him if anybody had opened the unlocked doors and had gone inside and ransacked the house. But she didn't ask Pa anything about the inside of the house. She asked him all about her trees, shrubs and birds. She even asked Pa if the big oak had fallen yet and Grandma had just been away three days.

"Mick, there's one thing I want you to do for me," Grandma said.

"What is it, Mother?" Pa asked.

"I want you to cut the tall green rye in your young apple orchard so I can see my house," she said. "If you'd do that I could sit in my room and look at my house from this window."

"Well, Mother," Pa said, "if you'll just wait about three weeks, I'll plow that rye under. I sowed it in my young orchard for a cover crop and I want it to get its growth and right now it's a-getting its growth. See, it's a fine crop to fertilize the roots of young apple trees."

"Don't think I can wait three weeks," Grandma said.

But Pa didn't want to turn it under, so he didn't say anything more to Grandma about it. Next day she asked him when he was going to turn it under or cut it and Pa said that he would do it soon as he plowed another field. And soon as Pa and Mom got off in another room to themselves, Mom told him to wait, that Grandma was a little childish and that she would soon forget about it.

But the next day Grandma asked Pa about when he was going to cut the rye or plow it under. And Pa said that he would do it as soon as he got his plowing done for corn. Grandma didn't like his answer and Pa could tell that she didn't. He didn't want to hurt Grandma and he didn't want to spoil the rye field in his young orchard so he called Mom into another room and talked to her about it. And Mom told him to leave it a few days. And the following day, Grandma told Pa that if he didn't do something about the rye that some morning he would get up and his rye would be blown flat on the ground by a windstorm. Pa wanted to laugh at Grandma's words but he was afraid he would make her mad.

"In three more days, I'll plow it under," Pa said.

But early next morning when Pa had fed his team and hitched it to the wagon, he looked at his rye in the young orchard and it was flat on the ground as if a log had been rolled over it. Pa ran inside the house and told Mom and they both went up to the orchard to see if the windstorm had hurt any of our young apple trees but not a tree had been hurt by the wind. Then they went up to Grandma's house to see if the wind had caved in the roof or had blown down the giant hulk of an oak in the front yard or had blown the gate down. There had been a windstorm all right but it hadn't hurt anything but Pa's rye.

"I'll tell you, Sal," Pa said just before he drove his team to the field, "I am all upset."

After Pa had taken our team to the field, I went into Grandma's room. She was homesick. She would look through our window at her house and still she couldn't see it very well for one of our apple trees was in the path of Grandma's eyes. She told me that she wanted me to cut this young apple tree so she could see her house. I told Mom about it and she told me not to do it.

"That's a pretty tree," Mom said. "I know your Pa doesn't want it cut. I know that I don't want it cut."

Our young apple orchard was eight years old and the trees had been carefully trimmed until their tops looked like big green bowls—but now they looked like big white bowls in the blue wind of April, for they were white with blooms and the honeybees were flying over their tops and fighting the bumblebees for the fragrance of the blossoms. I wanted to see Grandma get what she wanted but I knew how hard Mom and Pa had worked to get this orchard and how they put fires near the orchard to make great smokes to keep the frosts away so they couldn't fall on the young trees and bite the fruit that was yet in the blossoms. I knew that our orchard was the prettiest thing on our farm in April and that it was our money crop. And that if one tree was cut it would hurt the looks of the orchard.

When Pa came home at noon and had fed his team he came into the house. He was worried about his rye and when Mom told him about Grandma's wanting the young apple tree cut so she could see her house, Pa sat down in his chair. He didn't say anything.

"I can't cut one of my flowerin' fruit trees," Pa said. "I've worked too hard to raise that orchard. To cut one tree would ruin the looks of my orchard."

"Ma will forget about it," Mom said.

"I'm afraid she won't," Pa said.

"Grandma is homesick," I said. "She wants to see her own house."

"I'll tell you what we'll do," Pa said, his face growing brighter, "we'll take Mother back to her house and let her look the place over and go around the house again."

"Why haven't we thought of that before, Mick?" Mom said.

And when Pa told Grandma that he couldn't afford to cut his young tree but that he would haul her back to the house and let her spend the day a-looking it over, Grandma was pleased. Mary and I went with Grandma and we spent the day. Mary took her by one arm and I took her by the other and we helped her every place she wanted to go. Grandma was happy and she laughed and talked to us about her house, her trees, shrubs and rose-vines. She had us to take her to this one and that one and she told us when it was planted and the person who planted it. When Pa came after us late in the afternoon, Grandma didn't want to go but we lifted her on the express-wagon seat and hauled her down to our house.

I think she'll forget about my apple tree now," Pa said. "She had a good day at her old home."

But the next day when Grandma tried to look at her own home, the tree was in her way and she talked to Mom about having me to chop it down with an ax. But Mom told her the tree was a pretty tree and that it looked good in the orchard white with blooms and when it had borne fruit this year that she would have Pa trim its long branches. But Grandma wanted it cut. And that night she told Pa she wanted him to cut the apple tree or to take her back to her old house to live.

Pa didn't think anything about the orchard until two days had passed and he had his team harnessed to try to plow the tangled rye under. And when Pa drove his team into the orchard, he stopped his team, threw up his hands and ran to the house.

"What's the matter, Mick?" Mom asked.

"Who cut that apple tree?"

"No one," Mom said. "Has it been cut?"

"See for yourself," he told Mom. When Mom went out with him to look at the tree, I sat in Grandma's room with her and watched her look out of the window at her old home. Grandma sat peacefully by the window as if nothing had happened.

I saw Pa and Mom standing by the tree. Pa was carefully examining it. And I left Grandma in her room and went to the tree. It had been uprooted by a windstorm that had just swept the corner of our orchard and hit this tree that Grandma wanted cut. Not a heavy leafed, blossoming branch had been molested on the other trees. And again Pa hurried to Grandma's old home to see if the wind had done any damage there but not a thing had been touched since her house missed the path of the wind.

"I don't understand," Pa said. "I think we'd better take Mother back to her own home. I don't know what will happen here next if we don't."

Grandma was sitting by the window looking at her own home when Pa and Mom asked her if she wanted to move back.

"I never wanted to move here in the first place," Grandma

said. "I don't like it here. I'll never like it here. Yes, take me back."

I was glad when Pa and Mom moved Grandma and her furniture back to the old house and my sister Mary and I went with her to stay. Will, Herbert, Effie and Carrie were glad too. Sister Mary and I hated to see our two weeks pass. We hated to go back home. We would rather have lived with Grandma all the time. But Pa and Mom wouldn't let us do this. And, often, Uncle Jason, Uncle Jake, Pa, Aunt Mallie, Aunt Phoebe and Mom came to see Grandma. But she never went to see one of them. She stayed in her own house, among her old pieces of furniture, her flowers, vines, shrubs and trees.

We spent the spring and summer with Grandma. And autumn came and the leaves started turning. They fell into the drainpipes and clogged them and I climbed on top the house and lifted the dead leaves from the drainpipes. Once when I stepped on the shingle-roof, my foot broke through. I had the best times I ever had in life when I did things for Grandma and I enjoyed the freedom that she gave me. But it made me sad to hear her say that she would never leave her house again—that she had left it once and that was enough. It hurt me to hear her say that she would die in this house.

That hot September night thunder shook the earth and streaks of lightning cut the dark sky into tiny bits. It was a terrible night—a great rush of wind came. And Grandma told Mary and me to leave the house. She said that she would follow us. We didn't want to go first but she told us to and we did as we were told. We hadn't more than

I was glad when Pa and Mom moved Grandma and her furniture back to the old house.

reached the sidewalk until we heard a mighty crash. Little pieces of oak twigs hit us. We ran out into the yard—out into the heavy darkness screamin' for Grandma. But she didn't come. The heavy-topped oak had fallen onto the decaying house and it had crashed through it. When the lightning flashed we could see parts of the hulk of the house standing. Even the doorway that we had come through was crushed.

"Let's tell Mom and Pa," Mary said.

We followed the path toward home by the lightning flashes and on our way we met Mom and Pa coming in raincoats and carrying lanterns.

"The old oak fell on the house," Mary screamed. "Grandma can't get out!"

Pa sent me with the lantern to run through the darkness and the rain that was now falling in torrents to tell Uncle Jake and Uncle Jason. And Uncle Jason sent Herbert to tell John Blevins and Uncle Jake sent Will to tell Enic Tabor what had happened. When I got back to the house, Pa had thrown pieces of broken shingles and joists back from the place where Mary had told him Grandma was when the crash came. And they found Grandma pinned to the floor beneath a joist. She was dead. She had died where she wanted to die and maybe the way she had wanted to die. She had died in her own house and the oak that Pa had often told her was dangerous and had wanted to cut for her, had killed Grandma. And even through the mighty storm that raged and out into the vast swirl of wind, darkness, and rain, her birds flew from the hollow of the oak, chirruping a pensive melancholy dirge for her.

WHOSE LAND IS THIS?

"I see somebody comin' up the path," Pa said, pointing with his long skinny finger at a man coming up the path. "Looks like Uglybird Skinner. Come see if it isn't Uglybird, Shan."

"That's Uncle Uglybird all right."

"Wonder what he's doin' way out on this God-forsaken ridge."

Uncle Uglybird climbed slowly up the little foxpath that wound like a snake up the steep bluff toward the ridge. He held to the bushes to pull himself up the little rock shelves. Then he'd stop to wipe sweat from his sliced-beet red face with his big blue bandanna.

I like to watch a man climb a hill," Pa said. "I like to listen to 'im get his wind. Like to watch him stop to wipe sweat."

The August sun beamed from the sky like a white agate marble. Leaves were wilted on the bushes. Big rock cliffs sprawled high upon the ridgetop in the blazing sun like sleeping scaly monsters. Slow winds rustled the wilted pods of leaves on the black locusts, yellow locusts, black oaks, white oaks, red oaks, blackberry briars, greenbriars, sawbriar clusters and spindly half-choked, half-starved grass.

"Howdy, Uglybird," Pa said as Uncle Uglybird Skinner reached the ridge road. "What are you doin' way out on this

God-forsaken ridge?"

"Prowlin', just prowlin', Mick," he grunted as he stopped to get his breath. I want to walk out this ridge again. I want to see the old places, Mick. I want to walk over land where things happened when I was a young man."

"Nothin' ever happened here, did it?"

"Young man, you're too young to know," he said.

Uncle Uglybird laughed like the slow-blowing lazy August wind. He put his big hand on his knee to brace his body as he leaned over to pick up a stick to use for a cane. He grunted as he picked up a long slab the lightning had gutted from a ridge oak.

"Ain't the men we ust to be, are we, Mick?" he said as he raised up with the tree slab in his big wrinkled hand. He put one end of it on the ground and caught the other end with both hands bearing most of his weight on it.

"We're slowin' down, Uglybird," Pa said as he pulled a twist of home-grown burley from his hip pocket.

"That terbacker raised on this ridge?" Uncle Uglybird asked Pa.

"Right out there at that barn," Pa said.

"I want another chaw of the good old fragrant weed raised from this land that I own down in my heart," Uncle Uglybird said. "I can't bite it, Mick. Cut me a hen-egg-sized chaw off with your pocketknife. Don't have teeth any more. Haf to gum my terbacker."

Pa sliced Uncle Uglybird a piece of the twist. He sliced himself a slice from the twist since he had his knife handy.

"Mick, I heard about your boy buyin' all this old land," Uncle Uglybird said. "It bore on my mind, Mick. Just like a rabbit, I had to come back to my old settin' place this mornin'."

Uncle Uglybird walked over to a big oak, leaned his back against it and supported himself with the oak slab lightning had torn from the tree. He squirted ambeer from his thin-lipped, toothless mouth. Pa sat down on the sawed top of a stump and faced Uncle Uglybird as they talked. Pa spat his ambeer farther than Uncle Uglybird. It spattered on the dark dusty ridge road and on the wilted woodgrass stems.

"You can allus tell when one of us old birds is gettin' old," Uncle Uglybird said. "We get so we can't spit fur as we ust to. Now look at me, Mick; look at you. I'm about ten years older than you; I can't spit near as fur. I've just been standin' here watchin' you. You spit a fur piece yet. I ain't got the power I ust to have. Hell, I ust to hit a snake's eye at twenty feet!"

"You ain't gettin' old," Pa said. "It's just in your head that you are old."

"No, it's not, Mick," he laughed. "It's in my old body. It's in my bones. My muscles are gettin' softer every day. That's why I've come back this mornin'. I wanted to show your boy where a few houses ust to be on this place before I go on to meet my Maker. Thought he might like to know. Thought he might like to know that he has a deed fer this land but I just wanted to tell 'im I have a deed in my heart fer this land. It's recorded there, Mick."

Uncle Uglybird's clear blue eyes looked at the finger of ridge that parted from the main backbone of ridge at my tobacco barn and sloped toward the main hollow.

"You wouldn't think it, young man," he said to me as he pointed toward a rough rocky point with his cane, "but there ust to be a house down there. Did you ever find a big rock pile there?"

"Found it when I was rabbit hunting," I said.

"Sperrys lived there, when I was a boy," he said. "I ust to go there and spark little blue-eyed Winnie Sperry. Sixty years ago young man! Now Winnie Sperry sleeps at Plum Grove beside Watt Lumpkin. She married him. Had ten children."

"I remember Winnie Sperry and Watt Lumpkin," Pa said.

"Shore you do, Mick," Uncle Uglybird said. "They were good people. Dug a livin' out'n these hills, but their youngin's all scattered like wild quails. All sailed off to the West. Went to Oklahoma to homestead."

Then Uncle Uglybird shifted his cane in the air, pointed to the hollow below this flat. "Right down there," he said, "ust to be two houses. Rock piles are there yet where the chimneys ust to be. I looked as I come up this hollow. Howards lived on the left side of the creek; Johnsons lived on the right side of the creek. Fit and joured all the time they lived there. Howards had eight youngins; Johnsons had nine. If a Johnson youngin' crossed that little creek, the Howard youngins went after 'im. They stood with peeled clubs, purty clubs, you know, to fight with—and dared one another across that creek. And they meant business. Crissie Johnson and Old Gertie Howard pulled one another's hair once. That started the war. Jim Johnson sprinkled Bert Howard with buckshot before the fight was over!"

"I don't remember that," Pa said. "I remember the old-timers talked about it when I first come to this country!"

"It's a little before your time, Mick," Uncle Uglybird said putting his oak-slab cane on the ground to rest his arm. "I guess they'd a thinned one another out like rabbits if it hadn't been fer that big fire we had here that burned their houses."

"Did they have a big fire once here?" I asked.

"Did they have a big fire?" Uncle Uglybird repeated. "Young man, I'll say they had a big fire. It burned fifteen houses right here on this place that you own! I saw that fire. It was like Hell that the preachers ust to preach about. You think you've got virgin timber on this farm because you've got big oaks. But you don't have virgin timber here. All this timber was cut into cordwood. Squatters come here from all over the country. They made houses out of logs, daubed them with mud, kivered them with clapboards and built big chimneys out'n field rocks. After they cut the timber, they left the brush that wouldn't make cordwood. There were mountains of fine brush left in the little dreans. It dried out. One windy March a wood chopper fired the brush to kill the snakes. That fire went fast as a horse could run. Wasn't any savin' the houses. People run fer their lives and left all they had behind 'em. Didn't have much but the fire got all they had. Had to go somewheres and start all over again. These ridges were mountains of white, black and gray ashes. Not a tree left. Just the big rocks showed everplace. One good thing that fire done, it burnt up all the blasted copperheads."

"I've heard the old people talk about that fire too," Pa. said.

"Right out there on that pint," Uncle Uglybird Skinner pointed his cane toward the west, "was the old Hylton house. You know where that is. The old well is there. Ninety feet deep. Went down eighty feet through solid rock to get water. I was married in that house. Uncle Jim Garthee lived there! It's one house the big fire didn't get fer Uncle Jim was a man that kept the brush back from his door. He was allus afraid of fire; he had dreams and a token that a big fire was comin' and he was prepared!"

"I remember the logs of that old house," I said. "When I was a little boy, Pa rented that piece of ground for tobacco. I remember when Pa and Mom used to let me come with them. Mom rode one mule and Pa rode the other. I rode behind Mom on the mule that wouldn't buck. Pa rode the bucking mule. I remember it was the first place I ever pulled a tobacco worm from the stalk—I pulled it in two and buried it in the soft black smelly dirt of the tobacco balk."

"Right over in the hollow below the Hylton house pint," Uncle Uglybird pointed with his oak slab, "was a house by that sweet-rustycoat apple tree. You don't remember that house, do you, Mick?" he turned and asked Pa.

"Nope, I don't, Uglybird."

"Harley Staggs lived there," Uncle Uglybird said. "He wasn't exactly a preacher. He was an exhorter; that was almost a preacher in them days. When the people shook with fear back in the churchhouse—when they heard the sermons of fire and damnation—the exhorter went back atter 'em and hepped 'em to the altar where they prayed fer fergiveness of their sins. Harley Staggs was a stout man. He was a cordwood chopper; used an ax all his life. It wasn't no trouble fer him to pack a big man up the aisle on his shoulder! He'd take 'em right to the altar, I'm tellin' ye."

"Don't remember Harley Staggs," Pa said. "Have heard o' 'im's all. But I do remember that sweet-rustycoat apple tree. Et many an apple off'n it. It's dead now—old stump still standin' and a bluebird builds her nest there every spring."

"Right out there's where they had the big double-log churchhouse," Uncle Uglybird pointed with his oak slab. "That's where I's headin' fer when I run into you here. I wanted to go back out there to see that old place where I come when I's a boy and brought Winnie Sperry to church. Watt Lumpkin was tryin' to spark 'er then. But he couldn't beat my time until I started drinkin' and carvartin' and carryin' on with the rest of the boys. Toted a pistil and shot at the snakes sunnin' on the rocks around this ridge. You know how we ust to do, Mick. That was Sunday sport—ride your horse around this ridge fast as he could go and let your pistil loose at a snake sunnin' on a rock or a lizard scalin' the bark of one of the tall pines!"

"Have done it a many a time, Uglybird," Pa said spitting ambeer on the wilted woodgrass. "Every young buck wanted the fastest hoss, the best pistil and the purtiest gal!"

"That's right, Mick," Uncle Uglybird laughed like the slow-moving wind in the brush, briars, and sprouts.

Uncle Uglybird walked in front; Pa and I followed him along the dusty path toward my tobacco barn.

"Right there was a house," he pointed. "Right where your barn is. Stabletons lived there. Old Hams Stableton was a great eater. Not many invited him to dinner—a little skinny man but he could eat three chickens at a mess besides the other grub he put away. He was a great church member—took in all the basket dinners and the footwashin's and he tried to keep peace around the old churchhouse here when us young fellars fell out and fit over the yard. He would stand back and say: 'Fair play, boys, is all I ast. Don't use your pistils. No knifin' now, fellars! Fight fair!' I can hear 'im yet!"

49

"And right here stood the double-log cabin," Pa said. "It was here when I come to this country fifty years ago. Hezzy Smith lived here!"

"That's right, Mick," Uncle Uglybird said, pointing with his slab toward the pile of chimney rocks. "I've et many a good mess of coon there. Ust to coon hunt with Hezzy's boys—Alf, Jim and Tom. Had a dog we called Sooner. Old Sooner put the coons up the trees!"

"No more coons here now," Pa said.

"Here's the place where the churchhouse ust to be," Uncle Uglybird said. "We're standin' on the exact spot."

Now we stood in silence while Pa and Uncle Uglybird looked at land where there wasn't a trace of a house. Uncle Uglybird took his oak slab and hunted among the smart weeds and the ragweeds for a foundation rock. But he could not find a rock. Clumps of shoemakes stood here; they were smelly in the wind. The slow wind moved their wilted pods of leaves. Sawbriar clusters had vined among their pithy stems.

"All gone," Uncle Uglybird said. "All gone now. But I'll tell you this was the meetin' place for all of us in the spring when they had the big protracted meetings and the footwashings. We come here and brought our gals. I brought Winnie Sperry then. I think every man here that wasn't a saved man carried a pistil. I've seen hosses tied all along this ridge. I've seen this road filled with surreys, buggies, joltwagons and hug-me-tights. People come from all over this country to this church. I've seen Harley Staggs go up the aisle many a night with a big broad-shouldered wood chopper squirmin' on his shoulder! He was under 'conviction' but afraid to confess his sins."

"No water here," I said. "What did they do about washing one another's feet?"

"Took their lanterns and pine torches and went down to that sulphur spring under the hill in the beech grove," Uncle Uglybird said. "There was a path worn over the hill to that spring in them days slick as the path to a groundhog hole."

Then Uncle Uglybird looked at the sprouts and weeds again. He couldn't hear the sighing wind for he was too deaf to hear it but he saw the wilted pods of shoemake leaves move in the wind and he felt the wind against his wrinkled face and his thin lips.

"We didn't know we had a good thing here when we had this churchhouse," he spoke loudly for he was so deaf he could hardly hear his own voice. "That churchhouse may've been standin' yet if the damned fool boys hadn't put hay in the door and fired it one night when church was goin' on. People come out'n the winders like bees out'n a hive. Never heard sich screamin' in all my life. Burnt it to a pile of ashes. Talk about tough people then; we had 'em. Fight you at the drop of a hat. Loved a fight. Fight you any way you wanted to fight. Fight with knives, guns, rocks, clubs, or fists. The women even fit. All worked in the cornfields and they were stout as men. Men chopped cordwood; you know men get good muscles when they chop wood the year around."

Now we walked away from the place where the Six Hickories churchhouse used to be. We walked around the high ridge, looking down on the timber tops as we walked along. When we reached the highest point on the ridge, we stopped.

"Now I can show you," Uncle Uglybird said, leaning on his oak slab and pointing with his hand. "On that hill where you have corn yander, was a house. You know where that rock pile is."

"Yes, it's a pill to plow around," Pa said.

"There was a house there," he said. "Tim Hammertight lived there. He was a wood chopper. Had twelve youngins. All mean as striped-tailed snakes. I ust to fight with 'em. I know what I'm talkin' about. Atter the fire, they went to Oklahoma. Right below them where that spring is under that oak tree was another house. It was a little two-room logshack. Ensor Pennington lived there. He had ten youngins; they were allus fightin' the Hammertight youngins. Got the old people into it. Right over on this pint where you see that clump of walnut trees was another house. Flem Spry lived there. He and his wife Lizzie lived alone. They didn't have no youngins. They went to the Six Hickories church, tithed, and behaved themselves. But above the spring under that oak tree was the old Leathers house. Bill Leathers lived there. Had nine youngins; then they were with the Pennington youngins fightin' the Hammertights. There was a big orchard on that hill over there. But the big fire run over crabgrass under the trees and killed 'em all. I was almost burnt to death in that big fire—down there tryin' to hep get the furniture out'n Flem Spry's house."

"I didn't know there was ever a house there," I said.

"But it was there, young man," Uncle Uglybird said. "You wouldn't believe me if I'd tell you there was a house right over on the bank from where your Pa lives now. When you cleared that land didn't you find an old road that went up the bank?"

"Yes, we did," Pa said.

"That road went to a house there," Uncle Uglybird said.

"Eif Morton lived there. He had so many youngins I don't remember their names. Guess there were sixteen youngins in that family. You know we lived in a double-log cabin right below where you live, Mick—right where your garden is! I ust to throw rocks at the Morton youngins across that hollow half the day; then I'd make friends with 'em and we'd play marbles in the afternoon. We had the best time together. There wasn't much to do but fight in them days. We loved to hunt and fight. I was born in that house—right where your garden is! And where that cedar stands in your pasture field, Uncle Charlie Skinner lived there and raised twelve youngins. Pap raised nine!"

"I thought I bought a wilderness when I bought this land," I said. "It was sold to me for land that had never been plowed; land where the timber had never been cut!"

Uncle Uglybird laughed like the ridge wind among the oak leaves.

"Land that had never been plowed," he laughed. "Timber that had never been cut. I've plowed over half of it myself! I've cradled wheat right down there where your giant oak trees stand! I've used a cradle many a day down there. Believe it or not, this old man you see chewin' his home-grown burley and usin' this lightnin' oak splinter fer a cane was one of the best cradlers in these parts in his young days. He led the pack of men in the wheat field. And young man, cradlin' is work. Ast the old men about it! We had one of the old-time threshin' machines where the bosses pulled a long sweep around and around like a cane mill and threshed the wheat! It set right back out there in front of the Six Hickories churchhouse where your barn is today!"

"I didn't know that hill was ever in wheat," Pa said. "I wouldn't a thought that land had ever been plowed!"

"The last man I cradled with in that field," Uncle Uglybird said, "was Finnis Jason. He lived over the hill yander," he pointed with his slab, "in that patch of persimmon sprouts. There was a house there. He's the man that pizened his wife when he fell in love with Ensor Pennington's wife. Give her enough rat pizen to kill twenty wimmen so the Doctor said atter they got suspicy and dug her up at Plum Grove."

Now the sun was high above us in the sky. I saw Pa step on his shadow. Then Pa pulled his watch from his overall pocket.

"My turnip says it's twelve," Pa said. "It's right with the sun. Time we's gettin' to dinner!"

Then Pa put his watch in his pocket. He turned to Uncle Uglybird and yelled, "It's dinner time, Uglybird. Go home with us to dinner!"

"Can't do it," he said. "Must get home. Effie's got dinner waitin' fer me."

"Better go home with us," Pa yelled.

"Nope, I'll be gettin' home to dinner," he said. "I want to go past that persimmon grove where Finnis Jason ust to live and look the old place over. I ust to take Mollie to church at Six Hickories before she married Finnis. I want to go there to look around awhile and to think! Just want to see a little more of the old place that I have a deed fer in my heart!"

"Here, take another chaw of this burley before you go," Pa said as he pulled the twist from his pocket and cut a piece with his pocketknife big as a hen's egg. Then Pa bit himself a chew from the twist.

"That's real terbacker," Uncle Uglybird said putting the tobacco behind his lean beardy jaw. "Thank you, Mick."

We watched him as he walked out the dusty ridge path, toward the persimmon grove.

He owns this land that I bought and paid money for, I thought. Has a deed for it recorded in his heart.

I followed Pa down the finger ridge that left the backbone ridge. As we walked the foxpath under the tall oak trees, I thought about how Uncle Uglybird used to swing a cradle and let the stalwart wheat fall from the cradle fingers where the big oak trees grew now. I wondered if he had stepped where one of the big trees stood. I wondered if the Pennington, Hammertight, and the Leathers children had played here, if they had fought here, and wherever they were, if they were still alive in the west, if they remembered these hills where there was once a civilization, the churchhouse at Six Hickories, when exhorter Harley Staggs carried the sin-struck wood choppers squirming on his back to the altar. I wondered if they remembered the dreams, joys, happiness, fight, work and all that go to make a civilization—now covered over with brush, briars and leaves on the earth. I wondered if they had deeds for my farm recorded in their hearts.

This town has been the center of his universe.

MY FATHER IS AN EDUCATED MAN

Yesterday I was in town with my father. This town has been the center of his universe. He has never traveled a fifty-mile radius from this town. He goes on Saturdays, dressed in his overalls, clean blue work shirt, overall jacket, his soiled weathered cap with a shrinking bill and his turned-at-the-toes stump-scarred brogan shoes. Often, he goes through the weekdays to town if he wants something from the stores or a bottle of beer. He walks a path four miles over the bony hills to the town as he has done since I can remember. And I can remember him for thirty-three years. He has dressed the same way, has walked the same path to the same town.

My father talked to a group of men on the courthouse square where the men from all over the county meet on Saturdays with the men from the town, where they talk, tell their stories, chew their tobacco, try to whittle the longest shaving with their pocketknives while they listen to the courthouse bell calling men inside the courthouse for justice. While they talked and chewed tobacco from long homegrown twists of burley and spit mouthfuls of ambeer spittle on the courthouse square, I heard a man say, who was standing in another group of men not far from my father's group, "There's old overalled Mitch Stuart. See 'im in town every Saturday." This fairly well-dressed man, teacher of a rural school, pointed to my father and the men in his group looked and listened while he talked. "Never amounted to anything in his life. Never will. But he's got smart children. His boy is a book-writer; you may've heard about him."

Pert Maldin didn't see me as he went on telling the men in his group how my father loved to come to town on Saturdays and loaf, just loaf and try to whittle the longest shavings, how he loved the sound of the courthouse bell and how he'd listened to it for a half century. And he told them he'd known my father that long and how my father had gone to the same little tavern, run by the same people for a half century and got his beer on Saturdays and after he had a few beers how he talked to his old friends and told them big windy tales. He told about his seeing my father have a few fights in his younger days and how time had now slowed him down. Since Pert Maldin talked confidentially to the men that surrounded him, I couldn't hear all he said. I did hear him say my father wouldn't know his name if he would meet it in the road, that he couldn't read a beer sign and he couldn't write his name.

I thought once that I would walk over to Pert Maldin and tell him a few things. One thing that I would tell him was my father would know his name if he'd meet it in the big road or saw it printed on a sign beside the road, but if it were in a paper he would not see it for I'd never seen him look inside a newspaper in my life. Yet, he knew his name, for my mother had taught him the letters in his name and that he knew these letters same as he knew from memory a rock cliff, an oak tree, beech, sassafras or persimmon. . . . And that if he saw his name, he would know it immediately since my mother had taught him letters in our alphabet, that he would slowly go over the letters in a word and piece them together and pronounce some of the hardest words correctly.

I thought about walkin' over and popping Pert Maldin on the nose when he talked about my father. But I stood silently and listened as long as I could and many thoughts flashed through my brain as the ambeer spittle flashed brown in the November sunlight from the mouths of the men in the group where my father was talking, where they were laughing at some story one of his group had told. I thought a pop on the nose would serve Pert Maldin right and then I thought, "What's the use? What does he know about my father? And what does he know about education though he is a school teacher?"

While I stood on the courthouse square watching these figures of the hill earth who came to town on Saturdays to swap their windy tales and try each other's twists of home-grown burley, I thought about the members of the human family I had known. I thought about my own people and the path they had come over the earth. I thought about my father and my father's people, beardy-faced, tall, figures of the earth, tillers of earth, men who had cut the timber, cleared the fields of brush and sprouts and who had plowed the root and rock-infested mountain slopes with oxen hitched to yellow-locust-beamed cutter plows. And the longer thoughts flashed across my brain, the more I knew Pert Maldin didn't know what he was talking about . . . for my people, my father's people, had helped to build the railroads up the Big Sandy and into the mountains of West Virginia. They had helped to build the coal drags of the nation.... They had helped to build the cities, though not any that I knew lived there now or had ever lived there. My father's people had helped to build the highways. And the schools where children only of the late generations have attended. They had helped to build churchhouses where but few attended since such limitations had been put on the kind of a life they had loved, tobacco chewing, smoking, drinking of wine, whiskey, and even beer.

Such would never suit his people. They raised their own tobacco and they used it; they made their own whiskey and they drank it. They carried firearms and used them in time of danger while they helped to build America. What did they know about letters of the alphabet? These little things didn't mean a lot to them! And what did they care about books? Why should they spend their time in a closed-up school-room, controlled by school authorities, and strive to learn to read secondhand life in books when they had firsthand life before them to live?

The older men in my father's family, now sleeping in the Virginia, West Virginia and Kentucky mountains, if they were alive today would pity their offspring, entangled in the spider web of civilization. They would despise and fight with all their might, if they could raise from their graves, any barriers that would confine their freedom.

What would they care about my books? They would not even read them. To them, I would be an oddling.

Though I belong to them, they would not claim me since I have had my chance and unlike them I have not killed one of my enemies. I am one of the book-educated ones and I have thought this thing through. And it took me many days and nights walking among the hills to make my decision that

I would not kill an enemy except in the time of war.... And even when I was going through these days and nights of walking the hills and thinking about what to do, my father was telling me that since he didn't have as many years to live as I had that he would take care of my enemies. I told him that I would do my own fighting. And when I thought these through, maybe it was the book education and the spider-web civilization his people didn't take to that helped me to make my decision.

Let Pert Maldin talk on the courthouse square. Let him talk about my father's not having an education, that he wouldn't know his name if he'd meet it in the big road. I could tell Pert that he didn't know about education. He was speaking about these secondhanded things called books when my father's people had lived an education while they were helping to build a nation and a civilization. Yes, they had taken the law in their own hands for they had to do it since the law didn't protect them while they fought their enemies; helped to build the railroads through the mountains, bridges to span the rivers and blast the turnpikes around the rocky slopes. They cleared the fields and broke the first furrows through the roots. They built the log cabins from the giant trees they didn't split into fence rails; they hauled giant sawlogs with yokes of oxen to the edge of the Big Sandy and waited for the spring rains when, with spiked boots and with long poles with spikes in the end, they took their log rafts down the Big Sandy and the Ohio River to the little town of Cincinnati, the Queen City of the West.

I could tell Pert Maldin that my father, son of these figures of the earth, with the blood of these men flowing through his veins, was an educated man. He was educated same as they were educated ... but maybe his education didn't fit the time he was living. He couldn't sit behind a desk wearing a white shirt, a necktie, a neatly pressed tailored suit and shined shoes, with a pencil behind his ear. He couldn't live in a world of figures and words. They would be playthings on the wind to him. All he'd say, even if his mind were trained to do these things is "To hell with this." I know him well enough to know that he would say these words. For what does he say about my books? "A lot of damned foolishness."

I could tell anybody that my father is an educated man. Though he is a small man with a wind-parched face the color of the autumn earth, my father has the toughness in his muscles of the hickory sprout. He has a backbone like a sawlog. In his make-up fear was left out. That word is not in his limited vocabulary. I never heard him say, in my lifetime, that he was afraid of anything.

My father can take a handful of new-ground dirt in his hand, smell of it, then sift it between his fingers and tell whether to plant the land in corn, tobacco, cane or potatoes. He has an intuition that I cannot explain. Maybe Pert Maldin, with all his education, could explain it. And my father knows when to plant, how to plant and cultivate and the right time to reap. He knows the right trees to cut from his timber for wood to burn and the trees to leave for timber. He knows the names of all the trees, flowers and plants that grow on his rugged acres. My father is able to live from sterile rugged mountain soil. He has raised enough food for his family to eat and his family has eaten about all he has raised. Money does not mean food to him as it does to many in America today. Money is some sort of a luxury to him. It is something he pays his taxes with. Money is something for him to buy land with. And the land and everything thereon is more than a bank account would be to him; land is something durable, something his eyes can see and his hands can feel. It is not the secondhand substance he would find in a book, if he could read.

I could tell anybody in America if my father isn't an educated man, we don't have educated men in America. And if his education isn't one of the best educations a man can have, then I am not writing these words and the rain is not falling today in Kentucky. If his education isn't as important as mine—this son of his he used to tell every day to go to school since he had found the kind of education he had didn't work as well this day and time in America as the kind of education where a man had a pencil behind his ear and worked in a world of figures, words, dollars and cents, when to buy, what to buy, when, where, and how to sell—then I am not writing these words.

And as I think of my father's autumn-colored face, of this small hickory-tough figure of the earth, I think of the many men in America still like him. And I say they are educated men.

Mom wanted John buried in earth that belonged to our blood kin.

BROTHERS

I remember when John died. I remember the spring-wagon drawn by one shaggy-haired mule. Bert drove the mule with a pair of rope plow lines, run through loops on the hames and tied to the bridle bits. He sat on the spring-wagon seat and backed the mule into our yard. Bert was dressed in overalls. The grass on the yard was dead. It was brown and the January wind moved it. The apple tree back of the house by the rock-chimney was leafless. Pa stood under the tree and saw Bert haul my brother John away. We followed over the muddy road three miles to the graveyard. It was on a hilltop on Grandpa's farm. Mom wanted John buried in earth that belonged to our blood kin. Grandpa was the only one who owned land. Pines stood above the yellow heap of dirt. They sighed in the wind. I remember. It was the last of my brother John. He sleeps there today, marked by a thin slab, surrounded by pine trees, a rusty woven-wire fence, and cattle that come to the wire fence and wish for the grass inside the lot.

I wanted another brother. I would say to Mom: "Mom, I want another brother. John is not here any more. John is dead. I have no one to play in the sand with me. I have no one to help me gather the hen eggs from the nests in the woods. I have no one to wade the creek with me and catch the crawdads."

I can remember how the tears would drop from Mom's eyes while she would be sitting before the fire. She would not speak. She would sit there and darn away on a sock heel. She would knit sweaters. She would cut dresses for the neighborhood women. She would get them to piece on her quilts while she cut their dresses. Mom was skilled that way. She would pattern their quilts. She would wait on their sick. They came to Mom for things.

I would go out into the woods that came down to our door. I would hear the wind rustle the leaves. I would look for my brother John. I didn't see how he could stay away so long. I would hear him in the wind. I could hear him speak. I would call to him. But no answer. Just the empty wind rustling the dead leaves on the ground. Just the wind rustling the green leaves on the tree. Life was so funny. It was strange. I could not understand how the earth could hold John so long and let me live. I didn't think it fair that he should sleep in the ground and I could go on playing in the sand forever— see the spring come with birds, green leaves on the willows, sweet Williams on the cliffs. Hens cackling. Geese chasing the butterflies. And John not there.

I said to Mom one day: "Why did John have to die? Why does anybody have to die? Why can't we live forever, Mom?"

And Mom said: "It is because of God, son. We are like the flower. We come for a season like the sweet William. See how it blooms in the spring. See how it turns brown and dies in the fall-time of the year."

And then I said: "God is not a fair man, Mom, or he would have let John play in the sand with me. John sleeps under the ground, Mom. You know how hard that is. I don't want ever to sleep under the ground. I want John back to play with me. I don't like to play dolls with Sophia and Mary over there under the grapevines where that old goose has her nest."

I remembered how the tears dropped from her eyes. I remembered how I went in swimming with the girls—how I hated to go in swimming with them. How I laughed when they slid over the slate rocks where the frogs had been, into the knee-deep water. I remember the minnows that took to the willow roots and hid when we jumped naked into the water. I remember how Mom walked down across the sweet-potato vines one day and said: "Jesse, you must find you another swimming hole and quit swimming with the girls."

I was the only boy in the Hollow then. I had to swim by myself. I had to live by myself. I didn't like their dolls. I didn't like to do what girls did. One day I saw a man riding up to our house. He rode a big sorrel horse that had its tail twisted up in a knot. Its legs were splashed with mud. The man carried a little leather bag.

I ran to the house to see who the stranger was. We very seldom saw a man pass our house. When we did we ran to the house and looked out the window. The stranger met me at the door. I remember. He put his hand on my head. He asked me to hug his neck. He said: "You will hug my neck when you see what I brought you." He went on toward the horse that was tied to the fence post. I ran into the house. I heard a cry. I said: "It is another John, isn't it, Mom?"

Mom was there in bed. She smiled. She pulled the sheet back. I saw the baby. "Here is your brother that the Doctor fetched you," said Mom. "Doctor Morris brought him."

"Where did he get him?" I said.

"From behind a stump over there on the hill," Mom said.

I looked at him. Then I took back to the hill where the sweet Williams grew. I looked behind every stump on the hill. I was hunting for babies. Funny, as many hens' nests as I had found behind those stumps and had never found a baby. I looked every place. I ran wild, hunting for another baby. I ran to the house and told Mom I'd hunted for babies and couldn't find any. Then Mom said: "Only doctors can find babies."

That night Pa said: "I want to call this boy James. It is a name my people have carried for generations. It comes from the country across the ocean, I am told. It is a name to be found in the Bible. It is a name I like. I have a brother named James. Four of my brothers have boys named James. I must have a James."

Mom said: "Add Mitchell to it. That is your name, the name of your father, your father's father, and your father's father's father."

So I had a brother James Mitchell. When he cried I put the cat into the bed with him. I remember when he crawled. I called him Rawl. When he started pulling up by steps I called him Awger. He crawled out to the sand-pile with me. Acorns would fall from the tree and hit his head. He would cry. He was little but he crawled under the floor one day. I had to pull him out by his dress tail. Mom couldn't go under after him. The hole was not big enough for Mom to get back under. I had to take some of the underpinning from under the house to get him.

Mom would say: "I cannot stand to live here any longer,

Mitch. John died in this house. You must move me out. We must go to another place where none of us have died. We must move to another place. I cannot stand it here any longer. It seems like I can hear John walking in the dead leaves when the wind blows. I can hear them hit the windowpanes at night and I think of John. He is with me too often here. Sticks he drove in the ground are still out there by the corncrib with the white string he tied to them. I've never pulled them up. I can't bear to."

Pa would say to Mom: "Soon as a house is emptied in the Hollow we'll get it. We'll move to it. I can get rent for the third, maybe, by having my own mule."

The last house in the head of the Hollow was emptied.

Pa rented it for the third. He had found work for himself and his mule at a dollar and a quarter a day, work for me at a quarter a day, and Mom got housework at a quarter a day. "We need the money," Pa said. I ain't paid for my baby's casket yet. That was fifteen dollars. Butler has waited a long time now on me. I never stole chickens to pay a debt yet. I ain't going to. I aim to pay my jest and honest debts."

I remember the house had blackberry briars growing at the rock doorstep. Owls hooted from the dark timber at midday. We found a house snake on the wall plate. Pa killed it with a corn knife. I remember the dark puddle of blood on the floor. Sophie couldn't scrub up the stain.

Mom said: "This is a God-forsaken place. Two graves under the plum tree in the garden. I can't stand it here. The owls make it lonesome."

We could hear the owls come and get our chickens at night. Pa would run out on the snow barefooted in the winter and fire the shotgun into the night as the big winged bird silently muffled the frosty wind with his wings. We could hear the foxes bark from the hills above the house. We could hear cats meow from the dense dark woods on warm winter nights. We could hear the wind break the limbs from the trees and ooze through the briar thickets.

James was four. He would take the spotted hounds down among the dead cornstalks. He would say to the dogs: "Sic 'em." There wasn't anything to hunt there in the open fields but the quails that fed on the corn grains and grass seed. But James followed the hound dogs at four. I hunted with my father at night. I carried the 'possums in a coffee sack, and the coons. I wouldn't carry a skunk. He couldn't hire me to. I didn't like the scent. But there was the money. It was in the skunk hides. We sold fur. We went over the hills in early spring and dug roots of mayapple, ginseng, and yellowroot and sold them to Dave Darby. Later, we picked wild strawberries, raspberries, and blackberries and peddled them from door to door in Greenup. We made enough to eat and buy our clothes for winter. We paid for the coffin John was buried in. I worked from before sunup until after sundown for my quarter. I was called Lazybones.

Pa said: "You must have book-learning, Son. You must not grow up like a weed. You must not grow up like I have. I can't write my name till you can read it." I remember seeing Pa try to read the words on tobacco pokes. He would spell the word first. Then he would call it something. He would work and work with a word like a dog at a groundhog hole, gnawing roots and rocks to get the groundhog.

I walked three miles out of the Hollow with my sister to

school after the corn was laid by. We met the foxes in our path many a morning. We saw the squirrels play over our heads in the tall timber. Sawmills had not come to the Hollow yet. We saw the rabbits hop across our path. We met other children. They were strange children, or else we were strange children. I wanted to outlearn the boys I was in class with. I wanted to turn them down in spelling and get the prize for the most headmarks. When I turned one of the boys down, I laughed. When one turned me down, I cried. My sister and I would hold school before we got to school to see if I had the spelling words down pat. I wanted to outrun anybody in school. I wanted to tell them what to do. I fought with them, whipped and was whipped. It was a great place to be. I loved school—no beans to pick, no corn to cut, no hogs to feed, no wood to get. I learned fast because I worked hard.

My sister learned fast. We were called: "Martha Stuart's youngins. They learn fast. They are mean brats. They fight like mad cats—claw, bite, and scratch. That boy. The girl is clean and pretty always. That boy's knuckles are dirty and tough." It was true I'd met the other boys and played hard knuckles. I'd rake my knuckle-skin against the rough bark on the oak to make it tough and outdo the other boys.

One day in spring, when I was cutting brush and James was piling it and carrying water to the field to me, Sophie hollered to me from the house. She said: "Come to the house and see what is here." I went to the house; I heard the baby cry. It was the weakest crying I'd ever heard. Its crying sounded like the tiny meows of a baby kitten. I knew I didn't have another brother.

"Another brother," said Mom. "But he's so little. So little I'll have to pin him to the pillow. I'm afraid of losing him in the bed. He's so little."

She called him Lee. "I have heard of Lee," Mom would say when Pa would speak about Grandpa fighting for Grant. "My people died fighting for Lee."

One day the doctor came to see Lee. He could not give him new life. He couldn't do anything to save him. He was so small. Mom had him tied to the pillow. The doctor walked out of the house. He said to Pa: "Just a matter of hours, Mitch. He's getting his breath with a gurgling sound now."

Fever killed him. Fever had killed John. James took the fever. I prayed that he would live. He was sick when the same express that hauled John away hauled Lee. It was in April. The roads were muddy. The wind was cold. We followed Lee to the same hill where John was still sleeping soundly under the pines and the oaks. Grandpa was there and cut the barbed-wire fence so that the teams could go up the hill and dodge the coal ruts where the wagons had hauled the heavy loads from the mines and the sulphur water oozed yellow in the ruts. Lee was planted beside John. I cried. Mom cried and cried. Pop shed tears down his leaf-brown cheeks. James was home with the fever. It was late spring before he could get out of bed. One leg was left lame. He hobbled with a stick. He would walk awhile and rest awhile.

Pa got on the railroad section. He made three dollars for ten hours. He walked five miles to work and five miles back. He was making big money. We farmed at home. I was big enough to plow now and get fifty cents a day for work. I would plow a half day. Mom, James, and Mary would hoe the corn. In the afternoon I would hoe with them to catch up with all I had plowed in the morning. James was still lame in one leg but he kept getting better. One day James took a match and set some broom sage afire. It caught the woods on fire. We had to rake a ring through the leaves and fire against it to stop the fire. After the fire had burned over the hill Mom took her hand and started to spank James. He was six years old then. He started spanking Mom as they went around in a tussle. When Mom got through with him he didn't want to fight her back. He squalled and pulled up ragweeds by the roots with his tiny hands.

I was told about a high school across the hills over in the valley. Pa said: "Son, you must go to school. You must go. Sophie must go. Mary must go. And James must go as soon as he gets old enough to take high school work. I want to give you something I didn't get and something nobody on earth can take away from you. That is book-learning."

I was big enough now to help cut timber. I helped Grandpa cut timber. I helped make railroad crossties from the toughcut timber, tough-butted white oaks, red oaks, chestnut oaks that grew on our Kentucky hills. I worked during the winters. I read all the books I could get which included the Bible, *Peck's Bad Boy, Reynard the Fox* and *The Three Black Brothers*. I would write things down on clean white chips when Grandpa and I were chopping down the trees.

One day Pa walked through the pasture field with a cigar in his mouth. He ran in and grabbed Mom. They went round and round. Mom said: "Are you drinking again, Mitch? What's wrong with you?"

"I bought us the old Jack Sennett place—fifty acres for

three hundred dollars. I took a chance. Other men were afraid because one of Jack's heirs is a little off. But I took the chance. The place is mine."

Mom smiled and said: "A big lot of money for poor people. Can we ever pay for it?"

Pa had been laid off the section, but he got a job pouring concrete in Greenup. They were putting in the first hard road in the county, up Main Street in the county-seat town. I worked with him as water boy at first. Later I was promoted. We got before a high school, and there I stopped. I threw down my shovel and cement sacks. I started to high school. Pa worked on. He was proud of my being in school. He would turn up his pocketbook and pour out the pennies for me to buy paper, books and pencils with. He would say, "My last penny, Son, but take it. This is all I'm able to give you. It's more than corn-bread and buttermilk—the book-learning is. Get all of it you can. You'll need it before you get through this world."

I found myself in school with well-dressed children. I couldn't lead them as I did back at the schoolhouse on the hill. I hated them because I couldn't beat them and lead my class. They had more training than I had. Lots of things I hadn't heard tell of. The gerundive in grammar, for instance. A + B = AB. That was crazy to me—just to think about adding letters.

I went home and told Mom about it. She said: "High school must be very different. You add figures in the school at Plum Grove. You add letters in the high school."

High school was a great place. I found books to read. I read them. I found boys to fight. I fought them. I walked five miles. My sister came with me. We plowed through the mud in winter. It was cold. The winds howled. The snows drifted. Not anything stopped us.

Four years and I had finished high school. When I left high school James had been kicked out of Plum Grove school for fighting with his dinner bucket. He bent it over a boy's head. He left there and walked seven miles to Johnson's Chapel. A boy spit in his lunch bucket. He stabbed him on the hand with a barlow knife and ran away from school through the woods. James was ten years old now. He had learned fast in school. Mom would say: "My children learn fast. I have two children in high school and another one nearly ready." James was freckled-faced as a guinea egg. He was thin, with a big head and little legs.

"That boy takes after my people," Pa said when James entered high school at ten. "W'y, he's even got a couple of his toes growed together just like I got. He's like my father. He had his toes growed together, too."

I worked at home during the summers. I farmed the hills. I had my own way. Pa got a job on the section again. He was paying for the fifty acres while I farmed the land. Mom helped me in the fields. James worked with us. Mary worked in the fields. Sophie cooked for us and cleaned the house. It was a struggle. But we didn't know it. We didn't mind. We just had to face the strong current of wind. After I got my high school diploma I went home and started farming again.

I thought:

"Here I am with a high school education. I am back among the stumps with a bull-tongue plow and two big horses. I must go out into the world. I must get beyond these hills."

James was working with me. When I turned the horses from the plow and drove them to the barn, I was left with memories I shall never forget. We were plowing the new ground back in the hollow west of the house. It is in grass now. Quails feed there during the winter in the tufted dead grass. James followed me to the house and cried. He was a little freckled-faced devil and I didn't know he cared anything about me.

I put the horses in the barn. I ran to the house. My shirt was wet with sweat. I put what clothes I had in a pasteboard suitcase and pulled out. Mom laughed and said:

"You'll come back, Jesse. You'll always return to lonesome waters. Chickens come home to roost. You have your fling. Go have it."

Mom was fine. It was Pa—he'd always say when James did the least little thing, "That boy takes after me. He's like my people." Well, James was like Pa. He had two of his toes grown together like Pa. He had Pa's nose, his high forehead, his blue eyes. He had his actions—his nervous temperament. I was not like Pa. I didn't want to be. I wanted to get away from him. I wanted to get away from the sight of the hill where my brothers were buried. I wanted to get away from the old house in the Hollow. I wanted to leave it with Pa and James. So I walked away. I left home. I looked from the ridge at the old house back in the summer sunlight. Milkweeds blooming close to the house. Bean vines climbing the porch beams. Morning-glories in the fence corners and in the garden. To hell with the morning-glories. I was leaving. There was a world of books beyond the bull-tongue plow and the fussing with Pa.

But there were the payments to meet on the place. Pa could do that. But James would have to plow. That was all right. Mom would have to help him in the field. She would have to work harder. It hurt me to think of the work I left on Mom and James and Mary. A crow flew over my head and cawed. A ground sparrow fed its young by a stump among the weeds. That was all right. I could cry. But I didn't have time. I was leaving.

I got a job with a street carnival. I was fired after two weeks. I went to a military camp. I had a book of Burns's and a book of Poe's poetry with me. My lieutenant took a liking for me and advised me to enter college. I had made good in my military drills. I did excellent shooting. I hated the discipline. I would hate the routine forever. And they taught me how to run a bayonet through the guts of a man I was not mad at. I couldn't get used to it.

I didn't have money to enter college. So I left the military camp for the steel mills. I learned to be a blacksmith. I saved my pennies. I wrote poetry. I saw the red-painted lips of women.

I longed for the fields at home. But Pa said to Mom and

she wrote to me: "Tell him to stay away." And I stayed away. I wondered about James and Mary. I wondered if the corn was clean when they laid it by. But I could not go home to see.

One night I caught a bus and slipped home. I saw the blue smoke coming from the chimney. I never went any closer to the house. I saw the cows in the pasture. I heard the dogs barking. I saw Pa in the woodyard picking up kindling. I saw James in the yard shooting marbles with Bill Hillman. I did not venture to the house. I ran through the cornfields, breathed the wind from the corn, heard the whippoorwill; then I left for the town across the hill where I caught a bus back to the mills.

I would go to college. I knew I would. Pa would be proud of me. I left the mills hitch-hiking. I had my clothes in the same pasteboard suitcase. I had paid off my debts with the money I'd made at the mills. Now I had less than thirty dollars in my pocket. I was on my way to college. I was refused admittance at two colleges. Then I started hitch-hiking to one where I heard I could enter if I'd work.

That school was Lincoln Memorial. I stayed three years, worked my way at cleaning manholes, digging sewer lines, digging water lines, sweeping floors, writing news for a local paper, crushing limestone rock at the quarry where my job was helping the other three on the "bull-gang" use the hand drill. The boss measured how many inches of limestone we had to cut through of a morning or an afternoon. Then we put off shots of power, broke up the slabs of limestone, crushed them in a crusher and sold them to the Tennessee Highway Department for roads. I worked half a day, attended classes half a day. I studied at night. I bought my first overcoat at Middlesboro, Kentucky, priced fourteen dollars in November. I waited till March and got it for eight. It was a pretty grey topcoat. I bought my clothes. I made my way.

Pa got proud of me. He would say to the men on the section: "My oldest boy is in college. Contrary as the devil. But he is a fine boy. He's a good boy to work. He fooled me. He's the first of my people to finish high school. He's the first to go to college ." Pa would smoke a cigar. He would say: "And my other boy James is in high school. He learns fast. He's been doing the plowing at home during the summer."

I took a notion to come home. Mom said it was all right in a letter she sent me. Don West, my classmate, loaned me a dollar. I started hitch-hiking from east Tennessee on a one dollar bill. It was dark when I got the letter. I left in a blinding rainstorm. It turned to sleet—later to snow. I was on the road three nights and two days.

Did they kill the fatted calf when I got home? And was home dear to me? The black oak trees on the hills were my brothers. The dogs jumped all over me. The crows flew high overhead through the icy air. James, Mom, Mary, Sophie, and that little new sister, Glennis, what a time, and the table wouldn't hold the food. I was a college student now. I would soon be through. I would be the first of my people! My brother asked me about college. My father asked me. He said: "Let's forget the little past. We have worked together so hard. I'd give you my last cent. You know it. I want to see you get farther in the world than a section man." I forgave. He forgave. I was proud to be his son.

When I finished college I came home and went back to the

cornfields. We were in the weeds. James and I worked by moonlight. Pa was still working on the section. He came in and took the lantern and worked by lantern light and walked through his corn on the rugged new-ground slopes when there was not a moon to light him between the corn rows. We plowed at night. We hoed during the day when we could see the weeds better. Pa said: "College ain't stuck him up a bit. Don't mind dirtying his hands. High school ain't stuck James up a bit. He works right with him. And how they're sweeping them weeds. Soon will have the fields clean as a pin."

It was the last field we were getting out of the first weeds. I drove the horse in—his flanks a white lather, his face and sides wet with sweat. We just lacked two rows having the whole thing done. We ate our supper of cornbread and milk and I said to James: "Are you ready to go back with me and finish that piece of corn?"

"I'm tired as hell," said James, "and I'm not going. If you want it finished, you can do it yourself."

Pa heard what he said and he came round the corner of the smokehouse.

"What is the matter, James?" he asked.

"I'm too tired to finish them two rows of corn. And I am not going to finish them. If you want it done, you can do it yourself. I'm not working day and night. Weeds can choke the corn."

"You will go," said Pa. "I never took words like that from one of my children in my life. I'll show you."

Pa made for the hickory tree to get a limb. He had never before whipped one of us. Mom had done the whipping. James saw Pa go after the whip and he took over the hill down across the pasture.

"Catch him for me," said Pa. "Get him before he runs away from home."

He was making for the Hollow that I slipped along when I ran away from home. I took over the bank, down through the milkweeds, around a beech tree. He was losing ground. I was about to catch him when he caught his toe on a rock and fell. I jumped over him to keep from stepping on his head.

By this time Pa had got there with his hickory limb. "Will you help finish the corn?" Pa asked.

"No," said James, "not a damn stalk will I hoe."

Pa went in on James with the limb. Every time he hit James, James would say: "No, not a damn stalk will I hoe." Pa wore the hickory out on him. It got so short he couldn't use it any more. James took every lick. He never flinched. His clothes were thin. We wore but little clothing in the hot fields. James had worked with me since he was six. He had worked in the fields when other children could go to the river and swim. He was a good worker. Now, he had refused.

We started walking up the hill toward the field. The moon had come into the June sky. The sky was blue as a bird egg. The wind blew through the green apple-tree leaves. We had just plowed the orchard to sow clover.

When we started walking across the plowed dirt silently, James reached down and picked up a last year's cornstalk that had been plowed up. The old roots were clogged with a ball of hard dirt. He swung overhanded with the cornstalk. It caught the top of my head like a maul on a fence post. I went staggering down to the earth.

When I awoke, James and Pa were tired out tussling

around in the plowed ground. It was a hard fight. I believe he'd a whipped Pa if I hadn't been able to hand James a slight left blow on the cheek. It felled him to his knees. I caught Pa and held him back. He was about gone. I hardly knew we were in a fight. I remember James said: "There'll come the time when I'll clean you."

James went to college on borrowed money. He was a thin, freckled-faced boy. "Got my grit," said Pa. At the middle of the year, when he came home, his pant legs were far above his ankles. He had traded off his clothes for bigger clothes. He was thin as a rail and around six feet tall. He was fifteen then. The last half of the year, he learned to smoke tobacco, and was notified not to return to college. He said: "W'y, they tell me that I can't do anything in life. They are a bunch of liars." He wrote an article and criticized the school. It echoed over the country. Students tried to imitate it. James got letters from every state in the Union but one, and from five foreign countries.

He reentered school in a different place—he just packed up and went there. They had heard he had a bad reputation. There was another row. He smoked in the wrong hall. "My father used tobacco all his life. My mother smoked her pipe for forty-four years and then it is harm for me to use the blessed weed."

James was soon back rabbit-hunting in the hills. He had grown now till he touched the tops of two of our doors and slept with his feet well over the end of the bed. He worked on the place. He farmed. He helped Mom. "No more school for me," he would say, "I am wrong or they are wrong."

"The trouble," said Pa who had stopped saying James

took after his people, "is that he had his way out here on this farm too long when I was away. He's nearly a ruint boy. He won't take a education. He's not going to amount to anything."

I'd begun to look him over now. Once he said he was going to put it on me soon as he got big enough. He was tall enough. He had the reach on me. I had more weight. I was a good two hundred pounds and six feet, one-half inch. James must have been a hundred sixty now.

One night the dog and I had been up after a polecat that had killed an old hen and chickens. We caught him by a rock and the dog killed him. When I came in James was sitting by the stove. Bill Hillman was pouring cold water on his head and washing off the blood.

"What's the matter?" I asked.

This woke Pa and he came into the kitchen in his long underwear.

"Jim cleaned Tuck Sneed," said Bill. "He really poured it on him. Left him in the yard cold." I knew that was more than I could do. He was the best man in the neighborhood. James was still mad. He was not talking. He was sitting there in the kitchen under the streams of cold water. It was running down his face on to the kitchen floor. The moonlight was shining through the kitchen window. The whippoorwills hollered from the pines. The wind blew the rag in the broken window. The cat purred at my leg.

"I'm through with guns. I am through with drink. I am through with women for a while," said James. "I'm going back to college. I am going to make good. Who is it that says I can't make good? He's a liar. I have been growing. I have been playing with life in order to get life. I'll meet you in college, sir. I am nineteen now. Good-by."

James came home for vacation. "How are you getting along at college, James?" Mom said. Mom was helping him all she could with cream money and egg and chicken money.

"I am just getting along fine," said James.

"I'll fix the longest bed upstairs for you," said Mom.

I measured James. He now stood six feet, four and one half inches. "I hope and pray that I don't get taller," said James. "It was growing tall that bothered me in school work. I have just read about growing. You can't do any good and grow."

When he was back in college, I wrote him a letter and said, "From the looks of your grades you must be growing again."

He wrote me:

"Send me fifteen dollars. I'll forget all about our trouble. We are brothers, after all. I just decided not to give you that thrashing I have always planned to give you the day I got twenty one.

"Yes, I made a couple of damned D's. There were just 273 students in this school that made them. All hell can't stop me. I'll get a college education. My stomach has been kinda empty on two meals a day. But I'll make it. I intend to pay you every cent I get from you. Don't think you are giving it to me. I don't want it that bad. I am going to pay you every cent I owe you—even that scrape you got me out of."

THANKSGIVING HUNTER

"Hold your rifle like this," Uncle Wash said, changing the position of my rifle. "When I throw this marble into the air, follow it with your bead; at the right time gently squeeze the trigger!"

Uncle Wash threw the marble high into the air and I lined my sights with the tiny moving marble, gently squeezing the trigger, timing the speed of my object until it slowed in the air ready to drop to earth again. Just as it reached its height, my rifle cracked and the marble was broken into tiny pieces.

Uncle Wash was a tall man with a hard leathery face, dark discolored teeth and blue eyes that had a faraway look in them. He hunted the year round; he violated all the hunting laws. He knew every path, creek, river and rock cliff within a radius of ten miles. Since he was a great hunter, he wanted to make a great hunter out of me. And tomorrow, Thanksgiving Day, would be the day for Uncle Wash to take me on my first hunt.

Uncle Wash woke me long before daylight.

"Oil your double-barrel," he said. "Oil it just like I've showed you."

I had to clean the barrels with an oily rag tied to a long string with a knot in the end. I dropped the heavy knot down the barrel and pulled the oily rag through the barrel. I did this many times to each barrel. Then I rubbed a meat-rind over both barrels and shined them with a dry rag. After this was done I polished the gunstock.

"Love the feel of your gun," Uncle Wash had often told me. "There's nothing like the feel of a gun. Know how far it will shoot. Know your gun better than you know your own self; know it and love it."

Before the sun had melted the frost from the multicolored trees and from the fields of stubble and dead grasses, we had cleaned our guns, had eaten our breakfasts and were on our way. Uncle Wash, Dave Pratt and Steve Blevins walked ahead of me along the path and talked about the great hunts they had taken and the game they had killed. And while they talked, words that Uncle Wash had told me about loving the feel of a gun kept going through my head. Maybe it is because Uncle Wash speaks of a gun like it was a living person that he is such a good marksman, I thought.

"This is the dove country," Uncle Wash said soon as we had reached the cattle barn on the west side of our farm. "Doves are feeding here. They nest in these pines and feed around this barn fall and winter. Plenty of wheat grains, rye grains, and timothy seed here for doves."

Uncle Wash is right about the doves, I thought. I had seen them fly in pairs all summer long into the pine grove that covered the knoll east of our barn. I had heard their mournful songs. I had seen them in early April carrying straws in their bills to build their nests; I had seen them flying through the blue spring air after each other; I had seen them in the summer carrying food in their bills for their tiny young. I had heard their young ones crying for more food from the nests among the pines when the winds didn't sough among the pine boughs to drown their sounds. And when the leaves started turning brown I had seen whole flocks of doves, young and old ones, fly down from the tall pines to our barnyard to pick up the wasted grain. I had seen them often and been so close to them that they were no longer afraid of me.

"Doves are fat now," Uncle Wash said to Dave Pratt.

"Doves are wonderful to eat," Dave said.

And then I remembered when I had watched them in the spring and summer, I had never thought about killing and eating them. I had thought of them as birds that lived in the tops of pine trees and that hunted their food from the earth. I remembered their mournful songs that had often made me feel lonely when I worked in the cornfield near the barn. I had thought of them as flying over the deep hollows in pairs in the bright sunlight air chasing each other as they flew toward their nests in pines.

"Now we must get good shooting into this flock of doves," Uncle Wash said to us, "before they get wild. They've not been shot among this season."

Then Uncle Wash, to show his skill in hunting, sent us in different directions so that when the doves flew up from our barn lot, they would have to fly over one of our guns. He gave us orders to close in toward the barn and when the doves saw us, they would take to the air and we would do our shooting.

"And if they get away," Uncle Wash said, "follow them up and talk to them in their own language."

Each of us went his separate way. I walked toward the pine grove, carrying my gun just as Uncle Wash had instructed me. I was ready to start shooting as soon as I heard the flutter of dove wings. I walked over the frosted white grass and the wheat stubble until I came to the fringe of pine woods. And when I walked slowly over the needles of pines that covered the autumn earth, I heard the flutter of many wings and the barking of guns. The doves didn't come my way. I saw many fall from the bright autumn air to the brown crab-grass-colored earth.

I saw these hunters pick up the doves they had killed and cram their limp, lifeless, bleeding bodies with tousled feathers into their brown hunting coats. They picked them up as fast as they could, trying to watch the way the doves went.

"Which way did they go, Wash?" Dave asked soon as he had picked up his kill.

"That way," Uncle Wash pointed to the low hill on the west.

"Let's be after 'em, men," Steve said.

The seasoned hunters hurried after their prey while I stood under a tall pine and kicked the toe of my brogan shoe against the brown pine needles that had carpeted the ground. I saw these men hurry over the hill, cross the ravine and climb the hill over which the doves had flown.

I watched them reach the summit of the hill, stop and call to the doves in tones not unlike the doves' own calling. I saw them with guns poised against the sky. Soon they had disappeared the way the doves had gone.

I sat down on the edge of a lichened rock that emerged from the rugged hill. I laid my double-barrel down beside me, and sunlight fingered through the pine boughs above me in pencil-sized streaks of light. And when one of these shifting pencil-sized streaks of light touched my gun barrels, it shone brightly in the light. My gun was cleaned and oiled and the little pine needles stuck to its meat-rind-greased barrels. Over my head the wind soughed lonely among the pine needles. And from under these pines I could see the vast open fields where the corn stubble stood knee high, where the wheat stubble would have shown plainly had it not been for the great growth of crab grass after we had cut the wheat, crab grass that had been blighted by autumn frost and shone brilliantly brown in the sun.

Even the air was cool to breathe into the lungs; I could feel it deep down when I breathed and it tasted of the green pine boughs that flavored it as it seethed through their thick tops. This was a clean cool autumn earth that both men and birds loved. And as I sat on the lichened rock with pine needles at my feet, with the soughing pine boughs above me, I thought the doves had chosen a fine place to find food, to nest and raise their young. But while I sat looking at the earth about me, I heard the thunder of the seasoned hunters' guns beyond the low ridge. I knew that they had talked to the doves until they had got close enough to shoot again.

As I sat on the rock, listening to the guns in the distance, I thought Uncle Wash might be right after all. It was better to shoot and kill with a gun than to kill with one's hands or with a club. I remembered the time I went over the hill to see how our young corn was growing after we had plowed it the last time. And while I stood looking over the corn whose long ears were in tender blisters, I watched a ground hog come from the edge of the woods, ride down a stalk of corn, and start eating a blister-ear. I found a dead sassafras stick near me, tiptoed quietly behind the ground hog and hit him over the head. I didn't finish him with that lick. It took many licks.

When I left the cornfield, I left the ground hog dead beside his ear of corn. I couldn't forget killing the ground hog over an ear of corn and leaving him dead, his grey-furred clean body to waste on the lonely hill.

I can't disappoint Uncle Wash, I thought. He has trained me to shoot. He says that I will make a great hunter. He wants me to hunt like my father, cousins and uncles. He says that I will be the greatest marksman among them.

I thought about the way my people hunted and how they loved their guns. I thought about how Uncle Wash had taken care of his gun, how he treated it like a living thing and how he told me to love the feel of it. And now my gun lay beside me with pine needles sticking to it. If Uncle Wash were near he would make me pick the gun up, brush away the pine needles and wipe the gun barrels with my handkerchief. If I had lost my handkerchief, as I had seen Uncle Wash often do, he would make me pull out my shirttail to wipe my gun with it. Uncle Wash didn't object to wearing dirty clothes or to wiping his face with a dirty bandanna; he didn't mind living in a dirty house—but never, never would he allow a speck of rust or dirt on his gun.

It was comfortable to sit on the rock since the sun was directly above me. It warmed me with a glow of autumn. I felt the sun's rays against my face and the sun was good to feel. But the good fresh autumn air was no longer cool as the frost that covered the autumn grass that morning, nor could I feel it go deep into my lungs; the autumn air was warmer and it was flavored more with the scent of pines.

Now that the shooting had long been over near our cattle barn, I heard the lazy murmur of the woodcock in the pine woods near by. Uncle Wash said woodcocks were game birds and he killed them wherever he found them. Once I thought I would follow the sound and kill the woodcock. I picked up my gun but laid it aside again. I wanted to kill something to show Uncle Wash. I didn't want him to be disappointed in me.

Instead of trying to find a rabbit sitting behind a broomsedge cluster or in a briar thicket as Uncle Wash had trained me to do, I felt relaxed and lazy in the autumn sun that had now penetrated the pine boughs from directly overhead. I looked over the brown vast autumn earth about me where I had worked when everything was green and growing, where birds sang in the spring air as they built their nests. I looked at the tops of barren trees and thought how a few months ago they were waving clouds of green. And now it was a sad world, a dying world. There was so much death in the world that I had known: flowers were dead, leaves were dead, and the frosted grass was lifeless in the wind. Everything was dead and dying but a few wild birds and rabbits. I had almost grown to the rock where I sat but I didn't want to stir. I wanted to glimpse the life about me before it all was covered with winter snows. I hated to think of killing in this autumn world. When I picked up my gun, I didn't feel life in it; I felt death.

I didn't hear the old hunters' guns now but I knew that, wherever they were, they were hunting for something to shoot. I thought they would return to the barn if the doves came back, as they surely would, for the pine grove where I sat was one place in this autumn world that was a home to the doves. And while I sat on the rock, I thought I would practice the dove whistle that Uncle Wash had taught me. I thought a dove would come close and I would shoot the dove so that I could go home with something in my hunting coat.

As I sat whistling a dove call, I heard the distant thunder of their guns beyond the low ridge. Then I knew they were coming back toward the cattle barn.

And, as I sat whistling my dove calls, I heard a dove answer me. I called gently to the dove. Again it answered. This time it was closer to me. I picked up my gun from the rock and gently brushed the pine needles from its stock and barrels. And as I did this, I called pensively to the dove and it answered plaintively.

I aimed my gun soon as I saw the dove walking toward me. When it walked toward my gun so unafraid, I thought it was a pet dove. I lowered my gun; laid it across my lap. Never had a dove come this close to me. When I called again, it answered at my feet. Then it fanned its wings and flew upon the rock beside me trying to reach the sound of my voice. It called, but I didn't answer. I looked at the dove when it turned its head to one side to try to see me. Its eye was gone, with the mark of a shot across its face. Then it turned the other side of its head toward me to try to see. The other eye was gone.

As I looked at the dove the shooting grew louder; the old hunters were getting closer. I heard the fanning of dove wings above the pines. And I heard doves batting their wings against the pine boughs. And the dove beside me called to them. It knew the sounds of their wings. Maybe it knows each dove by the sound of his wings, I thought. And then the dove spoke beside me. I was afraid to answer. I could have reached out my hand and picked this dove up from the rock. Though it was blind, I couldn't kill it, and yet I knew it would have a hard time to live.

When the dove beside me called again, I heard an answer from a pine bough near by. The dove beside me spoke and the dove in the pine bough answered. Soon they were talking to each other as the guns grew louder. Suddenly, the blind dove fluttered through the treetops, chirruping its plaintive melancholy notes, toward the sound of its mate's voice. I heard its wings batting the wind-shaken pine boughs as it ascended, struggling, toward the beckoning voice.

"We're different people," says Pa.

THE STORM

"I can't stand it any longer, Mick," Mom says. "I'm leaving you. I'm going home to Pap. I'll have a rooftree above my head there. Pap will take me in. He'll give me and my children the best he has."

Mom lifts the washrag from the washpan of soapy water. She washes my neck and ears. Mom pushes the warm soft rag against my ears. Drops of warm water ooze down my neck to my shirt collar. Mom's lips are drawn tight. Her long fingers grip the washrag like a chicken's toes clutch a roost-limb on a winter night.

"We're different people," says Pa. "I'm sorry about it all, Sal. If I say things that hurt you, I can't help it."

"That's just it," Mom says as she dips the washrag into the pan and squeezes the soapy water between her long brown fingers. "Since we can't get along together, it's better we part now. It's better we part before we have too many children."

Mom has Herbert ready. He is dressed in a white dress. He is lying on the bed playing with a pretty. Mom gave him the pretty to keep him quiet while she dressed me. It is a threadspool that Pa whittled in two and put a stick through for me to spin like a top. I look at the pretty Herbert holds in his hands. Herbert looks at it with bright little eyes and laughs.

"Mom, he has the pretty Pa made for me," I say. "I don't want him to have it."

"Quit fussing with your baby brother," Mom says as she puts my hand into the washpan and begins to scrub it.

"Pa made it for me," I say, "and I want to take it with me. I want to keep it."

Pa looks at the top Herbert has clutched in his young mousepaw-colored fingers. Pa moves in his chair. He crosses one leg above the other. He pulls hard on his pipe. He blows tiny clouds of smoke into the room.

"You're not going to take all the children and leave me alone!" he says.

"They are mine," says Mom, "and I intend to have all three of them or fight everybody in this hollow. They are of my flesh and blood and I gave them birth, as you well remember, and I'm going to hold them." Mom looks hard at Pa as she speaks these words.

"I thought if you'd let Sis stay," says Pa, "she'd soon be old enough to cook for me. If it's anything I hate, it's cooking. I can't cook much. I'll have a time eating the food I cook."

"Serves you right, Mick," says Mom.

"It doesn't serve me right," says Pa. "I intend to stay right here and see that this farm goes on. And if I'm not fooled an awful lot, you'll be back, Sal."

"That's what you think," Mom storms. "I'm not coming back. I do not want to ever see this shack again."

"It's the best roof I can put over your head," Pa says.

"It's not the roof that's over my head," Mom says. "Mick, it's you. You can be laughing one minute and the next minute you can be raising the roof with your vile oaths. Your mind is more changeable than the weather. I never know how to take you, no more than I know how the wind will blow tomorrow."

"We just aren't the same people," Pa says. "That's why I love you, Sal. You're not like I am. You are solid as a mountain. I need you, Sal. I need you more than anyone I know in this world."

"I'm leaving," Mom says. "I'm tired of this. I've been ready to go twice before. I felt sorry for you and my little children that would be raised without a father. This is the third time I've planned to go. Third time is the charm. I'm going this time."

"I'm ready, Mom," says Sis as she climbs down the ladder from the loft. "I'm ready to go to Grandpa's with you."

Sis is dressed in a blue gingham dress. Her ripe-wheat-colored hair falls over her shoulders in two plaits. A blue ribbon is tied on each plait and beneath the ribbons her hair is not plaited. Her hair is bushy as two cottontails.

Pa cranes his autumn-brown neck. He looks at Sis and blows a cloud of smoke slowly from his mouth. Pa's face is brown as a pawpaw leaf in September. His face has caught the spring sunshine as he plowed our mules around the mountain slope.

"Listen," says Pa, "I hear something like April thunder!"

Pa holds his pipe in his hand. He sits silently. He does not speak. Mom squeezes the washrag in the water again. Now she listens.

"I don't hear anything," says Mom. "You just imagined you heard something."

"No, I didn't," Pa answers.

"It can't be thunder, Mick," says Mom. "The sky is blue as the water in the well."

Pa rises from his chair. He walks to the door. He cranes his brown neck like a hen that says "qrrr" when she thinks a hawk is near to swoop down upon her biddies.

"The rains come over the mountain that's to our right," Pa says. "That's the way the rains come, all right. I've seen them come too many times. But the sky is clear—all but a mare-tail in the sky. That's a good sign there'll be rain in three days."

"Rain three days away won't matter much to us," says Mom. "We just have seven miles to walk. We'll be at Pap's place in three hours."

"Listen—it's thunder I hear," Pa says loudly. "I didn't think my ears fooled me a while ago. I can always hear the fox-hounds barking in the deep hollows before Kim and Gaylord can. Can't beat my ears for hearing."

"I don't hear it," says Mom as she takes the pan of water across the dog-trot toward the kitchen.

"You will hear it in a few minutes," says Pa. "It's like potato wagons rolling across the far skies."

"Third time is the charm for me," says Mom as she returns from the kitchen without the washpan. "Ever since I can remember, the third time has been the charm for me. I can remember once setting a hen on guinea eggs. A blacksnake that you kept in the corncrib crawled through a crack to my hen's nest. He crawled under the hen and swallowed the eggs. He was so full of eggs that when he tried to crawl out of the nest he fell to the ground. I saw him fall with his sides bulged in and out like wild frostbitten snowballs. I took a hoe and clipped his head. Then I set my hen on goose eggs and soon as they hatched my old hen pinched their necks with her bill like you'd do with a pair of scissors. I set her on her own kind of eggs—and she hatched every one of the eggs and raised all her biddies. Third time was the charm."

"See the martins hurrying to their boxes," says Pa. "Look out there, Sal! That's the sign of an approaching storm."

The martins fly in circles above our fresh-plowed garden. They cut the bright April air with black fan-shaped wings. They chatter as they fly—circle once and twice around the boxes and alight on the little porches before the twelve doors cut in each of the two big boxes. Martins chatter as they poke their heads in at the doors—draw them out once and chatter again—then silently slip their black-preening feathered bodies in at the small doors.

Mom looks at the long sagging martin boxes—each pole supported by a corner garden post. Mom watches the martins hurrying to the boxes. She listens to their endless chatter to each other and their quarreling from one box of martins in the other box.

"Listen, Sal—listen—"

"It's thunder, Mick! I hear it."

"Will we go, Mom?" Sis asks.

"Yes, we'll go before the storm."

"But it's coming fast, Sal, or the martins wouldn't be coming home to their nests of young ones like they are. Are you going to take our children out in a storm? Don't you know as much as the martin birds?"

I know what Mom is thinking about when she looks at the martin boxes. She remembers the day when Pa made the boxes at the barn. She held the boards while he sawed them with a handsaw. She remembers when he cut the long chestnut poles and peeled them and slid them over the cliffs above the house. They slid to the foot of the mountain like racer snakes before a new-ground fire. She held the boxes when Pa nailed them to the poles. Mom helped him lift the poles into the deep post holes and Mom helped him wrap the baled-hay wire around the poles and the corner garden posts to hold them steady when the winds blew. I'd just got rid of my dresses then and started wearing rompers.

Mom turns from the front door. She does not speak to Pa. She walks to the dresser in the corner of the room. She opens a dresser drawer. She lifts clothes from the dresser drawer. She stacks them neatly on the bottom of a hickory split-bottomed chair. She looks at the chair as she stacks the clothes there.

"I know what Mom is thinking," I think, as she looks at the chair. "She remembers when she grumbled about the bad bottoms in the chairs and Pa says: 'Wait till spring, Sal—wait until the sap gets up in the hickories until I can skin their bark. I'll fix the chair bottoms.'"

And when the sap got up that early spring in the hickories, Pa took a day off from plowing and peeled hickory bark and scraped the green from the rough side of the bark and laced bottoms across the chairs. I know Mom remembers this, for she helped Pa. I held the soft green, tough slats of bark for them and reached them a piece of bark as they needed it.

Pa fills his pipe with bright burley crumbs that he fingers from his hip overall pocket with his rough gnarled hand. His index finger shakes as he tamps the tobacco crumbs into his pipe bowl. Pa takes a match from his hat band and strikes it on his overall leg and lights his pipe. I never saw Pa smoke this much before at one time. I never saw him blow such clouds of smoke from his mouth.

"The sun has gone from the sky, Sal," Pa says. His face beams as he speaks. "See, the air is stilly blue and yonder is a black cloud racing over the sky faster than a hound dog runs a fox."

Mom does not listen. She lifts clothes from the dresser drawer. She closes the empty dresser drawers. Mom never opens the top dresser drawer. That is where Mom puts Pa's clothes.

"Bring me the basket, Shan," Mom says.

I take the big willow basket off the sewing-machine top where Mom keeps it for an egg basket. When I gather eggs, I put them in this basket.

"Where will Pa put the eggs, Mom?" I ask.

"Never mind that, Shan," she says. "We'll let him find a place to put the eggs."

Mom stacks our washed and ironed clothes neatly into this big willow basket. I see her looking at this basket. I remember when Mom told me how long it took Pa to make this basket. It was when Sis was the baby. Every Saturday Mom and Pa went to town and took this willow basket filled with eggs and traded the eggs at the stores for salt, sugar, coffee, dry goods, thread, and other things we needed.

"Listen to the rain, Sal," Pa says. "Hear it hitting the clapboards!"

Big waves of rain driven by puffs of wind sweep across

our garden. We can barely hear the martins chattering in their boxes now. Their chattering sounds like they are hovering their young birds and talking to them about the storm.

Mom has our clothes in the big willow basket. She has Herbert's dresses on top of the basket. Herbert is asleep now. He does not hear the big rain drops thumping the dry-sounding clapboard roof. It sounds like you'd thump with your knuckles on the bottom of a washtub.

Mom walks to the door. She looks at the clothesline Pa made from baled-hay wire. He carefully put the pieces of wire together so that they wouldn't hook holes in the clothes Mom hung to dry. Mom watches the water run along the line and beads of water drop into the mouths of the fresh spring growing grasses. The clothesline is tied to a plum-tree limb on one end and a white-oak limb on the other. There is a forked sourwood bush that Pa cut and peeled for a clothesline prop between the plum tree and the white oak. It is to brace the clothesline when Mom has it loaded with the wet clothes.

The rain pours from the drainpipe in a big sluice into the water barrel Mom keeps at the corner of the house. "You won't wash my hair in rain water any more," says Sis. "Will hard water keep my hair from being curly, Mom?"

"I don't know," says Mom.

"You used to say hard water would hurt my hair," Sis says.

"I don't care whether Mom washes my hair in hard water or not," I say. "I'd as soon have it washed in well water as in water from the rain barrel."

Mom walks from the front room to the dogtrot. She looks at the rock cliffs over on the mountainside. I know Mom remembers holding the lantern for Pa on dark winter nights when the ewes were lambing in these cliffs and they had to bring the baby lambs before the big log fire in the house and warm them.

Mom looks at the snow-white patches of bloodroot blooming around these cliffs. She sees the pink sweet Williams growing by the old logs and rotted stumps on the bluffs. Mom is thinking as she looks at these. I know what she is thinking. "Mick has picked bloodroot blossoms and sweet Williams for me many evenings with his big rough hands after he'd plowed the mules day long around the mountain slopes. Yes, Mick, bad as he is to cuss, loves a wild flower."

Mom walks from the dogtrot into the big kitchen.

"Aren't we going to Grandpa's, Mom?" I ask as I follow Mom.

"Bad as it is raining," Mom answers, "you know we're not going."

"If we go, Mom, who'll cook for Pa?"

Mom does not answer. She looks at the clapboard box Pa made for her and filled with black loam he gathered under the big beech trees in the hollow back of the house. Pa fixed this for a nasturtium seed-box for Mom. Pa put it in the kitchen window where it would catch the early morning sun.

"I have my little basket filled with my dollie's dresses," Sis says as she comes running across the dogtrot to Mom. "I'm ready too, Mom. I'm not going to leave my doll. There won't be anybody left to play with her. You know Pa won't play with her. Pa won't have time. Pa plays with the mules and pets them and calls them his dolls."

"Yes," Mom says, your Pa—"

The sky is low. The rain falls in steady streams. The thin tender oak leaves, the yard grass, the bloodroot, sweet Williams, and the plum-tree leaves drink in the rain. They look clean-washed as Mom washed my face, hands, neck and ears.

"God must have turned his water bucket over so we couldn't get to Grandpa's, Mom," I say.

It never rained like this before. It's raining so hard now we cannot see the rock cliffs. We cannot see the plum tree and the clothesline wire. We cannot see the martin-box poles at the corners of the garden.

"It's a cyclone, Sal," says Pa as he walks across the dogtrot into the kitchen. "I told you a while ago when I saw the martins making it for their boxes a storm was coming. Now you see how much sense a bird has!"

"Yes, Mick, I see—"

"What if you had taken little Herbert out on the long road to your pap's place—a tree with leaves as thin as they are this time of spring wouldn't have made much of a shelter and there aren't any rock-cliff shelters close along that lonesome road."

Mom looks at the dim blur of wood-ash barrel that Pa put under the big white-oak tree where Mom washes our clothes. Pa carries the wood ashes from the kitchen stove and the fireplace and puts them in this barrel for Mom. She makes lyesoap from these wood ashes.

"Don't talk about the road," says Mom.

"Where is my pretty, Pa?" I ask.

"Herbert is asleep with it in his hand," Pa answers.

"When we go to Grandpa's I'm going to take it with me. Pa made it and I intend to keep it."

Damp cool air from the rain sweeps across the dogtrot.

"The rain has chilled that air so," says Pa, "a person needs a coat."

Through the rain-washed windowpane, Mom sees the little bench Pa made. Mom and Pa would sit on this little bench at the end of the grape-arbor and string beans, peel potatoes, and shuck roasting-ears. They sit here on the long summer evenings when the katydids sing in the garden bean rows and the crickets chirrup in the yard grasses. Pa smokes his pipe and Mom smokes her pipe and we play about them. We hear the whippoorwills singing from mountain top to mountain top and we hear the martins chattering to one another in their boxes. We see the lightning bugs lighting their way in the summer-evening dusk above the potato rows and we hear the beetles singing sadly in the dewy evening grass.

"The sun, Mom," I say. "Look, we can go now."

Pa looks at the red ball of sun hanging brightly in the blue April sky above the mountain. It is like a red oak ball hanging from an oak limb by a tiny stem among the green oak leaves. A shadow falls over Pa's brown, weather-beaten face.

"The third time," says Mom, "that I've got ready to go something has happened every time. I'm not going."

"Aren't we going to Grandpa's, Mom?" Sis asks.

"No, we're not going."

"What will I do with my basket of doll clothes?"

"Put them back where you got them."

Pa puts his pipe back in his pocket. His face doesn't have a shadow over it now. Pa looks happy. There is a smile on his September pawpaw-leaf-colored face.

"Come, Sal," says Pa. "Let's see if our sweet potatoes have sprouted yet."

Mom and Pa walk from the kitchen to the dogtrot. They walk up the bank where Pa has his sweet-potato bed. Pa has his arm around Mom. They walk over the clean-washed yard grass as green and pretty as if God had made it over new.

"I think the potatoes have sprouted," I hear Pa say.

Sis starts upstairs with her basket of doll clothes and her doll. I go into the front room to see if Herbert has my top in his hand. It is my top. Pa made it for me.

I Remember Mollie

"It happened here, Shan," Uncle Uglybird Skinner said as we put our baskets down on the buff-colored October pasture grass under a persimmon tree.

Uncle Uglybird used his sourwood cane to push away the dead grass from a corner stone; then he moved slowly along hunting for more stones. "Well as I can remember," Uncle Uglybird said, turning toward me, "here is where the door was. Here's where I come that mornin'. I walked right up the path, all kivered over now by pasture grass, that use to come right up the pint. I thought somethin' was wrong that mornin' since Finnis hadn't come to cradle wheat."

Uncle Uglybird put his big wrinkled hand in his pocket. He pulled out a twist of home-grown burley and started gumming a chew. With the other hand, he held to his cane. He had been a mountain of a man, but now time had got the best of him. His face was wrinkled like a withered shoemake leaf; his hair was white as milkweed furze bursting from the pods in late September. His nail-keg stomach and his broad shoulders and fence-post arms were a load for his soft-muscled legs to carry up the steep bluff to the persimmon grove.

"And I found Finnis right about here," he said, pointing with his cane. "I pushed the door open, stuck my head in like I'd allus done. And right there is where he lay on the floor beside Mollie. She had her head on his arm. I'll never forget how poor Mollie was moanin' and carryin' on."

"What's the matter with Mollie, Finnis?" I ast.

"Wish you'd quit goin' around and pokin' your head in other people's affairs," he said to me. "If you don't you're liable to get your head shot off, Uglybird! Don't you know my wife is awful sick?"

"Hadn't heard a thing about it," I said, 'I'll go get Doc Saddler soon as I can."

"No you won't," he said. "She'll be all right. You get away from here."

"I thought it wasn't Finnis Jason's nature to act like that as I walked down the path. He couldn't be jealous of me now since Mollie had married him instead of me. I was too ugly to get Mollie. That's why I never married; that's why people called me Uglybird."

As Uncle Uglybird talked, I picked up the first frost-riped persimmons and put them in my basket. The late October wind rustled the few bright-colored persimmon leaves on the persimmon boughs.

"That was forty-three years ago," Uncle Uglybird said. "I was a powerful man in them days. No one could beat me usin' a cradle. It was on Saturday. I cut wheat all day by myself. And every time I'd swing my cradle, I thought about Mollie and Finnis. I'd heard about Finnis bein' in love with Ensor Pennington's wife. But I couldn't believe it. Ensor's wife, Mattie, had a nest of ten youngin's, mean as young copperheads. By noon when I went home to dinner, I thought, maybe, there might be somethin' to it."

Uncle Uglybird sat his basket down. He leaned against

108

the rough bark of the persimmon tree, held his cane in one hand, with the other hand he gestured as he talked. "Right there is the place that I saw all this," he said, pointing with his cane. "It's your cow pasture now but there was once a house here. There was once life here. Things happened here. But you'd never know it now for time and the seasons hide old scars. The grass kivers them in the spring."

"Well, what did happen?" I asked.

"Just goin' to tell you, young man," he said as he spit ambeer on the pasture grass where the bright persimmons covered the ground, "that I worked all day in the wheat field. It was just about quittin' time when Flem Spry rode out the ridge just about where your terbacker barn stands now. He was norratin' Mollie Jason's death. He was tellin' all the wood choppers' families that Mollie Jason was dead. Flem was ridin' a little mule and his long legs nearly dragged the ground. He told me there would be a wake.

"You know when all the wood choppers, their wives and oldest youngins crowded that night into the double-log cabin that stood there, I was among 'em," Uncle Uglybird continued. "The house was full and part of us stood out in the yard. Ensor and Mattie Pennington stood in the corner of the house, right about here," he pointed with his cane. "Mattie just took on somethin' awful about Mollie's death. Tears run down the black beard on Finnis' face. He carried on somethin' awful, to hisself. All their youngins screamed. I thought all the cryin' Finnis and Mattie were doin' was put-on. But it was a sad thing—Mollie there nailed up in her oak-board coffin so none of us could see her. There was so much weepin' goin' on that I got outten the house. I walked right down there by that rock-cliff. I sat down on that spur of rock that you see stickin' out there."

"Is that the place where you sat?" I asked, pointing at the rock where we salt our cattle.

"That's right," Uncle Uglybird said.

"And over there where the oak trees now stand, is where you had the wheat?" I asked.

"Right," he answered, then he started to talk again. "I wondered about who'd made that coffin," he said. "I got more suspicy when I thought about it. He had already had it made—or he'd made it in a hurry. Then I wondered about who had dressed her—if Finnis had done it hisself, or if the neighbor wimmen had. And it was a funny thing that he would have her nailed down hard and fast so no one could see Mollie.

"As we went home, Pap told me Finnis told 'im to tell me to take charge of diggin' the grave the next mornin' at Plum Grove. Said Finnis he'd have me a quart of good moonshine bright and early. That's what we allus got in them days when we dug a grave. I thought he's bein' mighty good to me fer he felt like I knew a lot and that I might talk. But I'd be there; and I'd see that her grave was dug. Mollie was purty as they come when she was a young woman. But her beauty faded soon after she married Finnis. Soon after she started bearin' his youngins, workin' in the fields with a hoe right before a youngin' come—goin' to the woods and choppin' wood. Poor Mollie had a hard life that took the beauty from her face."

Uncle Uglybird spat another bright sluice of ambeer and wiped his stained lips with his big blue bandanna.

"I drinked that quart of moonshine, young man," he said, "while I trimmed the shale-rock and blue-slate with a sharp coal pick so Mollie's grave would be smooth. I had it done by noon. By one o'clock the funeral procession was there. Flem Spry hauled Mollie to Plum Grove with his little mules that strained to pull the big jolt-wagon with that heavy oak-board coffin and Mollie in it. Flem sat upon the coffin and rode over the chugholes. There was a whole army of weepin' people followin' the wagon. It was a sight to see them. They'd been splashed with mud from the chugholes and they were two hours late."

"Atter the funeral was over, I bought a quart of moon-shine," Uncle Uglybird said. "Moonshine made me feel wonderful back in them days. I took a nigh cut through the hill paths home to keep away from the funeral crowd. Before I started home I saw Flem Spry load Finnis and Mollie's little weepin' youngins on the wagon. I saw Ensor and Mattie Pennington get on the wagon and Mattie was talkin' honeysweet words to Mollie's little youngins to hush their cryin'. That made me feel more than ever about the whole affair. I guess I's the only one that felt this way about it."

"Atter I got home and et my supper," Uncle Uglybird said, "I put a little more moonshine down my gullet. I lit out. Pap ast me where I's goin'. I told 'im I didn't know. And I didn't know. I thought there was work to be done. And there was work to be done. I went up the holler, crossed the creek, struck out up this pint and come to this house. I knocked on the door of this house. Tim Jason, Finnis' oldest boy, come to the door. I ast 'im if Finnis was at home. He said that his Pa had been gone about an hour. I ast 'im the way he went. Said he went down the pint the way I'd come. I hurried back down the pint, crossed the gap, went up the other pint toward the top of the hill where Ensor lived. What do you think I found before I got there?"

"I don't know," I said.

"I heard a whisperin' in the brush," he said. "I slipped through the brush toward the sound. It was Finnis sittin' on a log beside Mattie Pennington with his arm around her. How Mattie'd got away from Ensor and the youngins I don't know. But it was over yander on that pint about where that tall pine stands. They were kissin' and sayin' sweet words to one another. I never heard sicha lovin' in my life. And to think how they'd wept at the funeral. I laid flat on my stummick and watched 'em until they parted. Mattie ran through the brush toward her shack; Finnis hurried down the path toward the gap. I was so close to Finnis, if I had been a copperhead I could've bit 'im. And that's just it. I was a copperhead."

"Let me tell you, Shan," Uncle Uglybird said, as the bright ambeer spittle flew from his mouth, "I never got so mad in all my life. I thought of all their weepin' at the wake and at the funeral. Then to think I'd find 'em out spoonin' in the moonlight before Mollie was cold under the Plum Grove clay. Mollie's poor youngins right here in this house by themselves. I went home and went to bed. I kept all that I'd seen to myself. I wondered if Finnis would be in the wheat field with me Monday mornin'."

"I didn't eat a bite of breakfast. The moonshine had died in me. I was in bad shape. Ma knew what was the matter with me. She thought I's takin' it hard over Mollie's death. She made me a biler of hot coffee. I took it to the wheat field with me. Finnis was there. He was talkin' a lot just like nothin' had ever happened. He never mentioned Mollie to me. Didn't say a word about how insultin' he was when I stuck my head in at his door and found him there beside Mollie when she was sufferin' death. Guess he'd forgotten all of this. But I hadn't."

"Goin' to put you in the shade today, Uglybird," he said to me. "Any man that drinks licker can't come to the wheat field and expect to keep his swath cradled beside the champion cradler."

"We'll see about that, Finnis," I said. "I drinked two quarts yesterday but that don't make no difference. I don't feel too good now but it takes a better man than you to put me in the shade."

Uncle Uglybird looked at the few persimmons in the bottom of his basket. He leaned over and started picking up persimmons. As he picked up persimmons, chewed his home-grown burley twist, he told his story fast as the words would come from his thin, wrinkled lips.

"Finnis took the lead swath with his cradle," Uncle Uglybird said. "I followed 'im right around that hill over there where the big oaks stand now. About every thirty minutes I'd go to my jug and get me a swig of strong coffee. Finnis thought I was still drinkin' moonshine. Finnis led in the first swath. When we had cut all the way around the field, Finnis was wet as sweat could make 'im. His wet clothes stuck to his body. I was dry as a chip in the sunlight. Before we started the second swath, I went to my jug to get more coffee. It made me feel better. Finnis didn't lead me ten yards like he did in the first round. He didn't lead me more than ten feet."

"As the bundles of wheat rolled from the fingers of our cradles, I said to 'im, 'Finnis, I guess your house was purty lonesome last night without Mollie.' 'Yep, it was awful lonesome, Uglybird,' he said. 'It was awful hard fer me to stay there with my youngins last night. I felt like cryin' all night.' Then I didn't say anythin' fer a while. I thought what an awful liar he was. Then I said, 'It was too bad Mollie had to die and leave her youngins.' 'Yep, it was,' he said. 'What kilt 'er, Finnis?' I ast 'im. He stopped cradlin' and looked funny at me. 'I don't know, Uglybird,' he said. 'She took somethin' like the collarmoggis and it took her outten this world like a flash of lightnin.'"

"By the time we had finished round number two, Finnis was gettin a little nervous," Uncle Uglybird whispered as he stood up and stretched his arms above his basket. "I was nippin' at his heels with my cradle. When we started another round, I went to my jug and got more coffee. I'll tell you I was crowdin' old Finnis as he cradled over that pint yander. 'Who made Mollie's coffin, Finnis?' I ast 'im. 'The Potter boys,' he said. 'Made it in a hurry, didn't they?' I ast 'im."

"Finnis' lips trembled until he could hardly speak. 'But they had the lumber,' he stuttered. 'The seasoned oak lumber that they were goin' to put into a barn this fall.' 'Who laid 'er out fer burial, Finnis?' I ast. 'None of your damned business, Uglybird,' he bellered at me. 'You're too damned nosy. You go around and put your long red nose into everybody's business.' 'I didn't know that it would've made you mad,' I said, 'er I wouldn't've ast you. I thought the coffin was made in a hurry. And I wondered who dressed 'er fer burial. And to tell you the truth, Finnis,' I said, 'I wonder why you spiked

114

that coffin lid down and never let Mollie's friends and your own youngins look at her.' 'Uglybird, you're a purty good fellar but you drink too much,' Finnis said. 'You're might nigh drunk again this mornin'.' 'Yep, nearly drunk on coffee,' I said. 'I've got coffee in that jug.'"

"We made eight rounds before noon," Uncle Uglybird said. "I drinked coffee and I bore down on my cradle handle with all the elbow grease there was in my muscled arms. In the seventh round I had to take the lead. Old Finnis was about pooped out. When the sun was high enough fer us to step on the heads of our shadder, Finnis said, 'Uglybird, I feel sick at my stummick. Got too hot this mornin' and drinked too much water. I won't be back this afternoon until it starts gettin' cool. Then I'll be back to work with you.' 'All right,' I said. 'I'll go on and cradle this wheat before it loses the grain.'"

"Soon as Finnis had crossed the pint fer home, I turned back toward Greenupsburg. I don't know what made me do it. I got to thinkin'. I thought that it was funny that he was goin' to take part of the afternoon off. And the way he climbed the pint he wasn't sick at his stummick either. I was lucky findin' Sheriff Blevins in Greenupsburg. I told 'im the whole story. Guess it took me an hour to tell it. 'We'll see what he's done to his wife,' Sheriff Blevins said. 'You go back to the wheat field and be workin' as if nothin' had ever happened.' I hurried back to the ridge—didn't eat a bite of dinner. I finished drinkin' my coffee. About four o'clock Finnis come back to the wheat field. I could see there was a big bulge under his overalls on the hip. He's brought his pistol here to kill me, I thought. I'm the man he thinks that's goin' to talk. If I can just keep peace with 'im until Sheriff Blevins and his men get here."

"Finnis ast me how I'd like to die and have my coffin lid spiked down," Uncle Uglybird said. "He told me I'd make a purty corpse. Ast me if I thought anybody would weep over me. I worked and prayed under my breath fer Sheriff Blevins to hurry. Finnis was tryin' every way in the world he could to start a fuss with me so he could plug me."

"I was a happy man," Uncle Uglybird said with a sigh of relief just as if he were goin' through it all over again, "when Sheriff Blevins and a posse of six men walked over the ridge. Soon as Finnis saw 'em he didn't waste any time, throwin' his cradle on the ground, runnin' over the hill, pullin' his pistol from his holster as he run. He put the long barrel over his shoulder and started shootin'. Sheriff Blevins told his men to fire. The wheat straws shook all around Finnis as he run over a high bank. He made fer the beech grove. Sheriff Blevins saw Finnis crawl into a hollow beech. His men surrounded the tree and began to put hot lead into its thin hulk. They shot until their guns got hot. One man lost a finger, another was shot through the foot. Finnis shot from a knothole. Finnis had brought plenty of cartridges to kill me but not enough to fight seven men. He tied a handkerchief on his pistol barrel and waved it from the knothole fer peace. They brought Finnis from the tree and took him to the Greenupsburg jail."

In the beech grove below us, Uncle Uglybird pointed with his cane to a limbless hulk that had once been a giant tree; it had been colored by the wind, sun and rain to wasp-nest gray and it trembled in each gust of autumn wind.

"That's the tree they took Finnis from," Uncle Uglybird said. "It's as old fer a tree as I am fer a man." And then he

Sheriff Blevins and a posse of six men walked over the ridge.

said, as he lowered his cane to the ground to support himself, "I wouldn't help take Mollie from her grave fer Doc Saddler to examine. I wanted to remember Mollie just like she was when I walked the ridge roads with 'er on Sundays when we were young. I wanted to remember the braids of crow-wing black hair down her back with red ribbons on 'em. I wanted to remember her pretty lips and her white teeth and the way she used to laugh."

"But did Finnis kill Mollie?" I asked.

"Doc Saddler found enough pizen in 'er to kill twenty people," Uncle Uglybird said.

"What did they do with Finnis?" I asked. "Give 'im life?"

"Atter Sheriff Blevins put 'im in Greenupsburg jail," Uncle Uglybird continued, "Finnis laughed and said, 'This wooden jail won't hold me.' Finnis broke jail but I guess he wished he'd a-stayed in. He walked right into the arms of a Plum Grove mob that had the jail surrounded. They'd come for Finnis soon as they'd heard he'd pizened Mollie. They took 'im to the hang-tree and swung 'im up and left 'im kickin'."

Uncle Uglybird spat his quid of chewed burley onto the carpet of powder-dry persimmon leaves. We picked up our baskets of copper-colored persimmons and started down the path.

"I didn't know that happened here," I said.

"Grass, sprouts and briars will hide old scars," Uncle Uglybird said. "Lips of the hills and trees and wind can't speak their secrets. They hold them forever. They never get to the courtroom."

FITIFIED MAN

"Sun is hot as blazes," says Pa. "I hate to stir on a day hot as this. I'll haf to be on my way."

"Where are you goin', Pa?" I asked.

"We've got a neighbor in distress."

Pa stands in the front yard and squints his blue eyes at the sun. He takes his bandanna from his hip pocket. He wipes the sweat from his red face. He puts the red bandanna back in his hip pocket. A slow July wind rustles the wilted leaves on the poplar tree in our front yard.

"Who is the neighbor in distress, Pa?" I asked.

"Haven't you heard about Jake Hunt?"

"No," I says.

"I can't believe it," says Pa. "I think I'll mosey over the hill and see if it's the truth."

"What's the matter with Jake?"

"Son, this isn't to be norrated over the whole district," Pa whispers, "but Gus Martin told me that Jake's a fitified man. Said he was out with 'em fox huntin' the other night and Jake tried to stand on his head. Said he tried to climb trees. Said he cut all sorts of fool shines. Said Jake wasn't drunk. I've lived by Jake Hunt all my life. I know he isn't a man to hanker after licker. I know Jake isn't off in the head. I went to school with 'im. Jake is a deep man. I can't understand. Do you want to go over with me to Jake's?"

"I'd like to go over to Jake's with you." Pa walks down the path in front of me. He pulls a bright burley leaf from his pocket. He crumbles a handful in his hand. He puts it in his mouth. He holds the quid of bright burley leaf behind his suntanned jaw. I fill my pipe with bright burley crumbs. I tamp the tobacco in my pipe with my index finger. I strike a match on my pant leg and light my pipe. I follow Pa down the yellow clay bank. We walk down the hollow to the Collins Hill. We walk up the hill under the dead chestnut trees, past the old coal mines and through the Collins apple orchard.

"Whooie," says Pa, as we reach the top of the Collins Hill, "I'm about winded. These old legs ain't good as they ust to be. But when it comes to a neighbor in distress, I've allus got to go." Pa pulls his red bandanna from his hip pocket and wipes the white streams of sweat from his beet-red face. He wrings the sweat from his red bandanna. He carries it in his hand for the sun to dry. I sling sweat from my forehead with my index finger. It leaves a little wet line across the dusty path.

"We'll soon be on Jake's place," says Pa. "Son, I just want you to look at Jake's farm. He's got the finest farm among the Plum Grove hills. If Jake is a fitified man, it would pay a lot more men at Plum Grove to be fitified. Jake Hunt is a good farmer and a good man. I can't believe all this I hear about Jake. We'll soon be at Jake's house. You be careful what you say. You let me do most of the talkin' until we see if it's the truth."

"All right, Pa."

Pa turns down the hill under the persimmon trees. I follow him down the little narrow path that is walled on each side by masses of wilted green-briar leaves, persimmon sprouts, and wilted sedge grass. The sweat streams from Pa's face. His brogan shoes kick up little clouds of dust along the path. Pa turns his head first right and then left. He spits bright ambeer on the wilted weeds.

"It's even too hot for a bird to fly," says Pa. "They are in the shade on a day like this takin' it easy. Guess we'll find Jake under the apple shade tree by the well box. That's where Jake allus hangs out on hot days."

We walk under a grove of wild plum trees. We reach the steps Jake has built over his fence. We see fields of grass and underbrushed woods pasture now.

"Look what a farm, Son," says Pa. "He's even put steps over his fences where the paths lead up to them so the people can cross his fences. Look at his woods! There's not purtier woods around Plum Grove than Jake's woods. Yet, Gus Martin tells me Jake's off in the head."

We walk down the path under the underbrushed woods. We walk into a grass field. We see Jake's cattle standing under a shade tree in the middle of the grass field. We walk over another pair of steps and cross his meadow. We see Jake's big log shack at the foot of a little hill. It is surrounded by locust trees.

"Look what a fine home Jake's got," says Pa. "Look how well he keeps it. I'll tell you there's a screw loose someplace. If Jake's gone a little batty somethin' powerful has had to happen to 'im."

We cross the bridge to the yard-palings. The wilted hollyhocks stand in rows along the fence. Jake's hound dogs sleep under the hollyhocks. They don't bark at us as we walk up to the gate. Jake's chickens wallow in dust piles in the middle of the road. Their tongues are out.

"Yander's Jake," says Pa. "As I expected, he's under the apple-tree shade by the well box."

"Howdy, Mick," says Jake. "You waked me up. I was about to take a nap o' sleep. Come on through the gate to the shade. Not any bitin' dogs around here."

"We'll be right in, Jake," says Pa.

Pa pushes the gate open. He holds the gate until I walk into the yard. The load of rusty plow-points and rocks tied to a chain and fastened to the gate pulls it shut soon as we enter.

"This gate's a handy contraption," says Pa. "Think I'll fix my gate like this."

"Yeh, it's all right, Mick," says Jake. "How you been keepin' yourself, Mick?"

"Okay, Jake," says Pa. Jake and Pa shake hands.

Jake is a tall clean-shaven man. His eyes are blue as the sky.

"That's your boy, isn't he, Mick?"

"Yeh, Jake, he's my boy."

"He's shot up like a bean pole," says Jake. "It's a sight how fast children grow. They remind me of sassafras sprouts. Sassafras sprouts and youngins are about to take the country, Mick."

Pa looks at me. Jake looks at Pa.

"Get you some chears," says Jake. "Let's sit under the shade and take it easy. Look like you're het up a little, Mick."

"Yes, Jake, I'm hot as a roasted tater. I thought I's goin' to ketch on fire I got so hot climbin' the Collins Hill."

"It's tough climbin'," says Jake.

Pa sits down in a hickory-split-bottom chair under the apple tree. Jake sits down in his chair. I lie down on the grass.

"Forgot to ask you fellars if you didn't want to fill your bilers with good cool well-water," says Jake. "Your bilers must be dry."

Pa looks at me. Jake gets up and goes to the well to draw water.

"He isn't talkin' nigh right," Pa whispers at me. "He's thinkin' o' sawmill bilers gettin' dry. Jake used to run a sawmill over at Cedar Riffles."

"Oh, yes, Mick," says Jake, "I'm all right. I know why you've come to see me, Mick. I'm glad you've come. I'll tell you the story. My head is all right."

Pa's face gets red. He didn't intend for Jake to hear what he told me. Pa whispers loud as a lot of people talk.

Jake carries the bucket of water to us. He reaches Pa the gourd dipper. Pa dips water from the bucket. He lifts the dipper to his lips. His Adam's apple works up and down on his red neck. You can hear Pa swallow the water.

"Aham," says Pa. "That's good water, Jake."

Pa tries to turn the subject.

"Yes, it cools your biler, Mick."

Jake carries the water bucket over to me. I get upon my knees from the quilt of cool yard grass. I dip water from the bucket with the gourd dipper. I drink and drink.

"Don't that water cool your biler, Son?"

"It's good water when a man is dry," I says.

Jake carries the bucket back to the well box. He empties the water left in the bucket on the yard grass. He puts the bucket back on the well box.

"I ain't off in the head, Mick," says Jake. "It must be norrated all over the deestrict that I am. I've had an awful time, Mick. I've had an awful fight on my hands. I've had to fight the Devil!"

"What do you mean?" Pa asks. Pa's eyes get big when he looks at Jake.

"I've had old Beelzebub to fight," says Jake, "and I live right under the shadder of the Plum Grove Church."

"Tell me about it, Jake," says Pa.

"You remember Esmerelda Sutton, don't you?"

"Yes, Jake," says Pa. "You was sparkin' her when I's goin' with my wife. We've double-dated together many a time. Don't you remember when we went to the Ashland Circus in my surrey together? That's when I drove that span of blazefaced ponies!"

"That's right," says Jake. "I remember it now. I've sparked Esmerelda all my life. She wanted me, Mick. She's been atter me ever since Ma died. She was atter me before Ma died. I couldn't marry her and bring her under the same roof with Ma. I told Esmerelda so. She said if we's ever goin' to marry it was time. Said we'd courted our lives away. When Ma died I was downhearted and didn't feel like marryin' fer a while. Esmerelda went atter me the wrong way. You won't believe me, Mick, when I tell you."

"Tell me," says Pa. Pa pulls another leaf of bright burley from his pocket. He crumbles the burley leaf in his hand and puts the handful of crumbs in his mouth. Jake fills his pipe from his burley tobacco crumbs from his hip pocket. He tamps the tobacco in his pipe with his index finger.

"I never noticed it," says Jake as he takes a match from his hatband and strikes it on his shoe, "so much until I went to feed the hogs one mornin'." Jake holds the partly burned match stem to his pipe and wheezes on his pipestem. He draws puffs of smoke from his pipe. "Mick, I poured the feed in the trough. I thought I was a hog. I couldn't believe I was a man. I got in the hog pen. I tried to eat with the hogs. I started to root with my nose. My hogs wouldn't let me. They had their mouths open. They acted like they's laughin' at me. Then they took back over the pint squealin' with their tails curled."

"Huh," says Pa. "Sounds like a dream to me."

"But it wasn't a dream," says Jake. "I bought a cow off'n Esmerelda about two weeks before I rooted with the hogs. I heard Esmerelda had a cow to sell. I heard she's hard up fer money. I went down to buy the cow. 'Jake, we ought to jump the broom,' she says. 'You live up there alone and I live alone down here. We've might nigh courted our lives away.' All she talked about was sparkin'. She didn't want to talk about the cow. 'I've come to buy your cow, Esmerelda,' I says.

"How much do you want fer her?' 'Forty dollars,' says Esmerelda.

"I pulled out my pocket book and shelled her two twenty-dollar bills off'n my roll. It was too much fer the old bony cow. I didn't ast her to sell the cow fer less. Atter she got the money and I took the cow she says, 'That cow won't do you any good, Jake. I'm goin' to make a little mouse that will stay with this cow. I'm goin' to make a little brown mouse that will tell this cow what to do. If the little mouse tells her to kick the bucket out'n your hand when you start to milk her, then she will do it. If the little mouse tells her not to eat, she won't eat. If this little mouse tells her to go dry, she will go dry. If this little brown mouse tells her not to calve, she won't calve. The little brown mouse will tell her what to do.' I jest laughed and laughed. 'You ain't gettin' batty, Esmerelda?' I ast. 'I'm tellin' you the truth,' she says. She didn't laugh when she talked to me. She looked at me with mean black eyes. As I drove the cow up the road, I got to thinkin' about what she said. I've been thinkin' about it ever since."

"How has the cow acted that you got from Esmerelda?"

"Jest the way Esmerelda said the cow would act," says Jake. "She hasn't done me no good. She takes spells, she kicks the bucket out'n my hand. Then she got so she wouldn't give her milk down. Now, she is dry."

"Did you ever see a little brown mouse around her?" Pa asks. Pa holds his quid of burley-leaf tobacco behind his suntanned jaw. Pa's eyes get big.

"Never have seen the mouse," says Jake, "but I believe the mouse is close." Jake blows a thin wisp of blue smoke from his clean-shaven lips. His blue eyes beam at Pa.

"Sounds like witchery to me," says Pa. "I remember that Esmerelda had two old maid aunts that ust to live here at Plum Grove. There was an awful lot of fitified people here in the deestrict then. Men said they's bewitched. Cattle, sheep, and hogs acted funny around here when Esmerelda's aunts were livin'."

"That's right," says Jake. "I think there's where Esmerelda got all her larnin' about witchery. I remember when Esmerelda's Aunt Phoebe died. She called Mort Higgins, Venny Seagraves, Don Caudile and Brother Baggs to her house. She told them, fer Don Caudile told me, that there was a pot of gold buried on Warfield Flaughtery's pint above the sycamore-tree bottom. Said if anybody went there to dig fer it, one of these four men would haf to be along. You remember how people tried to dig fer it. They'd dig and dig and they couldn't get anyplace. Dirt would fall back in the hole fast as they shoveled it out. You remember that big rock cliff on that pint—right where that grove of pine trees stood—you remember that big pine tree that rooted over the cliff—well; when people started to dig there they could see a big bull walk up this pine tree and he had a head on each end and a big pair of horns on each head. People saw 'im and they'd break runnin' fer their lives. When they'd start runnin' then the chains would begin to rattle. There was somethin' funny about all the Suttons. Esmerelda has nearly had me skeared to death, Mick. I get to thinkin' about 'er and I want to run and hide. I know what you have heard. You've heard that I was a fitified man."

"Yes, I have, Jake," says Pa. "I've said you couldn't be a fitified man unless somethin' had happened to you. I remember you in school. You was a pert boy. You was sharp as a shoebrad. I know it's not the Hunt nature to be fitified."

"I've been fitified, Mick," says Jake, "but I want to tell you how it all worked out. I wasn't shore about Esmerelda even atter I bought the cow and she told me about the little brown mouse. I wasn't sure she was causin' my fits atter I got down and tried to eat with the hogs. But I thought somethin' was wrong. I would do things that I couldn't help. I didn't have any control over myself. I was havin' an awful time here. My bull wouldn't notice my cows. My cows wouldn't give their milk down. My hound dogs thought they were foxes when I took them out to hunt. They'd get in front of the fox hounds and bark like foxes. My mules stood on their hind feet and tried to walk like men. They got to thinkin' they were men. I'll tell you, Mick, I was livin' in a different world. I began to wonder if I's asleep or awake. But the thing that brought me to my senses was one evenin' when Lute Puckett passed by here goin' to the coal-bank. He called me out to the palings there and started talkin'. 'Jake, I got somethin' to tell you,' he says. 'I know that I'm not dreamin' about it either. I know this is the truth. I pass the Plum Grove graveyard every mornin' but Sunday mornin'. One mornin' I heard a woman's voice. She was cryin' out to the Devil. She was offerin' 'im her soul if he would hep her do the things she wanted to do. I'll tell you the cold chills ran up my backbone. But I walked up closer and I saw the woman there among the tombstones. She was lookin' at a red ball of sun that was jest startin' to rise. She was cussin' the Lord. This happened fer three mornin's, Jake. We've got a witch in the Plum Grove deestrict jest as shore as God made little green apples.' 'Glory,' I hollered, 'I'm not a fitified man. I know what's the matter with me now, Lute.' 'What's the matter with you, Jake?' Lute ast. 'I wasn't shore what was the matter with me,' I says, 'I've been be-witched, Lute. My livestock has been bewitched. I'm havin' an awful fight. I'm glad to know this.' 'It's the first time I've told it to anyone,' says Lute. 'I was afeared they'd laugh and says I's afeard to pass that graveyard so early in the mornin'. I know that Esmerelda has been workin' for Beelzebub. It's hard to work against the Devil and a woman, Mick."

"It must be," says Pa.

"But I did know what to do," says Jake. "I had an awful time doin' it. I had to find one of Esmerelda's pictures. That was the job. I looked through everything on this place. I finally found a picture we had made together years ago. It was in the bottom of my trunk. I remembered what Grandma told me to do about a witch. I hated to do Esmerelda that way. I jest hated to think that she was a witch."

"I thought a witch had to give you somethin'," says Pa, "before she had the power to bewitch you."

"That's right," says Jake.

"What did Esmerelda give you, Jake?"

"Many kisses," says Jake.

"And you gave her money for the cow," says Pa.

"Yes," says Jake. "I gave her money for the cow."

"Then how did she bewitch your livestock?" Pa asks.

"Murt Hensley passed here one day," says Jake, "when I was in town. She saw Esmerelda saltin' my cattle. That's been since Lute Puckett heard her on the Plum Grove graveyard pint swearin' her faith to the Devil and cussin' the Lord. She saw Esmerelda feedin' corn to my hogs from a sack. She saw Esmerelda givin' my foxhounds bread. The reason I know it is, Murt thought we'd jumped the broom. She norrated it all over the Plum Grove deestrict. She norrated that we's married and Esmerelda had moved in the house with me. Mick, one little thing has jest led up to another."

"I see, Jake," says Pa. "Now you say you are all right."

"The last spell I took was one night I's out with the men fox huntin'," says Jake. "Charlie Gipson come along and ast me to go along. I called the dogs and went. That was before I found Esmerelda's picture. I didn't more than get with the fellars until I tried to stand on my head."

"Gus Martin was there, wasn't he?"

"Yes, Gus was there," says Jake. "Guess he was the one tellin' you about me."

"I don't mind tellin' you now since you've got all this stopped," says Pa. "Gus told me you tried to stand on your head on a whiskey jug."

I did," says Jake. "I tried to stand on my head on the jug's stopper. The men tried to hold me. They couldn't do a thing with me. I cussed and laughed. I called my dogs. I tooted my fox horn. I cut some rusty. That's not all. My dogs come to me. They cut all kinds of fool shines. They stood on their hind feet and tried to walk like I did. They would yap-yap like a fox and take through the brush—one bitin' at the other's tail. Did you ever hear of foxhounds doin' that?"

"Never did, Jake," says Pa. "A good foxhound isn't of that nature."

"And my foxhounds are the best among these hills," says Jake. "I ain't braggin', Mick, when I say this. I won't have any other kind of foxhounds. I've fox-hunted all my life. I love to hear a fox chase. I love to follow the hounds. I was terribly plagued the way my hounds acted that night. I was over my spell when my hounds started actin' funny. I guess Esmerelda, wanted me to be in my right mind so I could watch 'em. The fox hunters didn't know what was the matter with me. They don't know yet. They think I'm fitified. I don't know how I'll ever explain it to all of 'em atter I've courted Esmerelda all of my life. They won't believe me."

"How did you get away from Esmerelda?" Pa asks.

"I took her picture and nailed it on a locust tree back yander in my cow pasture," says Jake. "It was in the afternoon when the sun was goin' down. I put the picture opposite to the settin' sun. There was Esmerelda's sweet face on that picture. I wouldn't let myself remember the good times we'd had together. I started to thinkin' about the fits she'd made me take. I started to thinkin' about that little brown mouse she talked about when I bought her cow. I started to thinkin' about that cow. She's never done me any good. She's kicked the bucket out'n my hand. She wouldn't give her milk down. Then, she went dry. I thought about myself tryin' to eat with the hogs. I got mad. I had my hog rifle. I had melted a silver half dollar fer the bullet. I put in an extra gram of powder. I tamped it good. I shot Esmerelda smack through— and the silver bullet battered in the hard locust wood. Right then it was over, Mick. I'd kilt the Devil in Esmerelda. I fixed her. I haven't had a fit since. Now, I'm a well man. My livestock is all doin' well. The cow Esmerelda sold me has started to give milk again."

"That wasn't bad," says Pa, "it jest cost you a half dollar

to get rid of Esmerelda."

"Not bad when it comes to cost," says Jake as he knocks the ashes out of his pipe against his leg. "It's not the cost that hurts me. It will take a long time to live down the crazy things I done Mick. I hate to have people starin' at me and thinkin' I'm a fitified man when I was only bewitched by a woman—"

"A woman you ust to love," says Pa.

"My childhood sweetheart," says Jake. "It's a sight what a woman will do when she loves a man. Now you look at Esmerelda. She sold herself to the Devil to get me, Mick. Esmerelda is still atter me. God knows what she'll try next. She won't have the hep of the Devil now."

"You are a good ketch, Jake," says Pa. "You're a good man fer a woman to look at and you have the finest farm at Plum Grove. I know you have money in the bank. Why wouldn't Esmerelda want you? She is about your age and she lives alone and you live alone." Pa takes the hen-egg-sized quid of tobacco from his jaw and throws it on the grass. He looks at Jake and Jake looks at him.

"Jest to think about it," says Jake. "Wimmen will be afeard of me now. They'll hear all about this. This news will cover the Plum Grove deestrict like a mornin' dew. Everybody will know it. Wimmen will think I'm a little batty now."

"Esmerelda won't," says Pa. "She'll know what was the matter with you."

"That's right," says Jake. "Esmerelda is a purty woman, too. I can't hep it if she did bewitch me. She's the purtiest of the old maids. There's not a widder woman in these parts as purty as Esmerelda."

"Then you are all right, Jake," says Pa as he gets up from his chair.

Look up there at the Plum Grove church house...

"Oh yes," says Jake. "I'm certainly all right now."

"If you have any more trouble let me know," says Pa. "I'm your neighbor and friend. I'll haf to be moseyin' over the hill. It's gettin' about time to do the milkin' and feedin'."

"Yes," says Jake. "The sun has started down."

"Have you finished with Esmerelda, Jake?" Pa whispers in a low voice.

"If you ever see me with 'er in the buggy," says Jake, "forget all I've told you, Mick. I've been thinkin' it over. She'll make a good wife. I've kilt the power of the Devil in her. A lot of wimmen have devils in 'em, you know. Don't think anything if you hear our farms are united as one."

"Come over and see me, Jake," says Pa. We walk across the yard toward the gate.

"I will," says Jake. "Come and see me, Mick."

I follow Pa across the yard. He opens the gate and I walk through to the road. Pa walks through the gate. It closes itself behind him. The plow points as the gate swings shut. I look back to see Jake standin' under the apple-tree shade re-loadin' his pipe. He is squintin' his eyes toward the sun that is settin' over the Plum Grove hills.

Pa laughs and laughs as we walk up the path across the meadow.

"What are you laughin' about?" I ask.

"Jake," says Pa. "Look up there at the Plum Grove churchhouse, won't you. Jake lives in the shadder of the church and yet a witch got atter Jake."

We walk toward Jake's hills of timber where the evenin' shadows are lengthenin' from the tall trees out across his grassy pasture land.

GRANDPA BIRDWELL'S LAST BATTLE

"Shan, now you hurry along and get up the Hollow to your Grandpa's," Ma said. "I hate to see your Grandma and Grandpa left alone in that old house after night. It might ketch fire and burn 'em up. Somebody might think they've got money and try to rob 'em. You hurry along and get there before dark."

"Mom, I'm gettin' tired of goin' up there every night," I said. "I get lonesome sittin' before the fire and hearin' Grandpa tell his big windy tales about fightin'. Grandma will sit there beside him and listen to him tell the same tales over night after night. When Grandpa gets through tellin' one of his big tales Grandma will say, 'That's the truth. Battle's tellin' you the truth.'"

"Your Grandpa has been a fightin' man. I don't see any harm in him tellin' about it. If you live long enough, you'll be doin' the same thing. But you'll never be the man that your Grandpa has been. The country doesn't need the kind of men now that it needed then. The early days of this country made your Grandpa a tough man."

Grandpa never wore any shoes. When he got to tellin' about one of his fights, and he had the man by the throat with his big hand, his toes started wigglin'. Then a frown came over Grandpa's face. He squirmed in his chair. And he took another drink from the jug. I didn't tell Ma about this. I didn't tell her how Grandma sipped moonshine with him from the jug. They called it "Honorable Herbs." Ma didn't know about it. I wouldn't tell anythin' on Grandma and Grandpa if I didn't like what they were doin'.

"Hurry along, Shan," Ma said. "The sun is goin' down and shadows are lengthenin' over the path. You might step on a snake."

I put my cap on my head and rolled my overalls to my knees. I started up the hollow to Grandpa's house.

As I went up the hollow, I walked under the shadows of the water birches. I thought that sticks across my path were snakes. I thought the big gnarled roots that hooved above the ground around the trunks of the big oak and slippery elms were piles of snakes.

"You're late, Shan," Grandpa said. "What's kept you so?"

"Was late gettin' my work done," I said.

"We've missed you," Grandma said.

When Grandma said this, I was sorry about the way I'd talked about Grandpa and Grandma. I looked at Grandma's white hair and her wrinkled face. Her dim blue eyes looked across the table at Grandpa. He was sittin' on the other side of the table with his legs crossed. He had his hand on the jug. His hair was white as cotton. Grandpa was sittin' back in his chair like the world belonged to him. I could tell that he was gettin' ready to brag about his fightin'.

The white whiskey jug with the brown neck was on the table between them. There was a cup on the table for Grandma to sip from. Grandpa wouldn't sip his Honorable Herbs from a cup. He had to drink from the jug.

"Glad to see you, Shan, my son," Grandpa said. He looked at me with his sky-blue eyes. The white beard covered the wrinkles on Grandpa's face. I don't know whether his face was wrinkled or not. I don't believe it was. I never saw his face shaved.

"Guess you get kind o' lonesome comin' up here and stayin' with us," Grandma said. "All the other boys air out foxhuntin', giggin' fish at the Sandy Falls and sparkin' at the big revival meetin's and kickin' up thar heels at the square dances."

"No, Grandma, I don't get lonesome," I said.

"I'll tell you where we miss it, Lizzie," Grandpa said. "We ought to take Shan into our company and let him drink with us. That's why it's lonesome for Shan here."

"He's too young, Battle," Grandma said. "His Ma would take the roof off the house if she thought we'd give him a dram."

"Guess you air right, Lizzie," Grandpa said as he reached for the jug.

Grandpa held the jug high in the air. He looked toward the newspapered ceiling as he drank. His Adam's apple worked up and down on his big beardy neck. Grandpa's big bare feet were turned toward me. The skin on the bottom of his feet was thick and tough where he had gone barefooted.

"I'll tell you that's good Herbs, Lizzie," Grandpa said. "Herbs like these wouldn't hurt Shan 'r any other young man. He's got a great experience comin'. That will be when he partakes of the Herbs and the world becomes his own."

"Yes, Battle," Grandma said as she poured a cup of Herbs from the jug.

"That doesn't look like it's got much power to me," I said.

"That looks like clear water, Grandma."

"Shan, Sonnie, it's everythin' in the world but clear water," Grandma answered. "Two cups of this would make me want to stand on my head."

Grandma held her cup to her lips and sipped. She sipped like a cat drinks milk from a saucer. Grandpa watched Grandma sip her Herbs. His mouth opened in a big smile. Grandpa laughed at Grandma the way she sipped her Honorable Herbs.

"Here's the way to take it, Lizzie," Grandpa said as he lifted the jug to his lips. His Adam's apple worked up and down on his big bull-neck. After each swallow, he made a gurglin' noise.

"Aham, aham," Grandpa said as he pulled the jug neck from his mouth. "I'll tell you that's wonderful."

He put the jug back on the table between him and Grandma.

"I wish he was older, Lizzie," Grandpa said. "I hate to have anybody around me too young to jine me when I have a drink of Herbs. I like to have my company to jine me with a drink of Herbs or a smoke of the fragrant weed."

"That reminds me, Battle," Grandma said as she pulled her long-stemmed clay pipe from her apron pocket. She tamped the terbacker crumbs in her pipe with her index finger. She held a stick of pine kindlin' over the lamp globe until the resin begin to ooze and it caught fire.

Grandma lit her pipe. She puffed a big cloud of smoke from her long-stemmed pipe.

"Wait a minute, Lizzie," Grandpa said. "Don't fan that stick of kindlin' wood yet. Let it burn. I need it."

Grandpa reached in his inside coat pocket and pulled out a long green taste-bud cigar. Grandma bent over the table and laughed until she got strangled on smoke.

"What's the matter with you, Lizzie? " Grandpa said. "Have you sipped too much of the Honorable Herbs?"

"I'll tell you what I was thinkin' about, Battle, if you won't get mad."

"Cross my heart and swear," Grandpa promised.

"I was just thinkin' about the good times we're havin' since all our children left us," Grandma said. "We thought we's goin' to get lonesome without 'em. We've never been lonesome. We've been havin' the best time of our lives since our dozen youngins left this nest."

"Now, Lizzie, that's not all you's laughin' about," Grandpa said. "I know you too well. I know the things that touch your tickle bone."

"I just thought," Grandma said, "when you's lightin' that cigar, what if you'd get your beard on fire and it would burn the beard off'n your face clean as a fire burns new ground. Wonder if your face would be burned black as new ground."

"That's what tickled you," Grandpa said. "I don't see anything funny enough to laugh about that. If my face was to get on fire it would be awful."

"You've done so much fightin' in your day," Grandma laughed, "could you fight the fire on your face?"

"You've sipped too many Herbs," Grandpa said. "I'm sittin' here thinkin' about my fight with Bill Sexton."

I looked at Grandpa's toes. When he spoke of Bill Sexton, he wiggled his toes.

"Don't tell me about that fight you lost," Grandma pleaded.

"Tell about fights you've winned."

"It's not fair always to be a winner, Lizzie," Grandpa said as he lifted the jug to his mouth again.

Gurgle, gurgle, gurgle, gurgle.

"Nothin' in this world like it, Lizzie," Grandpa said as he put the jug back on the table and wiped the beard around his mouth with the back of his big hand. "It's powerful stuff, Lizzie. Watch your sippin'."

"Tell us about Bill Sexton," I said. "What did he do to you, Grandpa?"

"What did he do to me?" Grandpa repeated.

Grandpa began to wiggle his toes. He jumped up from his chair and stood in the middle of the floor. He looked like a giant. His big arms swung down at his side. His big gnarled hands looked like shovels. His blue eyes beamed in the yellow lamplight. He looked straight ahead of him at the wall. His big feet flattened on the floor like a blowin' viper's head when it hisses.

"Show Shan the scars on my head, Lizzie," Grandpa commanded.

Grandma stood up. She couldn't tiptoe and reach Grandpa's head to find the scars. She climbed up in her chair where she could part the white hair, thick and clean as a sheep's wool. She parted the hair until she found the big scar.

"Look where Bill Sexton hit your Grandpa with a coalpick that time," Grandma said. "Look what a scar he will carry to his grave."

"And to think I let him skip the country," Grandpa stormed. "I let him get away. I didn't follow him. I get so mad now that I could bite a ten-penny nail in two when I think of that man.

I'd a got 'im but he knocked me out. I didn't wake up for two days."

Grandma climbed down out'n the chair and Grandpa sat down in his chair.

"I'll tell you," Grandpa said, "I've been a fightin' man. I could stand a good fight right now. I ain't afraid of hell and high waters."

"Don't let Bill Sexton rile you," Grandma said. "He may be dead, you don't know. You run'im out'n this country and we've never heard tell of 'im."

"Let 'im die," Grandpa shouted and wiggled his toes. "Let Bill Sexton die. He fouled me in a coal mine and you know it."

"You didn't have any business goin' in that coal mine on Bill Sexton," Grandma answered. "You went in that coal bank to whop him and didn't have anything to fight with but your fist. He had a coal-pick to fight you with and he used it. Hit you three times in the head with it. He could see you comin' for the light was behind you. You couldn't see him for he was against the coal-vein."

"Yep that's the way he got me," Grandpa said. "If I'd a knowed he's goin' to use a coal-pick I'd a got me a slab of coal-bone and I'd a caved his ribs in; that is what I'd a done."

"You've had too much Herbs, Battle," Grandma said. "You air a-gettin' riled."

"I'm not gettin' riled," Grandpa said. "I'm already riled. I hope and pray to the Almighty that he comes back here one of these days. I'll whop him shore as the Savior made little green pawpaws."

"It's been fifty-three years since you fit him, Battle," Grandma said.

Grandpa sat and wiggled his toes. He looked mean out'n his eyes.

"Think I'll get me a drink of water," Grandpa said.

"I'll get the water for you, Grandpa," I said.

"I'll get my own drinkin' water, thank you," Grandpa said. "I'm able to wait on myself yet."

"Battle's riled," Grandma said softly to me. "I tried to get him to talk about the men he had whopped instead of the man that whopped him."

Grandpa got up from his chair and started toward the kitchen. He had to cross the entry. The entry was once a dogtrot through Grandpa's house. They took the floor up and left a dirt floor. They used this entry in winter for a place to stack wood. The kitchen was on the other side of the entry.

I looked when Grandpa stepped down from the door into the entry. He was carryin' a burning stick of kindlin' wood for a light. The last thing I saw above his head was the lighted torch. The next thing I heard was Grandpa holler.

"Dad-durn you," he shouted. "I'll kill ye; I'll kill ye!"

"Battle's in another fight," Grandma shouted. "It may be Bill Sexton."

Grandma grabbed the lamp in such a hurry that the globe fell off and smashed in the floor. I followed Grandma toward the entry.

"Fetch the light, Lizzie," Grandpa hollered. "Come here, Lizzie."

"Oh my lord, it's a snake," Grandma hollered as she saw the dark entry and Grandpa fightin' a snake. He was stompin' it with one foot and it was holdin' his other foot with its fangs.

"He's got his teeth hung in my britches leg," Grandpa

shouted. "Durn ye, you low-down sneak. You air as unfair as Bill Sexton. Crawl from under a man's floor and try to bite him."

"Kill him, Battle," Grandma shouted as she put the lamp on the floor and started clappin' her hands. "Kill him, Battle! Tear him to pieces."

"He needs more light," I said as I picked the lamp up and held it so Grandpa could see.

"You air right, Shan," Grandpa said as he bent over and reached for the snake.

Before Grandpa could bend over and reach the big copperhead with his hand, it had let loose of his foot.

"Watch 'im, Battle," Grandma shouted. "He wants to bite your hand, Battle!"

"I'll get 'im, Lizzie," Grandpa said. "Don't you worry. I'll get this low-down copperhead."

The snake writhed on the ground floor. Grandpa raised up and jumped two feet into the air to come down on the snake with both bare feet. When he came back to the ground the snake was coiled like a well-rope around a windlass. Grandpa missed the snake.

"Watch 'im, Battle," Grandma shouted. "Don't step on him and get snake bones in your feet. You won't live twenty-four hours if you do."

"I'll win this battle," Grandpa shouted to Grandma and looked up at her.

"Whip—"

The copperhead struck Grandpa on the other leg and let loose to get ready and strike again.

"Oh my Lord, Battle," Grandma pleaded. "Leave that snake

alone. It's riled and it isn't a-goin' to quit fightin'. It's atter you, Battle. It will finish you."

"I haven't begun to fight," Grandpa said. "I'm not whipped. I'll never let a little thing as a copperhead crawl into my house and start a fight with me. I feel like fightin' tonight. This snake is the spirit of Bill Sexton—the only man I didn't whip."

"Whew—" Grandpa stomped at the copperhead and missed. It struck again at Grandpa and missed.

"Come on, Battle," Grandma clapped her hands and started over to help Grandpa.

"You can't do that," I said. I held her wrist with one hand and with the other I held the lamp.

"Bite me, you low-down scamp," Grandpa shouted. "I'm as full of pizen as you air."

Before the snake had time to make up his mind, Grandpa took a run and jumped at the snake. His big heel caught the copperhead on the flat head and squashed it. The snake writhed on the dusty floor with its head mashed into the dirt and its big bright body still alive.

"I told you I'd whip this snake," Grandpa said proudly. "Bill Sexton is dead and his spirit had to go into somethin' and it couldn't go into anythin' higher than a snake."

"I'm so proud of you, Battle," Grandma said.

Grandpa reached down and picked up the squirmin' snake. With his big hands he pulled the snake in two. He took these parts and pulled them in two again. Then he took each part and tore it in two again. That made eight pieces of copperhead he piled in a pile on the entry floor.

"I'm glad you didn't stomp that snake," Grandma said.

"What if you'd a got them pizen copperhead ribs in your feet?"

"I'm bit all over nohow," Grandpa said as he climbed up the steps into the front room and Grandma took him by the arm.

"Do you want me to get you a drink of water, Grandpa?" I asked.

"Nope, I'll drink from my jug.

"That's right, Battle," Grandma said. "You need plenty of pizen in you."

Grandpa got the jug. I put the lamp back on the table.

Gurgle, gurgle, gurgle, gurgle, gurgle.

"Drain the jug, Battle," Grandma said. "You've got a lot of pizen in you."

Gurgle, gurgle, gurgle, gurgle, gurgle.

Grandpa put the jug on the table long enough to get his breath.

"Hurry, Battle, and get the Herbs down you," Grandma warned.

"Give me time, Lizzie."

"I need to put the turpentine bottle to the places the copperhead bit you," Grandma said. "You'll wake up in the mornin' and you'll never know you battled with a copperhead."

Gurgle, gurgle, gurgle, gurgle, gurgle.

"I'm seein' darkness, Lizzie," Grandpa said. "Lower me to the floor. Don't let me fall."

While I steadied Grandpa, Grandma put a quilt down on the floor and she put a pillow on the quilt. We lowered Grandpa to the quilt. He didn't speak after we got him down. He was lifeless as a tree.

"I'll get the turpentine," Grandma said.

By the time Grandma got back with the turpentine, I had found the two places where the copperhead had socked him.

"I'll get the light down there," Grandma said. "I want to see where the snake's teeth went in Battle's legs. It'll look like briar prints."

"Here's one place, Grandma. See right here by Grandpa's ankle!"

"I can see the prints of its fangs."

Grandma put the unstopped bottle-neck down over the bite.

"Put the lamp up close, Shan," she said. "See if you can see any green stripes of pizen goin' up into the turpentine bottle."

I got down on my all-fours. I stuck my face up against the bottle. I held the lamp close so I could see.

"I can see it, Grandma," I said. "I can see green stripes goin' up in the turpentine bottle."

"I'll haf to hurry so I can draw the pizen from Battle's other leg."

"Here's the other bite, Grandma," I said. I showed her the place on Grandpa's shin bone.

Grandma put the bottle over the place.

"Watch for the pizen, Shan."

"I see plenty of it."

"I'll take the bottle away now," Grandma whispered. "It's about full of copperhead pizen. Think I got about all the pizen. All I didn't get the Herbs will get. Now you fetch me a quilt and I'll spread it over Battle and let him rest the night here."

I got a quilt off'n one of the beds for Grandma. She spread it over Grandpa.

"Battle's a brave old warrior," she said as she spread the quilt over him. "He'll fight anythin' that walks, crawls or flies."

"Look, Grandma, his toes are wigglin' under the kiver."

"He's fightin' in his dreams."

"Reckon he's all right?"

"Of course he's all right," she said. "He's been bit before by copperheads. We know how to fight 'em."

We sat there and watched Grandpa's chest heave up and down as he got his breath and let it go again.

"Do you reckon that was Bill Sexton's spirit in that snake?" Grandma asked. "He was a sneak and the snake sneaked from under the floor and bit Battle near the ankle. That's the way Bill Sexton fought."

"I don't know whether it was Bill Sexton or not," I said. "I don't know whether a man can go into a snake or not when he dies."

"I believe he can," Grandma whispered. "That snake had the countenance of Bill Sexton."

We sat awhile by Grandpa's pallet.

"It's gettin' late, Shan," Grandma said. "We'd better turn in and get a little sleep. I'll sleep here in the room where I can wait on Battle if he wants anything. You sleep upstairs where you've always slept."

"All right, Grandma."

I didn't sleep well. I dreamed of snakes runnin' from a newground fire. I saw them go over the steep hill slope with their heads high in the air and their tails barely touchin' the ground. Grandpa was after them with a club. When Grandma called me down to breakfast, Grandpa was sittin' at the table.

"We had some night last night, didn't we?" he said.

"Yep we did, Grandpa."

"I never had a better night's sleep than I had last night. I feel like a two-year-old today."

"Battle, you winned a good fight last night."

Grandpa looked at Grandma and smiled.

"I believe it was Bill Sexton that I fought."

"It might have been Bill Sexton, Battle."

"If that snake was Bill Sexton," Grandpa said, "I'll be able to die happy when I die. I'm good for twenty more years yet."

Then Grandpa took a big sip of coffee from his saucer.

BURY YOUR DEAD

"I'd rather see Ceif dead and in his coffin as to be married to Portia Pratt," Pa said between puffs on his cigar. "Just to think my own flesh and blood married into that family. Urban, you break the news to your Ma."

Pa held his head down and whittled fast as his strong arm would shove the hawkbill knife blade through the sassafras stick. He made the long rainbow-curved shavin's fly like wind blows leaves from a September sassafras. Anybody followin' the path could track us by the shavin's Pa left. As we walked along, I kept thinkin' how hard it would be to tell Ma.

Soon as we reached our log shack, Pa walked toward the barn. He didn't want to be around when I told Ma.

"Got somethin' to tell you, Ma," I said as I opened the door.

"What news do you bring, Urban?" Ma asked. Ma's worryin' about Ceif a-meetin' Portia Pratt someplace every time he could had put new wrinkles in her face.

"I know the news you bring," Ma said before I had time to tell her. "You are goin' to tell me that Ceif has married Portia Pratt."

"Squire Screech Horsley married 'em," I said. "He told Flem Spry. And we met Flem ridin' his mule around the ridge road a few minutes ago. He told Pa and me."

Ma held one hand in the air over her quilt. It just looked like her arm was froze that way. Her eyes were just as much set on me as Eif Porter's eyes were set on me when the last breath left him. Ma didn't move. She didn't speak. Not a tear fell from her eyes. I thought she's takin' it better than we had expected.

"What do you think about it, Ma?" I asked her.

Ma didn't answer. She kept her hand raised above the quilt with the needle in it. Her eyes were fastened on me now just like Eif Porter's dyin' eyes had been. She didn't make a sound. I thought somethin' funny. I asked her again what she thought about Ceif. She didn't answer me. I thought Ma was dead.

I hurried to the kitchen.

"Sister Carrie, the camphor bottle," I screamed. "Ma's dyin'.'"

Sister Carrie grabbed the bottle from the cupboard shelf. We hurried to the front room, turnin' over the chairs as we went. Ma hadn't changed a bit. She was sittin' there just like she was when I left her. Sister Carrie rubbed her arms and I held the unstopped camphor bottle to her nose. Ma walled her eyes back. She was coming to. Soon as she got so she could speak she said, "It can't be so, Urban. Ceif's not married to Portia Pratt. It's a dream that we've dreamt."

Soon as Pa had fed the mules, he came to the house.

"Adger, Ceif's gone," Ma screamed, wavin' her wrinkled arms high in the air. "Our Ceif is gone. Married to that Portia Pratt. Married to a Pratt. I'd rather see him dead and in his coffin!"

"I've said the same thing already," Pa said, whittlin' big

shavin's on the hearth as he sat down in a chair before the fire. "Raise a boy up near the Pratts as we have. He knows what a set of people they are. He knows the trouble we've had with 'em. He knows a Pratt never sticks his foot on Dry Fork where the Wamplers live. And thank God, a Wampler would be too proud to dirty his shoe leather by steppin' his foot on Shackle Run where the Pratts live."

Pa's big arm shook as he whittled. He was nervous as a white-oak cluster of dead leaves in the January wind. He had smoked his cigar so short that we couldn't see it for his mustache. I wondered why the cigar didn't set Pa's mustache on fire.

"We know the Pratts, Adger," Ma said. "They've allus been a thorn in the Wampler flesh! Now they've got our Ceif. He'd be better off in his grave among his people."

"He'll be in his grave in five years," Pa said puffin' faster on his cigar.

When Pa said that Ceif's life was a matter of a few years, he stomped his big boot-heel as hard on our floor as you hit a number twenty nail to drive it in a seasoned beech plank. Pa's blue eyes danced fire. Ma held her wrinkled hands over her eyes and wept.

"Look what's happened to the boys and girls that's married into that tribe," Pa said as he threw the short cigar stub in the fire. "The Pratts made Pratts out'n 'em or they kilt 'em. But here's one set of people they never could bully. That's why they hate us. Now, we stand even—eight Pratts honorably kilt by Wampler guns; eight Wamplers bushwhacked in the foulest way by Pratts' clubs, rocks and guns. If we didn't stand even, there wouldn't be any peace."

Pa took another cigar from his vest pocket and lit it.

"But Ceif was never good to work," Ma wept. "Poor little Ceif was no good to help me about the house. He never was stout enough to break a hoe handle hoein' in new ground. He wasn't stout enough to sink a double-bitted ax to the eye in locust wood. He couldn't even lift the end of a small sawlog on the hind couplin's of a jolt-wagon. What will he do with a Pratt wife to keep?"

"He'll haf to work," I said.

"He's driven his goose to a bad market," Pa said. "Wonder how he'll like diggin' his bread from Pratt hillsides. Wonder if he'll get thirsty for the sweet waters he ust to drink from a Dry Fork well?"

"All married now but Carrie and Urban," Ma said. "All married where I darst set my feet on their ground and drink water from their well. Seven married now and I can only visit six. Six can come home if Adger or me was to die. But Ceif can't come."

We didn't go to bed that night. Not one of us could've slept if we had gone to bed. It hurt me to think about poor Ceif. Snort Pratt would talk about the lazy Wampler that his Portia had married. He'd hold Ceif up as an example of the Wamplers.

When Ma started to get up from her chair to put a fire in the stove to get breakfast, Pa said, "I've allus said if one of my youngins married and got hisself blistered, he'd haf to sit on the blister."

When Pa and I went to the fields, we missed Ceif. We missed hearin' his chair without rockers bumpin' on the plank floor when we come home from the fields. There was never one of us missed like Ceif when he left our house. It wasn't the same place. Ma missed Ceif more than any of us.

Spring passed away; summer came and passed. Though Ceif was only seven miles from us, we never saw him. There was a backbone ridge that separated Shackle Run and Dry Fork. And it was good that it did. There was only one place where a path went from their domain to ours. It was a big gap in the backbone ridge where the waters of Dry Fork started from a spring on the east side and flowed toward the sunrise. On the west side of the gap, Shackle Run started from a spring and flowed toward the sunset. Right here was the only place we had to build a line fence between our domain and the Pratt domain.

Flem Spry told Pa in December that he saw Ceif. Said Ceif was askin' all about us. Said Ceif looked bad. Said he had little dark half-moon crescents under his eyes. And he said Portia was with him when he saw Ceif. Said he believed that Ceif would soon haf to be rockin' one of his own youngins in a chair without rockers.

It was in January that Portia had her first baby. It was a man child. Ceif called him Snort, atter his Pappie-in-law, Snort Pratt. It made Pa so mad that he could've bit a tenpenny nail in two, to think that a baby of Wampler flesh and blood would ever be called Snort. He smoked one cigar atter another. And you could track Pa for two weeks along the paths by the shavin's he'd whittled with his hawk-bill knife.

Eif Sperry told us that the Pratts had it in for Ceif, until he called his first-born man-child, Snort. Flem said the Pratts didn't think Ceif was loyal to them. Atter he called his boy Snort, they accepted Ceif in good faith. They fox-hunted with him and shared their terbacker and drinks with him.

"I don't know how the Pratts treat their in-laws that are no good to work," Pa told Eif Sperry, "but I know when they get a mule that isn't good to work they kill the mule or make it work. And knowing the Pratts as I know 'em, I'd think they'd be as mean to a man as they are to a dumb brute."

Another spring and summer had passed; autumn was nearly gone when Lonnie Tremble walked down the path and told Pa that Portia and Ceif had a pair of twins at their house.

"If one's a man child," Pa said, "I guess Ceif will call 'im Snort number Two. If both his twins are man babies I guess he'll call 'em Snort number Two and Snort number Three."

Lonnie told Pa that the were both girls.

"He'll call 'em atter some of the Pratt wimmen," Pa grumbled.

We heard later that he called one Pollie atter Portia's mother and the other Mollie atter Ma. Ma smiled when Pa told her about it. She was pleased. She would have given all the teeth she had left in her mouth just to've seen the twins one hour. She wanted to see Ceif too since he'd been away from home nearly two years.

Eif Sperry told Pa he had heard when he fox-hunted on the Pratt domain, that the Pratts were hell-fired mad at Ceif because he called one of the twins Mollie atter Ma. When Pa told Ma about it, fire danced in Ma's eyes. "Why didn't he name 'em all atter the low-down viper Pratts," Ma said. "Two of Ceif's three youngins are named atter 'em now."

When spring came again, Pa and I plowed and planted our fields. We often talked about Ceif. Gilbert Tremble passed our way and said he'd seen Ceif and talked with him. Said Ceif told him to drink a quart of our sweet well water for him. Said Ceif looked like a pile of skin and bones since Snort Pratt was workin' him hard. Gilbert said Snort made each of his six sons-in-law farm as many acres as he told them to farm. Said he told them how much to plant, when to plant and how to plant. Since Ceif was his youngest son-in-law, he had to take the rootiest, poorest, steepest ground and give the older ones their choice.

"Ceif can't sit on his blister much longer," Pa said. "He can't live under that petticoat govern-mint."

Atter we had corn and terbacker laid by that summer, I thought I'd kill a mess of squirrel on the backbone ridge between our domains. While I was waintin' for a squirrel in a tall hickory tree, I saw a man come down the hill who walked like Ceif. But it can't be Ceif, I thought. He was too small for Ceif. But it was Ceif. We shook hands with one another. I was glad to see Ceif; he was glad to see me.

"Why did you marry a Pratt, Ceif?" I asked. "Why did you forsake your own people?"

"It was love, Urban," Ceif said. "Love will make you forsake your own people; it will make you live with your enemies."

As I looked at poor Ceif I wanted to cry. He was nothing but a skeleton of skin and bones. I thought about what Pa said. Ceif wouldn't last five years the way he was losin' flesh from his bones. He wouldn't be alive three years.

"Do you feel well, Ceif? " I asked him.

"All right, Urban," he said. "I do miss the sweet water from our well though."

"But it's not drinkin' water that causes you to lose weight," I said.

"You know, Urban, I don't mind hard work and losin' weight," Ceif said. "I never think about it since I've got three babies to rock. Little Snort, Mollie and Pollie."

This was too much for me. I couldn't stand it any longer. I couldn't stand to look at my brother who was a walkin' corpse if I had ever seen one. I picked up my gun without sayin' good-by and left the squirrels in that hickory tree for him to shoot.

I never told Pa, Ma and Sister Carrie about seein' Ceif. I kept that to myself. Autumn had come again; we cut the corn and housed the terbacker. Then we heard somethin' that surprised us. Portia had triplets. It was hard to believe. But Lonnie Tremble said he stopped at Ceif's home and looked at them. Said they were strong babies. And then we heard what that Ceif had named the two boys, Urban and Adger atter Pa and me. And he called the girl, Alice, after my oldest sister.

When we heard that the Pratts were more than hell-fired mad at Ceif over his namin' the triplets atter the Wamplers, Pa puffed his cigar and laughed. But Pa didn't laugh very long. It was in October when the leaves left the trees that Ceif took sick. Eif Sperry told us about it. But none of us went to see Ceif.

Every night atter we heard that Ceif was sick, Ma turned a coffee cup and read the coffee grounds. Every time Ma would scream and say that she saw a coffin with Ceif in it. Ma would scream and wring her hands. "Poor Ceif," she'd say, "he hasn't been married three years yet and he has six youngins to rock. But poor Ceif won't get to rock 'em much longer. Ceif will die."

The dogs barked all night but I didn't pay mind to their barkin'. I thought the strange noises I heard were the high winds among the October trees around our house. But when Pa got up to feed before daylight that mornin', I heard him fall on the porch. Then I heard Pa get the lantern from the nail on the porch where it hung. I heard him get a hatchet and start pryin' boards loose. I wondered what was wrong. Then I heard him scream. I hurried downstairs and Ma and Carrie had got out'n bed. We hurried to the porch. There stood Pa with a lantern in one hand and a hatchet in the other.

"It's Ceif, Mollie," Pa wept. "They put 'im in the coffin and brought him back to us."

"It's not as much shock to me as the day Urban told me Ceif was married," Ma said without sheddin' a tear. "I'd rather see him in his coffin, as to be Snort Pratt's lackey-boy-son-in-law."

"But he can't be buried here," Pa said.

"Why didn't Pratts bury him on Shackle Run?" Carrie asked.

"Because he give four of his babies Wampler names," Ma said. "He's my Ceif and he's dead but I'd as leave he'd be buried among the Pratts where he belongs."

We carried the poplar-plank coffin to our back room. There we closed the door and left Ceif. Pa smoked hard all day and he whittled hard. He made shavin's three feet long fly from a poplar stick.

"We'll take him back tonight," Pa said. "You go down the creek and get Tim, Snyder, and Lon. We'll need 'em to help us carry Ceif back to Shackle Run."

When I went atter my brothers I told them what Pa said. They said they'd come and help for Pa was right. And that night, we carried Ceif back to them. We carried him to their house and put him on the porch. While we carried him, none of us spoke. Their dogs barked but that didn't matter.

"I guess old Snort will soon find out, that he can't make us bury their dead. Ceif's my son but he's a traitor."

We thought now that the Pratts would understand and bury Ceif in their graveyard. We thought that Portia might want to be buried beside Ceif someday and she could never be buried among us Wamplers in our dirt. Our dead couldn't rest with a Pratt in our graveyard.

The next day passed. We worked most of the day. The sun came out and it was hot. That night, atter our work was done we went to bed. But we didn't talk about Ceif. The next mornin' we got up, fed and milked. Ma allus fed the chickens and when she went to the hen house, she screamed and we hurried to the hen house to see what was wrong.

"They've brought Ceif back," Ma said.

"They are bull-headed," Pa said, turnin' white around his eyes as he spoke. "Old Snort wants his way but this is one time that old copperhead won't get his way!"

We put Ceif in the backroom again and locked the door. I went after my brothers again. And when dusk came, we carried Ceif back to Snort Pratt's shack. We didn't put him on the porch for fear that Snort would be expectin' us. We put Ceif in Snort's corncrib where he'd be sure to find him soon as he fed that mornin'.

This time we thought Snort Pratt would keep Ceif. We

thought it was time to bury him for the days were hot. Next mornin' atter Pa fed, he started to draw a drink from the well. He stumbled over Ceif's coffin left at the well.

"I won't be outdone by that low-lifer," Pa said.

And that night we carried Ceif back and set his coffin by old Snort Pratt's springhouse door. We put it where they would find it. We got home at three in the mornin'. We never went to bed that day. Pa said he'd stay awake that night to watch for the low-lifed Pratts with a double-barreled shotgun. Ma didn't want him to do it. She said one dead already and unburied was aplenty.

We heard Pa shoot both barrels at the Pratts. We heard them screamin' and shootin' back as they ran. Pa didn't follow them for he knew they'd bushwhack him. Their buckshot sprinkled our roof like sandgrains as they hotfooted it up the hill. They left Ceif by our cellar door.

"We'll take him back to them," Pa said. "We'll fool 'em. They'll be watchin' for us with guns now. They think we'll come tonight. We'll take Ceif back tomorrow night."

"The Bible says you shall bury your dead," Ma said with tears in her red-wrinkled eyes.

"And we should bury our dead," Pa said. "But Ceif's not our dead. He can't sleep with us. He belongs to the Pratts."

"Bury 'im someplace on the farm," Ma said. "We've over a thousand acres of land."

"But not one inch for a traitor," Pa snapped like a turtle.

That day the sun was hot. The crows flew over our house in swarms. They lit in the trees by the spring.

"We must bury Ceif," Ma wept as she heard the crows cawin'. "I can't stand this any longer."

But Pa had his way. On the second night, at two o'clock in the mornin' we took Ceif back and left him in the yard. Not even a dog barked when we left him there and hurried away, each man with his hand on his pistil.

"Now the thing for us to do," Pa said, "is to guard this gap tonight. It's the only way they can bring Ceif home."

With rifles and shotguns by our sides and pistils in our hands, we guarded the narrow pass. We got behind rocks and trees and waited. We guarded the pass all that day. We could see the flock of crows above old Snort's shack. We could see swarms of crows sailin' in the sky. We knew that Ceif was there. Before the day ended, we saw the crows swarmin' toward us.

"They're pullin' one," Pa said. "They're goin' to try to slip Ceif back today. But they'll never do it."

As we held our posts, Pa slipped up to the gap and looked over.

"Boys, hold to your rifles and pistils," Pa said. "I see a whole army of Pratts comin' with Ceif. I'll get behind this rock in front. I'll halt 'em at the line-fence."

Soon as they reached the gap, Pa yelled, "Halt, there, Pratts, if you don't want to lose your brains!"

They stopped still in their tracks.

"Set that coffin down right there," Pa ordered as he stepped from behind the rock and pulled his long blue .38. "Don't one of you pull a pistil. I've got a army of men behind these rocks. And now will be a good time to get rid of a few Pratts."

Snort Pratt, the old man with the long whiskers, stepped out in front of the Pratts.

"Adger Wampler, what will we do with Ceif?" Snort asked. "He's your boy."

"Boys, hold your rifles and pistils," Pa said.

"He's a traitor to the Wamplers," Pa said. "You took him. Now you bury him."

"He wasn't a true-blue Pratt," Snort said. "He can't sleep among the Pratts."

The men stood still, afraid to reach into their pockets and get handkerchiefs to wipe the sweat from their eyes and faces. While they stood there and we stayed behind the rocks and trees outnumbered five to one, the crows swarmed over us and cawed.

"Bury half of him on your side the fence and other half on our side of the fence," Pa said thoughtfully.

"Since he's been out'n the ground this long," Snort said, "I guess that will be all right. You send one of your men back and tell your people. I'll send one of my men back and tell our people. And you bring tools and dig your half o' the grave and we'll bring tools to dig our half of the grave."

"Then let us have peace while we bury Ceif," Pa said.

We stacked our guns; the Pratts stacked their guns.

Brother Lon went to norrate the truce that Pa and Snort had made. Only Pa and Snort talked when something had to be said. They dug their half of the grave; we dug our half of the grave. We slid the coffin under the fence. Ceif's feet was on our side of the fence toward the sunrise; his head was on their side the fence toward the sunset. Only Ma and Portia shed tears. I think Portia was the prettiest girl I ever saw. I didn't blame Ceif for marryin' her. Not a Wampler spoke to a Pratt nor a Pratt spoke to a Wampler at any time durin' the funeral nor as we gathered our guns and parted at the gap.

DEATH HAS TWO GOOD EYES

"It's funny when you go to visit kinfolks you've never seen, you have to carry a pistol," I said.

"But it's best to play safe," Finn said.

The Big Sandy train was screeching around the curves up the single-line track. Finn and I looked out the window at the Big Sandy River that wound between the Kentucky and West Virginia Mountains like a big silver-bellied cow-snake. We'd heard Pa talk about this river—how Grandpa had taken big trains of log rafts down the Big Sandy to the Ohio River to Cincinnati and Louisville.

We'd heard Pa tell about how the Kentucky boys used to shoot it out with the West Virginia boys across the Big Sandy River to test their pistols. Pa told how they'd make for cover when they heard a bullet whiz about their heads or when a bullet plowed the dirt under their feet. Pa said if there wasn't a cliff close for them to git behind, they'd fall flat on the sand and empty their pistols at the men across the river. Said you couldn't tell whether you hit a man or not. Said sometimes you'd hear a fellow scream and then you'd see a crowd take for cover behind a cliff.

I thought about all this as we looked from our coach window at the engineer across the curve from us.

"Blanton, Blanton, all out for Blanton," the gray-headed

conductor came through our coach yelling.

"That's our station," Finn said. "Wonder where we'll find Cousin Frank."

When Finn and I got off the train, we saw a big man riding a bare-backed mule. He was leading two mules that were saddled.

"He must be Cousin Frank," Finn said, pointing to the big beardy-faced man.

"Are you Frank Powderjay?" I asked.

"Shore am," he said.

"I'm your Cousin Shan Powderjay," I said. "This is your cousin, Finn Powderjay."

"Glad to meet you," Frank said. "I've heerd a lot about ye, boys, but this is my first time to lay my eyes on ye. Git on these mules; we've got to hurry home. We're a-havin' a lot of trouble at home."

I climbed on one mule; Finn reached me our suitcase. Then Finn ran from behind the other mule, slapped his hands on the mule's rump and leaped to the middle of the tiny cowboy saddle.

"Never seen a man mount a mule like that," Frank said. "Ye're more active than I thought ye'd be."

Finn's mule followed Frank's mule and my mule followed Finn's mule from the big crowd gathered around the tiny railroad station. Soon as we left the Big Sandy Valley, we were among the rugged hills on a road filled with chugholes and deep jolt-wagon ruts.

"What's the nature of the trouble we're going to have?" Finn asked Cousin Frank as our trotting mules leaped the chugholes and ruts.

"Ye'll see soon as ye git thar," Frank said. "I don't like to talk about it. We'll haf to fight our bloodkin. Much as we hate 'em, we respect 'em enough to put our pistols and knives aside to fight with fists, clubs, and rocks."

Finn turned and looked at me; I looked at him as our mules dashed up the narrow road behind Frank's mule. Soon we left the narrow wagon road for a mountain footpath between thickets of brush and briars. We wound around this mountain path until we reached the ridge path and then it was faster going. Our mules were wet with sweat, flecks of foam fell from between their legs and foamy slobbers dripped from their hanging lips.

"It's a right fur piece over here from the station," Frank said. "It's eleven miles by crossin' this mountain. Fifteen miles if we go around it."

Now Frank spurred his mule to a trot and our mules followed. I was getting a little sore riding on a small cowboy saddle. Finn was having a little trouble with the brush switching across his face since he was tall and was riding a longlegged mule."

"It's a shame that none of us have never seen none of ye before," Frank said. "I heerd ye's a mighty stuck-up people since ye boys went to high school. Heerd ye's eddicated and soft."

"Tell me more about that trouble you're having," Finn said.

"Wait till ye git home," Frank said. "Then ye'll see what it is. I don't like to think about it. I tell Ma that we ought to use guns and knives and git it over with. A body can't finish a piece of trouble with fists, rocks, and clubs."

"Will the other fellows fight?" Finn asked.

"Ye damned right they'll fight," Frank said.

When we reached a big double-log house down at the foot of the mountain, Frank rolled off his sweaty steaming mule. Finn jumped off his mule and threw our suitcase to the ground. And I rolled over the bony side of my mule. Soon as I hit the round, I stretched my arms and legs and looked around for Uncle Melvin. But there wasn't anybody around but young men I took to be my first cousins.

"Where's Uncle Melvin?" I asked.

Everyone was silent.

I want ye to meet my brothers," Frank said. I want ye to meet some more of yer first cousins that ye have never seen."

Finn and I met Dobie, Erf, Tim, Gullet, Don, and Van, our first cousins. They were husky, strong, tough-looking as tough-butted white-oak saplings. The palms of their hands were hard as brogan shoe-leather where they had been gripping mattock handles, double-bitted ax handles, saw handles, broad-ax handles, pitchforks, and one-eyed sprouting hoes. Erf and Tim had heavy black beard on their faces. Don and Van were too young to shave; they had white fuzz on their faces that needed to be shaved.

"Come to the house and meet Ma," Frank said, sadly.

Seven of us followed Frank toward the house while Van took the mules to the barn. When we reached the house, we walked through the dog-trot between the two big log pens. Aunt Mallie met us at the door wringing her hands and crying.

"Ma, here's Finn and Shan," Frank said.

"Glad to know you, Aunt Mallie," I said, shaking her hand.

"Glad to know you," Finn said, shaking her hand quickly.

"Sorry ye boys come right in the midst of all this trouble," Aunt Mallie said, weeping again. "But I don't know of any time ye could come here lately when we weren't a-havin' trouble."

I looked at Aunt Mallie's wrinkled face and the gray wisps of hair stringing over her face. I didn't think she ought to look as old as she did.

"How's Brother Micky?" Aunt Mallie asked.

"He's getting along as well as common, Aunt Mallie," Finn said.

"I'd like to see 'im," she said, her face brightening some when she spoke of Pa. "It's been nigh twenty years since I seed 'im. I'll bet he's changed a lot."

"I don't know how he looked twenty years ago," Finn said. "That was before I was born."

"I don't think he's changed much," I said. "I believe you'd know 'im if you were to meet 'im in the big road."

"Where's Uncle Melvin?" Finn asked.

"Oh, Oh," Aunt Mallie screamed, "he's not here. Hain't ye heerd about our trouble? Hain't Micky told ye?"

"No," Finn said.

"He's over the hill yander a-livin' with that old thing," Aunt Mallie screamed, then she dropped to her chair.

"Never mind, Ma," Frank said, "we're a-goin' to clean that place up today. We'll fetch Pa home."

"Be keerful, boys," Aunt Mallie warned between sobs. "They'll do anything to ye. They are liable to bushwhack ye, use knives 'r pistols 'r anything they can use to git ye with. Anybody that will try to pizen yer well-water will do anything."

"But we got two more to put into the fight today," Frank

said. "I think Finn and Shan can hep us out. I think two more men can decide the fight. We've been too evenly matched before—seven of them and seven of us. Today, it will be nine of us and seven of them."

Finn looked at me; I looked at him.

"I hate fer Brother Micky's boys to come to see us and haf to fight the first day," Aunt Mallie said between sobs.

"Ah, we don't mind, " Finn said.

We followed Frank to the woodyard. He called his brothers around him."

"Shan, I didn't know that you and Finn didn't know about Pa," Frank said. "But he's a-livin' with an old hag over that mountain yander. He's been a-goin' to see 'er fer the last twenty-five years. He's got a fambly over thar too. We've got seven half brothers and two half sisters. Here lately he spends more time over thar than he does with Ma. That old frowsy-headed hag is younger than Ma. It's damned nigh a-puttin' Ma in 'er grave. We've got to do something about it. We aim to bring Pa back dead 'r alive."

I looked at my first cousins. Their beardy faces got red as Frank talked. They looked mean as snakes as they kicked the ground with the toe of their brogans. They twitched their nervous fingers.

"Cousin Finn and Shan, do ye mind dirtyin' yer hands and maybe gittin' yer noses mashed flat in a fight to hep yer Big Sandy cousins?" Frank asked us.

"When we came to see you," Finn said before I had time to speak, "your fight is our fight. We'll stay with you until the fight is finished."

"That's the speret," Erf said.

"What do ye say, fellars?" Erf said, spitting ambeer at his feet, wiping his beardy lips with his shirt-sleeve.

"Let me tell Cousin Shan and Finn a leetle about the way we fight," Frank said. "See the mountain yander. We'll climb the path to the ridge road. We'll scream like wildcats and cuss Pa's youngins by that old hag with every kind of rotten cuss word we can lay our tongues to. They may be up thar on the mountain a-layin' fer us and jump from the bushes and grab us soon as we git upon the mountain. Seems like they've allus got spies up among the trees like crows a-watchin' everthing we do down here! Now if ye hear war whoops and see 'em a-comin' from the bushes at ye, go right after 'em."

Frank walked in front down the path like he was going to a funeral. All of our first cousins looked that way as they went to battle their half brothers. Before we got to the end of the garden, Aunt Mallie opened the door.

"Frank, do be keerful," Aunt Mallie hollered. "I feel like somebody is a-goin' to die."

"Okay, Ma," Frank yelled.

"I believe they've got a spy a-sittin' up in one of these trees," Frank said as we started up the mountain. "Thought I heerd 'im give a signal whistle."

They must have had a spy someplace. Before we reached the mountain top, seven husky men met us.

"Ye would come to take the advantage o' us," Frank snarled as he singled out the biggest of our half first cousins by unlawful wedlock.

"Where ye git yer hep?" he snarled back at Frank. "Hit'll jist be too bad fer yer strangers. We'll give 'em a double dose of all that we've been a-givin' ye."

"The devil ye will," Frank said.

Before Frank's words had left his mouth, Finn had met his man and upended him the first lick.

"Jesus Christ, ye've got a wallop fer a eddicated man," Cousin Erf told Finn.

"I've got the difference too," Finn said, "in case I have to have it. They'll never whip us."

Frank and his big half brother had tangled. They were clinched-arms around each other, and like logs tied together with big brown cables, they were rolling down the mountainside, cussing, biting—fighting—like old enemies. We were all fighting—nine men against six now for Finn had knocked one man out the first lick he struck. I wasn't mad at the man I was fighting until he stuck his broken discolored teeth into the fat of my ear. That made me a little sore and I fought him a little harder. But I thought Uncle Melvin wasn't worth all this fighting. I had never heard as much swearing in any fight I'd ever seen. I had never seen such fighting. Frank and his half brother were standing up pounding one another with big fence-maul fists. The blood was dripping from their ears where they had bitten each other and it was flying from their noses where they were pounding each other—but Frank was pushing him up the mountain.

"Get in there and fight," Finn screamed as he was getting hot under the collar. "Everybody fight! Come on, you first cousins! You are not fighting!"

Finn upended another man. He looked to be their youngest but it was another one out of the way. When our first cousins saw what Finn had done, they started fighting harder.

If Uncle Melvin's boys by his unlawful wife had just known to have clinched Finn, he was easy to throw down. But long as he could stand up and maul with his long gorilla arms, he'd knock 'em out fast as he got to them. They didn't know how to fight Finn.

"Ye brought yer damned first cousins in here to hep ye," one shouted. "Ye couldn't whip us by yerselves. One is a prize fighter!"

"Yer a liar," Erf shouted as we drove them closer to the mountain ridgetop with two already on the ground—nine of us were fighting five now.

"I'll break the rule when ye foul us," one of Uncle Melvin's boys by his unlawful wife yelled as he whipped a pistol from his hip pocket.

"No, you won't," Finn said, drawing his pistol to cover him. "If you move, I'll let you have it."

"Don't kill 'im, Finn," I yelled. "Don't have trouble the rest of your days over Uncle Melvin."

"Drop that pistol or you die."

He dropped the pistol. Erf ran in and grabbed it. Finn put his pistol back in its holster and Erf stuck his captured pistol down in his hip pocket. Now we had them backed on the mountain ridgetop. We would soon be fighting more to our advantage for we would be backing them down the other side of the mountain toward the shack where they lived.

I don't believe I could have whipped my man if it hadn't been for Erf helping me. When Erf started to fight him, I thought it looked bad to have two men on one that was smaller than I was. I dropped out of the fight and just let Erf fight him. I sat on a stump and watched the fight as everybody tangled on the ridge road.

"Ye tried to pizen us," Frank said to the half brother that he was fightin'. "Ye passed our house when we's all out in the field at work and ye tried to throw a hunk of meat in our well. Ye missed the well and our dog got the meat. He was dead in three hours after he et it. This lick is fer that piece of meat ye throwed at our well."

Frank stood on his tiptoes and threw all the weight of his powerful shoulders against his fist. It connected with his half brother's beardy chin and upended him. He lay sprawled on the ridge road with blood running from his nose, mouth and eyes.

"Think that old hag sent 'im to pizen Ma on our wellwater," Frank said, "while we's out in the field."

Finn was about to get the best of his third man. He had clinched Finn because he was tired and Finn was pounding him with little short uppercuts to the chin and to his short-ribs.

"Oh, my God, ye brothers stop yer fightin'," a woman screamed just as I was getting ready to light my pipe. She came up the mountain path from the other side of the ridge, wringing her hands and screaming. "No ust to fight now. My poor Melvin is dead."

"Did ye pizen 'im?" Erf shouted.

"Oh, no, I loved 'im too much," she wept, wringing her bony calloused hands and then pushing the crow-wing black wisps of hair back from her face. "My true love is dead."

Everybody stopped fighting and started wiping blood from his face, except the three boys that were sprawled cuckoo on the ground. Everybody was too dumbfounded to speak. I didn't light my pipe. I remembered that Aunt Mallie had a feeling that somebody would be dead before this fight was over.

"We're a-takin' Pa home dead 'r alive," Frank said. "Let's go git 'im, boys."

We followed Frank down the path toward the shack down in the valley. She followed behind us weeping and her boys followed her—helping one another down the mountain path and wiping blood from each other's faces. There wasn't any cold water to throw on their faces on the mountain top.

When we reached the three-room mountain shack, all the doors were open. Frank looked in at each door. He couldn't find Uncle Melvin. Then he went inside and looked but Uncle Melvin wasn't in the house.

"He's not in here, boys," Frank said.

"Wonder where the hell he is," Van said.

"God, I'd like to know," Erf said. "Wait till she comes and we'll find out."

"We ought to burn down this shack" Dobie said.

"No sir, the trouble will end if Pa is dead," Gullet said. "No ust to burn the shack. We don't want this bunch to come over the mountain to live offen us."

When Uncle Melvin's unlawful wedded wife walked down the path with her seven boys crippling along the path, their two sisters were following them.

"Where did they come from?" Don asked pointing to his half sisters.

"Must've taken to the brush when they saw us a-comin'," Erf said.

"Where's Pa?" Frank asked soon as she reached the yard.

"Out thar," she said, pointing.

"Out where?" Frank asked.

"The privy."

"Did he die out there?"

"Yes, poor Melvin did," she said weeping. "He complained about his heart this mornin'. And when the boys went upon the mountain, he went outside. He stayed a leetle long and I went to see about 'im and found 'im dead."

"My God," Frank said as he walked toward the toilet that was built over a little creek.

"Love of two wimmen is too much fer any man's heart," Dobie said.

We followed Frank.

"He's here all right," Frank said.

"Ain't this awful," Erf said.

"Wonder what Ma'll think?" Van said.

"She jist won't think," Dobie said. "Ma'd rather have 'im on our side of the mountain dead than to let that old Hag out thar have 'im alive on this side the mountain."

"It's a disgrace fer Pa, to die in her privy," Gullet said.

"Death has two good eyes," Erf said. "He can find a man in the privy same as he can find 'im in a house 'r a cornfield."

"I'd've loved to've seen Uncle Melvin alive," Finn said.

"He'd a liked ye, Finn," Gullet said. "Ye're a fighter."

Frank stuck Uncle Melvin's legs out the privy door. Erf took one leg, I took the other. Frank carried his head and shoulders through the door. Uncle Melvin was a big man with broad shoulders and a big white mustache. He looked like he was still alive but he wasn't, for his big eyes had set under his ferny eyebrows. When Frank squeezed his shoulders through the door, Van took hold of one arm, Gullet got the other and Frank carried his head to keep it from sagging down on his limber neck.

When we left the house all the boys were weeping over their father. And his unlawful wedded wife was carrying on something awful. The two girls were weeping.

"Cry all ye damned please," Frank said, "he don't belong here. He's a-goin' back where he belongs. And ye be damned shore ye stay on this side the mountain when we bury 'im. We'll be prepared at the funeral with powder that is dry enough to burn."

He'll be a load to carry up this side of the mountain and down the other side, I thought as we moved along the path more slowly than the lazy mountain wind that fingered its way through the thickets of brush, briars, sprouts, and trees on the rugged mountain slopes.

We walked along the narrow path with Uncle Melvin, while our first cousins bragged about what a fighter Finn was, said he took after the Powderjays while I must have taken after my mother's people.

"Pa's been dead seven years now," I said.

WEEP NO MORE, MY LADY

"Tomorrow will be a bad day to have the funeralizing," I said as I put more wood on the fire.

"How do you know that it will be a bad day?" Ma asked.

"Look how the smoke is blowing toward the ground," I said. "Last night, there was a ring around the moon. The mules have played in the barnlot all day. These are sure signs of fallen weather."

"Yes, I know, Eif," Ma said as she started churning.

"Pa's been dead seven years now," I said. "I don't see any use having his funeral preached every year. It brings back old memories. And it brings back old griefs."

"I know it brings back things that you children would as leave forget," Ma said, sopping milk from the churn that the dash had sprayed through the churn-lid hole. "But I want you to know that your Pa was a Mountain Baptist. And if we didn't have the funeral preached every year, he'd turn over in his grave."

"You don't want me to norrate to the people that we won't have the funeralizing tomorrow", I said.

"Regardless of weather we'll have the funeralizing tomorrow," Ma said as she sopped more milk from the churn lid with her index finger.

I felt bad about it. I'd talked to my brothers and my sisters and they felt bad about it. They wanted me to talk to Ma and if I couldn't get her to stave off the funeralizing until next year. They thought since I was the oldest child that Ma would listen to me. The reason we felt so bad about it was Ma had married again. We wondered what Jason would think of the funeralizing since he wasn't a Mountain Baptist. We knew how Brother Cyrus W. Seagraves would preach about what a good man Pa was.

That evening after the work was done, Jason hurried to bed. I could tell that he was worried. He'd never been to a funeralizing. And tomorrow he'd hear about what a good man Pa had been. I wondered how Jason would take it. Since he'd been married to Ma, he'd been like a father to Pa's children. He just wasn't a Mountain Baptist like Pa was. He was a Free-Will Baptist.

When I went to bed that night, I laid and thought a long time about what would happen at the funeralizing. I couldn't get it off my mind. I heard the lonesome winter winds howl over the house. It reminded me of the lonesome day when we buried Pa. I thought about the deep snow and how we had to haul Pa on a sled with our surest-footed mule to the top of the mountain. Pa got a token that he was going to die; he chose the place where he wanted to be buried and cleared a place in the thicket a week before he died. Then Pa went to the barn and made his own coffin out'n seasoned boards that he'd kept ten years in the barnloft for that purpose. He always kept seasoned lumber so if one of us died he wouldn't have to split a green tree to make a coffin.

Next morning it was just as I told Ma it would be. We had had fallen weather and plenty of it. It was a snow that was as deep on the ground as it was the day we buried Pa. Everything was buried in snow. The snow was over a tall man's knees.

"Just like the day we buried Dave," Ma wept at the breakfast table as she supped her coffee from the saucer. "It brings back the day seven years ago that I'll never forget."

Jason didn't say a word. He supped his coffee and got up from the table. He went to the barn to feed and milk.

"I wouldn't weep so, Ma," Sister Effie said. "Pa's dead and gone now."

"He's dead but he's not gone," Ma sobbed. "Mountain Baptists never go. Dave is with me still."

Eustacia and Lucretia didn't say a word.

"Do you suppose anybody will be here on a day like this?" Brother Tim asked.

"There'll be a lot of people here," Ma said. "You remember how full the house was on the day we laid poor Dave under the ground. So many here and the day so cold part of the men had to go to the barn and stay."

"I remember it," Brother Prince said.

"There'll be as many here today," Ma sobbed. "All of the people that came to his funeral seven years ago will be here today. All but the ones that have died and time has disabled. If any Mountain Baptist is able, he'll be here. This is a place where the Mountain Baptists rule. Not the Free Willers."

I got up and left the table. I thought I'd better help Jason with the work. I didn't want to sit around the table where Ma was weeping about the past. I loved my father. But I didn't want to hear Ma going on about him as if he had just died.

"I'll tell you the Mountain Baptists are funny people," Jason said. "I don't have nothing against anybody's religion. Let people belong to the church they like best. I can't understand the Mountain Baptist."

"It's the only church I've ever known, Jason," I said.

"Your mother ast me what I was," Jason said. "I told her I was a Baptist. Right then she said she loved me. I guess she thought I was a Mountain Baptist. But I was a Free Willer. We don't have these funeralizings."

"If you're a Free Willer you're a son of Satan among the Mountain Baptists," I said.

"I've found that out," Jason said.

I looked at Jason as he blew his warm breath on his knuckles so he could get his fingers limber enough to milk the cows. Jason was a good-looking man. He was a better-looking man than Pa was. Ma had done well to marry Jason. He'd never been married before. He was tall, blue-eyed with hair black as a crow's wing and not a gray hair in his head. There was not a line in his smooth face. I don't know why he wanted to marry Ma and try to help her raise seven children when he could have married a younger woman.

Just as we had finished doing the work, people started coming to the funeralizing. They waded through the deep snow. Men with felt arctics and high-topped boots walked in front and broke paths through the drifts so the women and children could come. They carried song books and Bibles. I never saw such crowds of people. Everybody came that wasn't sick, too young or too old to wade through the deep snow. Jason just had time to get dressed in his best clothes for the day. The house was jammed full of people. All were in the front room but my sisters. They were getting dinner for the people. The people were shaking hands with Ma. They were making things worse for Ma when they spoke about the big snow on the ground seven years ago. Ma was weeping and shaking hands with all the people.

Jason acted funny when he got among the crowd of Mountain Baptists. He acted like a sheep that was in the wrong pasture. Jason tried to pretend that he was at home with them. He shook hands with Brother Cyrus W. Seagraves. Brother Cyrus talked to Jason for a few minutes before he announced that services would begin at nine o'clock. Brother Cyrus told us that we were late getting started.

The old people got all the chairs we had. The next oldest sat on the sides of the beds. The young people sat on the floor or stood and leaned against the wall. The front room was full of people; doors that led to the kitchen, dining room, and the other three rooms were opened so the heat would go in from the big fireplace. And these rooms were filled with people. They were all filled but the kitchen and the front part of the kitchen was full.

Jason had his chair pulled up beside of Ala's chair. But around Ma and Jason were many of the old Mountain Baptists. The men had long gray hair, beards on their faces and big horns of mustaches. Jason's face was clean-shaved. They would lean over and whisper to Ma and cup their hands over their ears to get Ma's answer when she whispered loud enough to them so everybody could hear. There were enough people gathered close to Ma and Jason to smother them. I noticed Jason's face was getting pale already.

"Before we really begin this service for a departed Brother," Brother Cyrus said in a strong, high-pitched voice, "we had better 'fellowship.' Now if any of you Brothers and Sisters know of anybody that you have anything against, if one of your Brethren or Sisters has wronged you, get up and tell us about it here. If anyone confesses he has wronged somebody, then we will 'Church' that person. He will no longer be a Mountain Baptist."

There was silence in the rooms. Not a person spoke. No one had wronged another. Brother Cyrus stood before them and waited.

"Then all is well among the Brothers and Sisters," Brother Cyrus said. "Now do any of you know of a Brother or a Sister who has been to a street fair, a circus, a picture show, a gambling? If you do, speak up and tell it here. If you do know and don't tell it, then that sin will be chalked against you in the Lamb's Book of Life."

There was silence in the crowd. Not a person made a sound.

How can anybody see a picture show that lives this far back, I thought while there was silence in the crowd. How can one see a circus back among these hills where there has never been a circus? Where is there a town big enough for a carnival to come? I didn't know about the gambling joints.

"It's mighty fine, children," Brother Cyrus said as he stood in the middle of the room with his Bible in his hand. His head nearly touched the joists in our house. His big hand covered both sides of the Bible he held. His black pants bagged at the knees; drops of snow-melted water stood over his long black coat. Ice-melted water dripped from the long horns of his white mustache.

"It's a wonderful world when men can leave other men's

wives alone," Brother Cyrus said. "It's wonderful when they put the worldly things behind. Wonderful when they can come together to iron out their troubles in good Mountain Baptist fellowshipping."

I looked at Jason. His face was getting red. He twisted in the chair where he sat beside of Ma. The people around Ma were still whispering to her. I guess Jason heard what they were saying. And I know that they were speaking about Pa. They were talking about what had happened seven years ago.

"Now let us sing that good old fellowshipping song, 'Leaning on the Everlasting Arms'," Brother Cyrus said. "Sister Ebbie, you read while we sing. Brother Amos will play for us."

Brother Amos Ratcliff sat in a chair in the middle of the front room. The crowd pushed back to give him room to work his arms and room for his long guitar. Brother Amos had little hands, slim fingers, and a long clouded face. He started plucking his guitar strings and moving his body and patting his feet. Sister Ebbie Patton read the stanza:

What a fellowship, what a joy divine,
Leaning on the everlasting arms;
What a blessedness, what a peace is mine,
Leaning on the everlasting arms.

Now Sister Ebbie's voice led the singing of what she had read. Everybody started singing in a high-pitched voice to the accompaniment of the wailing guitar. Brother Amos sat with the guitar in his lap and plucked the strings with his long fingers while with the other hand he held his pocketknife with the back side of the big blade open and chorded the strings on the long, battered guitar neck. He pushed the knife blade up and down the strings to make the guitar wail. There was enough sound in our house to jar the pictures from the walls. I saw some of the small children sitting on the floor put their hands over their ears for the sound was deafening.

Soon as the words that Sister Ebbie had read were sung, the singing and the music died until Sister Ebbie read again:

Leaning, leaning, safe and secure from all alarms;
Leaning, leaning, leaning, on the everlasting arms.

Then everybody sang again to the wail of the guitar.

Soon as they had finished singing the chorus, I looked at Ma and Jason. Jason's face was red as a turkey's snout; he acted like a chicken with the gaps. I knew that Jason couldn't stand it much longer; neither could Ma the way she was taking on. I knew that she was going to have another sinking spell.

When Sister Ebbie started reading:

Oh, how sweet to walk in this Pilgrim way,
Leaning on the everlasting arms;
Oh, how bright the path grows from day to day,
Leaning on the everlasting arms,

I slipped out from the crowded house and walked the path to the cellar. I was needing something to revive me and I got it in the cellar. As I walked back carrying a gallon jug my path had grown brighter in twenty minutes. The wailing guitar and the singing in the house sounded much better. When I got inside, I saw Ma's face was getting white.

"She's having a sinking spell," Martha Hailey said, holding to Ma's hand. "Her hand's getting cold."

The singing stopped. I rushed over to Ma. I put the jug to her lips. And she drank. In a few minutes her eyes opened and color came to her face. Then I turned to Jason.

"I believe you're having a sinking spell too," I said. "Looks like something is wrong."

I put the jug to his lips and he drank like he was thirsty. I knew that this funeralizing was more than Jason could bear. I put the jug to his lips the second time he drank; I put it to his lips the third time and he just sipped a little. Then I saw color come to his face. I passed the jug around to the people that felt lousy. Most all of the men and many of the women drank and they felt much better. Now everybody sang. It was a different service altogether.

At eleven-thirty dinner was ready. Grub was stacked on the table and the people walked into the kitchen and helped themselves. Ma wasn't weeping so much now. Her face looked brighter. Jason wasn't trying to get away from Ma. He was holding her arm and leading her around. He was waiting on Ma more than I had ever seen him. And even now the Mountain Baptists were making him feel quite at home. He was getting right into the spirit of funeralizing. He wasn't thinking so much about what Brother Cyrus was saying about Pa and what all the people were whispering in Ma's ear about what had happened seven years ago.

There wasn't room around the table for everybody, so no

one sat down at the table. The people loaded their plates,
found a place to sit down to eat. Many stood up and ate.
Many refilled their plates three times. I'll tell you it took a lot
of grub to feed as many people as we had in our house. When
dinner was over, everything had been cleaned up until there
wasn't enough scraps left for our two hounds. But everybody
would need food now. The hardest part of the day was yet
to come. We had to get up on the mountain where Pa was
buried. We had to go and stand by his grave and sing again.
And it was beside his grave that Brother Cyrus would have
to preach his long sermon.

Strong young men led the way breaking the path through
the snow. And the old people and the women folks followed
up the snow-broken path. I went along and carried another
full gallon of spirits. I thought there might be more sinking
spells. Somebody might get too cold and need warming. I'll
tell you it was hard to climb to the top of the mountain. But
we made it. The young boys and girls helped the old men
and women up the path. Sometimes a whole bunch would go
down in the snow together but they'd get up one by one and
brush the snow from one another. Finally we reached Pa's
grave. It was snowed under, but there was a mound of snow
about it. We stood around this mound of snow while Brother
Amos sat on his haunches and strummed his guitar. Sister
Ebbie read the words:

From Greenland's icy mountains,
From India's cor-al strand,
Where Afric's sunny fountains,
Roll down their golden sand;

From many an ancient river,
From many a palmy plain,
They call us to deliver
Their land from error's chain.

Now to the tune of the wailing guitar and the lonesome wind high on this mountain, everybody sang. Brother Cyrus stood in front of the crowd and lifted his hands high, holding his Bible in one hand. His great voice roared louder than the wind. Brother Amos's hands trembled for they were thin and long and the cold wind chilled them. After we sang this verse, I offered Brother Amos spirits to warm him. And he drank freely.

Then Sister Ebbie read:

What though the spicy breezes
Blow soft o'er Ceylon's isle;
Though ev-'ry prospect pleases,
And only man is vile:
In vain with lavish kindness
The gifts of God are strown;
The heathen in his blindness
Bows down to wood and stone!

Before we had finished singing these words, I had to give the people spirits. I didn't have to give Jason any more. Sweat had broken out in big white drops that stood like white soup-beans over his face. Ma wasn't weeping now. She held to Jason's arm as they stood together on the steep snowbanks She was looking at the mound of snow. I guess she was thinking about how time had changed everything. Soon as Sister Ebbie had finished reading and we'd finished singing "From Greenland's Icy Mountains," Brother Tobbie Lennix prayed a long prayer.

Then Brother Cyrus started his long sermon. He preached about Pa from the time he was a small boy riding a mule to the water mill barefooted with a turn of corn to grind for meal. He took Pa all through his young days, what a sinner he was then and how he finally knelt at the altar where Brother Cyrus was still a young preacher. Then he preached about the change that had come over Pa, how he married Ma, a pretty young girl of seventeen summers from Beaver Branch. He preached about how they had replenished the earth with seven fine children, all saved but one, and that was me, and how they had earned a living by the sweat from their brows on the steep rocky mountain slopes. But he didn't leave me out there. I had helped dig the living from the earth too. Then he brought Pa's life up to the day of his death. He spoke of what a powerful man Pa was when he worked in the fields or when he worked for the Lord.

As Brother Cyrus continued his sermon, I passed the spirits to the old men and women whose lips were getting blue and whose teeth chattered when the icy winds blew, not from Greenland's icy mountains, but from Kentucky's rugged hills. And when they drank the warm spirits from the jug, they were revived. I know that some of the people at this funeralizing would have passed out if I hadn't taken something along. Brother Amos had kept his fingers limber so he could pick the guitar. But the cold didn't freeze Sister Ebbie's voice. She could still sing like a lark and she wouldn't drink.

Brother Cyrus didn't need anything, for he preached so hard that he was sweating.

Jason stood it well until the close of Brother Cyrus's sermon, when he preached that no man could ever take the place of the man that was buried seven years ago beneath this snow. He said that it was impossible to find a man to fill his shoes, to run his farm and all of that. And when he said these words, Jason almost wilted, though he had been getting pretty well into the spirit of a Mountain Baptist funeralizing. When I saw that Jason was hurt, I went over and handed him more spirits. He drank freely from the jug. Soon he was himself again. I gave Ma more spirits for I didn't want her to have a sinking spell and have to carry her down the steep hill from Pa's grave. It had taken Brother Cyrus nearly four hours to finish his sermon.

"Now, Sister Ebbie, sing the greatest song ever written," Brother Cyrus said.

Though all of us knew this song by heart for we had heard it since we were old enough to listen to anything, Sister Ebbie read the words and we sang them for it was in accordance with our church.

Amazing grace, how sweet the sound!
That saved a wretch like me
I once was lost, but now I'm found,
Was blind, but now I see.

There was a lot of weeping when we sang this song to the wail of the lonesome winter wind that swept through the leafless tree-tops in this mountain top. It was a sad song to all of us for it had been sung at so many funeralizings. Even Jason shed tears. Ma started weeping again when we reached the last stanza.

When we've been there ten thousand years,
Bright shining as the sun;
We've no less days to sing God's praise
Than when we first begun.

Now the funeralizing was over. I hated to see Ma weeping. But Jason was weeping with her. I didn't mind seeing them weep together. Many were cold as we left the hill. I gave Ma and Jason another sup of spirits and they felt better. I passed the jug until it was emptied.

There was a lot of handshaking and slapping each other on the back. Everybody tried to talk and everybody was happy in fellowship and human love. As the short winter day was coming to a close and trains of crows flew above our heads going to a pine grove on a mountain crest to roost, we formed a chain of fellowship, holding each other's hand to get back safe down the steep mountainside. And two of the strongest links in this chain of fellowship, I believe, were Ma and Jason.

RAIN ON TANYARD HOLLOW

"Don't kill that snake, Sweeter," Mammie said. "Leave it alone among the strawberry vines and it'll ketch the groundmoles that's eatin' the roots of the strawberry plants."

Mammie raised up from pickin' strawberries and stood with one hand in her apron pocket. Drops of sweat the size of white soup-beans stood all over her sun-tanned face and shined like dewdrops in the sun. Mammie looked hard at Pappie but it didn't do any good.

"Kill that snake," Pappie shouted. "It must a thought my knuckle was a mole. It ain't goin' to rain no how unless I kill a few more black snakes and hang 'em on the fence."

Pappie stood over the black snake. It was coiled and a-gettin' ready to strike at 'im again. It looked like the twisted root of a black-oak tree rolled-up among the half-dead strawberry plants. It must a knowed Pappie was goin' to kill it the way it was fightin' him back. It kept drawin' its long black-oak-root body up tighter so it could strike harder at Pappie. It stuck its forked tongue out at him.

"You would fight me back," Pappie shouted as he raised a big flat rock above his head, high as his arms would reach. "You would get me foul and bite me. That's just what you've done. Now I'm goin' to kill you and hang you on the fence and make it rain."

Pappie let the big rock fall on the black snake. The rock's sharp edge cut the snake in two in many places. Its tail quivered against the ground and rattled the dried-up leaves on the strawberry plants. Its red blood oozed out on the dry-as-gunpowder dust. Mammie stood and looked at the pieces of snake writhin' on the ground.

"Old Adam fit with rocks," Pappie said. "They air still good things to fight with."

Pappie stood with his big hands on his hips. He looked at the dyin' black snake and laughed.

"That black snake didn't hurt your hand when it bit you," Mammie said. "Sweeter, you air a hardhearted man. You've kilt a lot of snakes and hung 'em on the fence to make it rain. They air still hangin' there. I ain't heard a rain-crow croakin' yet ner felt a drop of rain. The corn is burnt up. You know it has. The corn ain't goin' to git no taller. It's tasselin' and it's bumblebee corn. If you's to drop any ashes from your cigar on this strawberry patch it would set the plants on fire. They look green but they are dry as powder. Where is your rain?"

"I don't know, Lizzie," Pappie said. "You tell me where the rain is."

"It's in the sky," Mammie said, "and you won't get it unless you pray fer it to fall. It's about too late fer prayer too. And the Lord wouldn't listen to a prayer from you."

When Mammie said this she looked hard at Pappie. Pappie stood there and looked at Mammie. What she said to him about the Lord not listenin' to his prayer made Pappie wilt. His blue eyes looked down at Mammie. The hot dry wind that moved across the strawberry patch and rustled the strawberry plants, moved the beard on Pappie's face as he stood in the strawberry patch with his big brogan shoes planted like two gray stumps. His long lean body looked like a dead snag where the birds come to light and the beard on his face and the long hair that stuck down below the rim of his gone-to-seed straw hat looked like sour-vines wrapped around the snag.

"Don't stand there, Sweeter, like a skeery-crow and look at me with your cold blue-water eyes," Mammie said. "You know you air a hardhearted man and the Lord won't listen to your prayer. Look at the harmless black snakes you've kilt and have hangin' on the fence and you ain't got rain yet. Sweeter, I'm lettin' the rest of these strawberries dry on the stems. I'm leavin' the strawberry patch."

Mammie slammed her bucket against the ground. She pulled her pipe from her pocket. She dipped the light-burley terbacker crumbs from her apron pocket as she walked toward the ridge top rustlin' the dyin' strawberry plants with her long peaked-toed shoes. By the time Mammie reached the dead white-oak snag that stood on the ridge top and marked our strawberry patch for all the crows in the country, Mammie had her pipe lit and there was a cloud of smoke followin' her as she went over the hill toward the house.

"Tracey, your Mammie talked awful pert to me."

"Yep, she did, Pappie."

"She talked like the Lord couldn't hear my prayer."

When Pappie talked about what Mammie said about the Lord not payin' any attention to his prayers, his beardy lips quivered. I could tell Pappie didn't like it. He felt insulted. He thought if the Lord listened to prayers, He ought to listen to one of his prayers.

"I'm just hard on snakes, Tracey," Pappie said. "I don't like snakes. My knuckle burned like a hornet stung me when that dad-burned black snake hid among the strawberry plants and bit me. It didn't come out in the open and bite me. Your Mammie got mad because I kilt that snake. I know the baby-handed moles are bad to nose under the roots of the straw-berry plants and cut their white-hair roots and the black snakes eat the moles. But that ain't no excuse fer a black snake's bitin' me on the knuckle."

"I don't blame you, Pappie," I said.

When I said this, Pappie looked at me and his face lost the cloud that was hangin' over it. The light on Pappie's face was like the mornin' sunshine on the land.

"It's a dry time, Tracey," Pappie said as he kicked the dry strawberry plants with his big brogan shoe. The leaves that looked green fell from the stems and broke into tiny pieces. Little clouds of dust rose from among the strawberry plants where Pappie kicked.

"We don't have half a strawberry crop," I said. "And if we don't get rain we won't have a third of a corn crop."

"You air right, Tracey," Pappie answered. "We'll get rain. If it takes prayers we'll get rain. Why won't the Lord listen to me same as he will listen to Lizzie? Why won't the Lord answer my prayer same as he will answer any other man's prayer in Tanyard Hollow?"

When Pappie said this he fell to his knees among the scorched strawberry plants. Pappie come down against the dry plants with his big fire-shovel hands and at the same time he turned his face toward the high heat-glimmerin' sky. Dust flew up in tiny clouds as Pappie beat the ground.

194

"Lord, will you listen to my prayer?" Pappie shouted. "I don't keer who hears me astin' you fer rain. We need it, Lord! The strawberries have shriveled on the vines and the corn is turnin' yaller. It's bumblebee corn, Lord. Give us rain, Lord. I've kilt the black snakes and hung 'em on the fence and the rain don't fall. Never a croak from the rain-crow ner a drop of rain. The black snake on the fence is a false image, Lord."

Pappie beat his hands harder on the ground. He dug up strawberry plants with his hands and tossed them back on the ground. He dug up the hard dry ground and sifted it among the strawberry plants around him. He never looked at the ground. His face was turned toward the high clouds. The sun was beamin' down on Pappie and he couldn't look at the sun with his eyes open.

"Send rain, Lord, that will wash gully-ditches in this strawberry patch big enough to bury a mule in," Pappie shouted. "Let it fall in great sheets. Wash Tanyard Hollow clean."

I didn't bother with Pappie's prayer but I thought that was too much rain. Better to let the strawberry plants burn to death than to wash them out by the roots and take all the topsoil down Tanyard Hollow too. Can't grow strawberries in Tanyard Hollow unless you've got good topsoil of dead-leaf loam on the south hill slopes.

"Give us enough rain, Lord," Pappie shouted, "to make the weak have fears and the strong tremble. Wash rocks from these hillsides that four span of mules can't pull on a jolt-wagon. Wash trees out by the roots that five yoke of cattle can't pull. Skeer everybody nearly to death. Show them Your might, Lord. Put water up in the houses—a mighty river! Put a river of yaller water out'n Tanyard Hollow that is flowin' faster than a hound dog can run. Make the people take to the high hill slopes and let their feet sink into the mud instead of specklin' their shoes and bare feet with dust!"

Pappie prayed so hard that white foam fell from his lips. It was dry foam the kind that comes from the work cattle's mouths when I feed them corn nubbins. The big flakes of white foam fell upon the green, withered strawberry plants.

"Send the thunder rollin' like tater wagons across the sky over Tanyard Hollow," Pappie prayed. "Let the Hollow grow dark. Let the chicken think that night has come and fly up in the apple trees to roost. Let the people think the end of time has come. Make the Hollow so dark a body can't see his hand before him. Let long tongues of lightnin' cut through the darkness across the Hollow and split the biggest oaks in Tanyard Hollow from the tip tops to their butts like you'd split them with a big clapboard fro. Let pieces of hail fall big enough if ten pieces hit a man on the head they'll knock 'im cuckoo. Let him be knocked cold in one of the biggest rains that Tanyard Hollow ever had. Let the rain wash the dead-leaf loam from around the roots of the trees and let the twisted black-oak roots lie like ten million black snakes coiled at the butts of the big oaks. Lord, give us a rain in Tanyard Hollow to end this drouth! Give us a rain that we'll long remember! I'm through with the brazen images of black snakes! Amen."

Pappie got up and wiped the dry foam from his lips with his big hand.

"I ast the Lord fer a lot," Pappie said. "I meant every word I prayed to Him. I want to see one of the awfulest storms hit Tanyard Hollow that ever hit it since the beginnin' of time. That goes way back yander. I ast fer an awful lot, and I hope

196

by askin' fer a lot, I'll get a few things."

"Pappie, I don't want to wish you any bad luck," I said, "but I hope you don't get all you ast fer. If you get all you ast fer, there won't be anythin' left in Tanyard Hollow. We'll just haf to move out. The topsoil will all be washed away, the dirt washed from around the roots of the trees and they'll look like bundles of black snakes. The big oaks will split from their tip tops to their butts, right down through the hearts with forked tongues of fightnin'. Trees will be rooted up and rocks washed from the hillsides that a jolt wagon can't hold up. There won't be any corn left on the hillsides and the strawberry patch will be ruint."

"Tracey, I've ast the Lord fer it," Pappie answered, "and if the Lord is good enough to give it to me, I'll abide by what He sends. I won't be low-lifed enough to grumble about somethin' I've prayed fer. I meant every word I said. I hope I can get part of all I ast fer."

"It's time fer beans," I said. "I can step on the head of my shadder."

Pappie left the strawberry patch. I followed him as he went down the hill. He pulled a cigar from his shirt pocket and took a match from his hatband where he kept his matches so he could keep them dry. He put the cigar in his mouth, struck a match on a big rock beside the path, and lit his cigar.

"When I was prayin' fer the rain to wash the rocks from the hillsides," Pappie said, "this is one of the rocks I had in mind. It's allus been in my way when I plowed here."

"If we get a rain that will wash this rock from this hill-side," I said, "there won't be any of us left and not much of Tanyard Hollow left."

"You'd be surprised at what can happen," Pappie said. "You can turn a double-barrel shotgun loose into a covey of quails and it's a sight at 'em that'll come out alive."

Sweat run off at the ends of Pappie's beard. It dripped on the dusty path. Sweat got in my eyes and dripped from my nose. It was so hot it just seemed that I was roastin' before a big wood fire. It looked like fall-time the way the grass was dyin'. Trees were dyin' in the woods. Oak leaves were turnin' brown.

Pappie took the lead down the hill. It was so steep that we had to hold to sassafras sprouts and let ourselves down the hill. The footpath wound down the hill like a long crooked snake crawlin' on the sand. When we got to the bottom of the hill, Pappie was wet with sweat as if he'd a swum the river. I was as wet as sweat could make me and my eyes were smartin' with sweat like I had a dozen sour gnats in my eyes.

"Whooie," Pappie sighed as he reached the foot of the mountain and he rubbed his big hand over his beard and slung a stream of sweat on the sandy path. "It's too hot fer a body to want to live. I hope the Lord will answer my prayer."

"I hope Mammie has dinner ready."

Mammie didn't have dinner ready. She was cookin' over the hot kitchen stove. Aunt Rett and Aunt Beadie were helpin' Mammie.

"Lord, I hope we'll soon get rain," Mammie said to Aunt Rett. She stood beside the stove and slung sweat from her forehead with her index finger. Where Mammie slung the sweat in the floor was a long wet streak with little wet spots from the middle of the floor to the wall.

"It's goin' to rain," I said.

"Why is it goin' to rain?" Mammie ast.

"Because Pappie got down in the strawberry patch and prayed fer the Lord to send rain and wash this Hollow out," I said.

Mammie started laughin'. Aunt Rett and Aunt Beadie laughed. They stopped cookin' and all laughed together like three women standin' at the organ singin'.

"We'll get rain," Mammie said, "because Sweeter has prayed fer rain. We'll have a washout in Tanyard Hollow fer Sweeter prayed fer a washout in Tanyard Hollow. We'll get what Sweeter prayed fer."

They begin to sing, "We'll get rain in Tanyard Hollow fer Sweeter prayed fer it."

"Just about like his hangin' the snakes over the rail fence to get rain," Mammie cackled like a pullet. "That's the way we'll get rain."

Uncle Mort Shepherd and Uncle Luster Hix sat in the front room and laughed at Pappie's prayin' fer rain. They thought it was very funny. They'd come down out'n the mountains and were livin' with us until they could find farms to rent. Uncle Mort and Aunt Rett had seven children stayin' with us and Uncle Luster and Aunt Beadie had eight children. We had a big houseful. They's Mammie's people and they didn't think Pappie had any faith. They didn't think the Lord would answer his prayer. I felt like the Lord would answer his prayer, fer Pappie was a man of much misery. Seemed like all of Mammie's people worked against 'im. They'd sit in the house and eat at Pappie's table and talk about gettin' a house and movin' out but they never done it.

They'd nearly et us out'n house and home. When they come to our house it was like locust year. Just so much noise when all their youngin's got to fightin' you couldn't hear your ears pop.

"It's goin' to rain this afternoon," Pappie said. "There's comin' a cloudbust. If you ain't got the Faith you'd better get it."

Uncle Luster got up from the rockin' chear and went to the door. He looked at the yaller-of-an-egg sun in the clear sky. Uncle Luster started laughin'. Uncle Mort got up from his chear and knocked out his pipe on the jam-rock. He looked at the sun in the clear sky and he started laughin'.

Uncle Mort and Uncle Luster hadn't more than got back to the two rockin' chears and started restin' easy until dinner was ready, when all at once there was a roar of thunder across the sky over Tanyard Hollow. It was like a big tater wagon rollin' across the sky. Mammie dropped her fork on the kitchen floor when she heard it. Aunt Rett nearly fell to her knees. Aunt Beadie set a skillet of fried taters back on the stove. Her face got white. She acted like she was skeered.

"Thunderin' when the sky is clear," Aunt Beadie said.

Then the thunder started. Pappie was pleased but his face got white. I could tell he was skeered. He thought he was goin' to get what he'd ast the Lord to send. The thunder got so loud and it was so close that it jarred the house. 'Peared like Tanyard Hollow was a big pocket filled with hot air down among the hills and the thunder started roarin' in this pocket. It started gettin' dark. Chickens flew up in the apple trees to roost.

When Mammie saw the chickens goin' to roost at noon,

she fell to her knees on the hard kitchen floor and started prayin'. Mammie thought the end of time had come. The chickens hadn't more than got on the roost until the long tongues of lightnin' started lappin' across the Hollow. When the lightnin' started splittin' the giant oak trees from their tip-tops to their butts it sounded louder than both barrels of a double-barreled shotgun.

"Just what I ast the Lord to send," Pappie shouted. Mammie jumped up and lit the lamps with a pine torch that she lit from the kitchen stove. I looked at Pappie's face. His eyes were big and they looked pleased. All Aunt Beadie's youngins were gathered around her and Uncle Luster. They were screamin'. They were screamin' louder than the chickens were cacklin' at the splittin' oak trees on the high hillsides. Uncle Mort and Aunt Rett got their youngins around them and Uncle Mort started to pray. All six of us got close to Mammie. I didn't. I stuck to Pappie. I thought about how hard he'd prayed fer a good rain to break the long spring drouth. Now the rain would soon be delivered.

Mammie, Aunt Rett and Aunt Beadie let the dinner burn on the stove. I was hungry and I could smell the bread burnin'. I didn't try to get to the kitchen. I saw the yaller water comin' from the kitchen to the front room. The front room was big and we had a big bed in each corner. When I looked through the winder and saw the big sycamores in the yard end up like you'd pull up horseweeds by the roots and throw 'em down, I turned around and saw Aunt Beadie and Uncle Luster make fer one of the beds in the corner of the room. Their youngins followed them. They were screamin' and prayin'. Uncle Mort and Aunt Rett and all their youngins made fer the bed in the other corner of the room. Mammie and my sisters and brothers made for the stairs. Mammie was prayin', as she run. I stayed at the foot of the stairs with Pappie. When he prayed in the strawberry patch, I thought he was astin' the Lord fer too much rain but I didn't say anythin'. I didn't interfere with his prayer.

The water got higher in our house. A rock too big fer a jolt-wagon to haul smashed through the door and rolled across the floor and stopped. If it had rolled another time it would have knocked the big log wall out'n our house. Uncle Mort waded the water from the bed to the stairs and carried Aunt Rett and their youngin's to the stairs. When he turned one loose on the stairs he run up the stairs like a drownded chicken. Uncle Luster ferried Aunt Beadie and their youngins to the stairs and turned them loose. Pappie had to take to the stairs. I followed Pappie.

"If we get out'n this house alive," Uncle Mort prayed, "we'll stay out'n it, Lord."

Uncle Luster prayed a long prayer and ast the Lord to save his wife and family. He promised the Lord if He would save them that he would leave Tanyard forever. I never heard so much prayin' in a churchhouse at any of the big revivals at Plum Grove as I heard up our upstairs. Sometimes you couldn't hear the prayers fer the lightnin' strikin' the big oaks. You could hear trees fallin' every place.

"The Lord has answered my prayers," Pappie shouted.

"Pray fer the cloudbust to stop," Mammie shouted. "Get down on your knees, Sweeter, and pray."

"Listen, Lizzie," Pappie shouted above the roar of the water and the thunder and the splittin' of the big oaks on the high slopes, "I ain't two-faced enough to ast the Lord fer somethin' like a lot of people and atter I git it, turn around and ast the Lord to take it away. You said the Lord wouldn't answer my prayer. You've been prayin'! Why ain't the Lord answered your prayer? You ain't got the Faith. You just think you have."

When the lightnin' flashed in at our upstairs scuttlehole we had fer a winder, I could see Uncle Mort huddled with his family and Uncle Luster holdin' his family in a little circle. Mammie had all of us, but Pappie and me, over in the upstairs corner. I looked out at the scuttlehole and saw the water surgin' down Left Fork of Tanyard Hollow and down the Right Fork of Tanyard Hollow and meetin' right at our house. That's the only reason our house had stood. One swift river had kilt the other one when they met on this spot. I thought about what Pappie said.

I could see cornfields comin' off'n the slopes. I could see trees with limbs and roots on them bobbin' up and down and goin' down Tanyard Hollow faster than a hound dog could run. It was a sight to see. From my scuttlehole I told 'em what I saw until I saw a blue sky comin' over the high rim of rock cliffs in the head of Tanyard Hollow. That was the end of the storm. I never saw so many happy people when I told them about the patch of blue sky that I saw.

"This is like a dream," Uncle Mort said.

"It's more like a nightmare to me," Uncle Luster said.

"It's neither," Pappie said. "It's the fulfillment of a prayer."

"Why did you pray fer destruction, Sweeter?" Mammie ast.

"To show you the Lord will answer my prayer atter the way you talked to me in the strawberry patch," Pappie said. "And I want your brother Mort and your brother-in-law Luster to remember their promises to the Lord."

The storm was over. It was light again. The chickens flew down from the apple trees. The big yard sycamore shade trees went with the storm but the apple trees stood. There was mud two feet deep on our floor. It was all over the bedclothes. There were five big rocks on our house we couldn't move. We'd haf to take the floor up and dig holes and bury the rocks under the floor. Trees were split all over Tanyard Hollow hillside slopes. Great oak trees were splintered clean to the tops. Our corn had washed from the hill slopes. There wasn't much left but mud, washed-out trees, rocks and waste. Roots of the black-oak trees, where the dead-leaf loam had washed away, looked like bundles of clean-washed black snakes. The big rock upon the steep hillside that bothered Pappie when he was plowin' had washed in front of our door.

"I promised the Lord," Uncle Mort said, "if we got through this storm alive, I'd take my family and get out'n here and I meant it."

"Amen," Pappie shouted.

"Sorry we can't stay and hep you clean the place up," Uncle Luster said, "but I'm takin' my wife and youngins and gettin' out'n this Hollow."

They didn't stay and hep us bury the rocks under the floor. They got their belongin's and started wadin' the mud barefooted down Tanyard Hollow. They's glad to get goin'. Pappie looked pleased when he saw them pullin' their bare feet out'n the mud and puttin' 'em down again. Pappie didn't grumble about what he had lost. The fence where he had the black snakes hangin' washed down Tanyard Hollow. There wasn't a fence rail or a black snake left. The strawberry patch was gutted with gullies big enough to bury a mule. Half of the plants had washed away.

"It wasn't the brazen images of snakes," Pappie said, "that done all of this. Tanyard Hollow is washed clean of most of its topsoil and lost a lot of its trees. But it got rid of a lot of its rubbish and it's a more fitten place to live."

...there was over a thousand people to meet the train.

ANOTHER HANGING

I'll remember the Bellstrase Hangin' to my dyin' day. We've had our hangin's! We've had the Sizemore Hangin', the Dimmer Hangin', Dillmore Hangin', Perkins Hangin' and the Reeder Hangin'. We never had a hangin' that would come up to the Bellstrase Hangin' in 1903. It was one of the best hangins this country has ever seen.

I was a boy in school then. We heard about Willard Bellstrase cuttin' old man Gullet's throat with a razor. It was with a big black-handled razor he pulled on Pa once. "Willard, you're goin' to pull that razor once too often one of these days and you'll be worse off'n a chicken thief," Pa said. "You'll go to the gallows. You know there's a law here agin razors more than anything else. When you pull a razor it's a dangerous thing in Kentucky. The people won't stand for a razor."

Willard shut the razor and let Pa be. He tried the same thing on Blaze Gullet. Blaze couldn't hold his temper. You know the Gullets. He hit Willard around the temple with a ear of corn. Willard yanked his razor and cut Blaze Gullet's throat. He left 'im on the hill where they were gatherin' corn till the next day. Folks at home thought Blaze was gallivantin' around—maybe fox huntin'. His boy found him dead the next day on the hill with frost all over his whiskers. His throat was slit from ear to ear. When John Keene and Amos

Blair went over to see Willard about it, he said, "Shore, I cut his throat. I cut it with a razor. What about it?"

"W'y, we're goin' to take you to the sheriff," John said.

"Take me with you," Willard said. "I want to go. Blowed out the lamp last night and there were devils just a-crawlin' around my bed. Skeered me to death. I've been skeered all night. Take me any place."

Pa allus said Willard'd cut somebody's throat. It kind o' tickled all of us when we heard about it. Tom, Big Aaron, Little Edd and Zulus—I wish you could a heard 'em. "We'll get to leave school. We'll get to go home for the hangin'. It'll be the biggest hangin' we've had in many a day! We'll get to go home! We'll get to go home fer the hangin'!"

And they ran all over the schoolyard and hollered. It made me feel ashamed of myself and of the folks at home. I know a man that pulls a razor there or steals chickens can't last long. Too many trees around there and too many ropes. I felt sorry fer poor old Bertha Bellstrase; there with seven little youngins. Just to think she married a man always pullin' a razor! He packed it with 'im to cut somebody's throat. He packed round rocks in his pocket to throw at men in a fight. He could throw a rock harder and straighter than some men can shoot a rifle ball. I never could be nice to 'im atter he jumped on Pa that time over two little white oaks on the line fence.

"Eif, poor old Willard's had a hard time," Pa told me. "He's one of sixteen children. Used to fight like dogs and cats in the family. He was one of the oldest children. Had to dig and hoe around on these old poor hills and try to help keep grub for the rest. Used to work him all day hitched to a plow."

Pa used to tell me this over and over and he tried to make me like Willard's youngins. I used to chase around with 'em before I went off to school. Didn't care nary bit when I heard old Willard was going to hang by the neck. It tickled me fer I thought he was gettin' what was comin' to 'im. I never said much to the kids around school since they were already makin' plans to go to the hangin'. All were a-gettin' new suits of clothes fer the Bellstrase Hangin'. "Boys will try to look better than I do at the hangin'," I thought. "I'll show 'em who looks good and who don't."

While they were gettin' their new suits, I just went a step further. I got a pair of high-heeled button shoes and one of the finest hats there was in the store. My suit was powder blue, double-breasted with peg-legs. I'll tell you when I got my new shoes, suit and hat on, people around the school didn't know me. I just wanted to let 'em know that I hadn't been away to school for nothin'. I wanted to let 'em know I had somethin' on my body as well as somethin' in my head. And when the excursion train got to Bear Branch at the Eight-Mile Station, I wanted the crowd gathered there goin' to the hangin' to see me. I intended to be one of the first to get on the train after I bought all my new clothes. I wanted to show some of the Burton boys at home who could dress and who couldn't. They could talk all they wanted about Pa's trappin' fer muskrats, polecats, coons and minks and buyin' my clothes. I just wanted to show 'em that I could come dressed better than anybody at home that ever come out to one of the hangins.

I'll never forget what Professor Brady Strickland said to us scholars, "The whole school is goin' on the excursion to the hangin'. I'm goin' to dismiss school and go too. Durned if I stay here and teach an empty schoolroom."

Well everybody at school was gettin' ready for the hangin'. It was to be on Saturday at sunrise. You'd a thought sure as the world it was a baseball game. Just a-runnin' wild to get the train that night. Lanterns and pine torches all lit up. People came in from the hills all rigged up to catch the train to White Rock and ride it to Bear Branch to the hangin'. I never saw so many people in all my life.

"W'y, the Old Line Special won't hold 'em all, will it?" some man said. "They've put on a couple of coaches and couple of boxcars extra. Guess that'll hold 'em all right."

The crowd was a-goin' wild around the depot! Poor old Professor Brady Strickland was all dressed up and talkin' to the girls. Professor Brady was not married. He was a bachelor, we'd heard. We'd heard he'd been married five times and all his women were in the West. He'd come out'n the West to teach our school. People thought it was funny he'd come from the West to these forsaken hills to teach school for forty-eight dollars a month. A lot of the boys were wantin' girls and a lot of 'em had 'em hangin' on their arms.

"Wait till I get to Eight-Mile Station at Bear Branch," I said to Big Aaron. "I'll get the best-lookin' girl at the hangin'. I'll have more than three counties to pick the girls from." And Big Aaron laughed at me. He thought I was funnin'.

I was goin' to show the folks at home I was somebody. I would see Pa and Ma and all the family there. They always come to the hangins. Big Aaron ran up and down the railroad tracks with me at White Rock. Where all that patch of ragweeds is along the railroad tracks, people had it tramped flat as a board. All goin' to Eight-Mile Station to the hangin'! Just like a thousand wild geese right above your head. All just a-goin' on and a-hollerin' and cryin' till you couldn't hear your ears. Screamin' louder than the train could whistle!

The moon came up over the railroad tracks and the rag-weeds. It was time fer love. I was without a girl fer the first time in years. I told Big Aaron we'd better wait and get us a girl at the hangin'. I was dressed to catch a girl too. Didn't know who she'd be and didn't care, just so she was good lookin'.

The train came up the tracks, a-huffin', a-puffin' and a-blowin', and it was about midnight. The train was already loaded and the passengers were a-hollerin' like a lost flock of wild geese. Passengers were wavin' handkerchiefs, and the boys were standin' on flatcars huggin' the girls. A thousand wonders to me some didn't fall off and break their crazy necks the way that train came rockin' around the curves. When it pulled up, we loaded on. Some of the boys were drunk as all get-out and had their pistols out. Their sweethearts were hangin' on to their arms tryin' to get 'em to put their pistols in their pockets—a-cryin' and a-beggin' 'em! Men were tryin' to fight on the train.

Professor Brady got on the train. He loaded on with the crowd. He was surrounded with a boozin' crowd of men singin' wild songs. We happened to get loaded in one of the coaches they'd kept fer the school. The flatcars were to haul the hill men on—the kind who get boozy every time they step outside of the house at night. It's a wonder that some didn't fall off the flatcars and break their necks—back there tryin' to fight and cut one another with knives, tryin' to break jugs over each other's heads.

"Everybody on B-O-A-R-D," the conductor shouted.

"Just a minute," some fellar said. I saw them throw a couple of drunks on a flatcar like you'd throw on a couple o' sacks of cracked corn.

"Okay," one of them said. They hopped on the flatcar. And the train started jerkin', and jumpin' and tearin' out up the track under the moonlight. The night wind was a-blowin' in at the winders. When you ride the Old Line Special you are jerked around and the wind hits your face. You get chilly and want somebody to stand close to you.

I'll tell you a night in May with a lively crowd on the train and a hangin' almost in sight is wonderful! Professor Brady's face was all lit up; pretty girls were all around him! The train was rollin' into the night! It was one of the prettiest nights I ever saw in my life. No wonder boys and girls were lovin' on the train. Arms were around one another's necks, and their cheeks against one another's cheeks!

Right up the track, huffety-puffety, huffety-puffety, and the smoke rolled in black rock-cliff mountains across the moon. Great streamers of black smoke, and the train's lonesome whistle against the cliffs on the sides of the river and the train a-windin' up around the rock-cliffs above the river like a snake, all headin' for the biggest hangin' that ever took place along the Old Line Special!

"I just feel like the train might jump the tracks," Big Aaron said. "I've got to the place I don't care if it does. Let her jump the tracks and throw us into the river!"

"I'll tell you this is a night," I said. "It is the greatest night in all my life."

Hootie, toot toot—right up the track! Hootie toot—and we rolled right up the track! Professor Brady walked over and said, "Girls, how about me sittin' down here by you and gettin' warm? This wind o' May is a little chilly for me."

"He's had a drink too," Big Aaron said. "Moonshine does me that way. I don't give a damn right now if the Old Line Special jumps the tracks clean into the river."

"Sit right down by us, Professor," some tall freckled-faced girl said.

I was afraid the train would wreck and I wouldn't get to see the hangin'. Then I'd take another notion and think it would be great to be in a train wreck and roll down from a cliff into the river, bumpety—bumpety—bumpety—bumpety! Right over the cliffs into the river and the boys on the flatcars a-goin' down through the air a-hollerin' and cavortin' and the moonshine jugs, horse quarts and fruit flyin' in the air. Right up the track we rolled, huffety—puffety—hootie—toot toot— hootie—toot—toot around the bend for Eight Mile Station.

When the Old Line Special rolled into the Station there was over a thousand people to meet the train. The whole hill was covered with boys, girls, men, women, children, and barking dogs a-waitin' for the greatest hangin' Bear Branch people had ever seen. People met the train with torches and lanterns! The whole hillsides seemed covered with boys and girls a-laughin', talkin' and having the biggest time in the world. All the schools in the county had dismissed to see the hangin'!

When I got off that train nobody knew me. Girls looked at me like I'd come from someplace far away. Big Aaron and I went out into the crowd together where there was a lot of hollerin', singin', laughin', talkin' and lovin' goin' on. I never saw hide-nor-hair of Pa and Mom and the rest of the family. They must have thought I wasn't comin'. Didn't know, maybe, that a hangin' within fifty miles was for our school too.

The moon was just goin' down over the Kentucky hills. The tired train was pantin' a little bit now after its long run up the river pullin' all that load of people. People were swarmin' over the hills and the railroad tracks like bees. Boys had their arms around the girls' necks.

"Let's go out to the jail and see Willard Bellstrase," I said.

"Do you reckon he'll break jail and come at one of us with a razor?" Big Aaron asked.

"You needn't worry about him ever takin' after another person with a razor," I said. "His cuttin' throats is over when he once gets in the Eight Mile Station jail. It's made of big rocks that it took twenty yoke of oxen to pull from the old furnaces. He can't get out of the jail for I live here and I know."

There was a big crowd around the jail. We went up to a winder where a lot of people were standin' around. I looked through the winder and I saw Willard in a cell. He had his shirt unbuttoned and his face looked pale as a flour-poke. It would a looked lot paler if it hadn't been for his beard. "He don't look like a mean man," Big Aaron said. "He's got a sad face."

"You'd have a sad face too," I said, "if you's goin' to leave this world and a wife and seven children soon as the sun come up from behind the hills."

Willard didn't know me the way I was dressed and he used to see me every day, too. It wouldn't be long now until poor old Willard would hang on the scaffold built out by the road on a sycamore tree. The watersprouts had been cut away and the first limb trimmed and a rope swingin' down from it like a grapevine swing. A little platform had been built upon four posts with a door fixed on top of it with a pair of leather hinges on one side and a big button on the under side. The rope fell down from the sycamore limb to the trap door, and under the platform the people would get to see Willard swing by the neck after he fell through the door. It was not fixed like a lot of gallows where they have the sides of the platform boxed till you can't see the man swing by the neck.

Of all the pitiful cryin' you ever heard in your life was when Willard's children come to the jail and looked through the bars and cried with Bertha, her screamin' at the top of her voice. Willard ought to have thought about that when he was packin' that razor around for somebody's juggler vein.

"It'll soon be time fer the sun," Big Aaron said. "See the light streaks a-breakin' in the east! It'll soon be time fer the hangin'!"

If you could have seen the crowds gettin' up off the ground! Some had been asleep and some had been down drunk. Some were just a-restin' after a tiresome trip to the hangin'! Every bush on the hillside had a mule or a horse tied to it. It was a sight to see. Wagons, buggies, hug-me-tights and surreys were on every level place where one could be left. It was the biggest crowd that ever had been to Eight-Mile Station. Hundreds of people were wavin' their hands into the air and a hollerin' every way we looked.

The whippoorwills were a-hollerin' and the roosters a-crowin' fer daylight! The crowd was goin' wild. I'll tell you I never got so excited in all my life. Big Aaron, Little Edd, Tom, Zulus, and I together. The moon was goin' down and it looked like it was tired after the way it had tried to run up a sky of white clouds to keep up with the train that brought us to the hangin'. Sorry the moon couldn't stay in the sky to see the hangin' but night was slippin' fast away like a shadow before sunrise. Night was slippin' off across the fields behind the Kentucky moon. Men and boys were a-drinkin' from their jugs, horse quarts, bottles and fruit jars again and a-fightin' all around Eight-Mile Station. They were gettin' ready for the hangin'.

"Bring on the man!" they screamed.

It was just about this time that I met Beadie Blevins. She was the prettiest girl I saw at the hangin'. It was just breakin' day but I could tell she was as pretty as a ripe peach. Her hair fell in long curls over her shoulders and her teeth were white as percoon petals. I just felt like hollerin' "goodie goodie" to the rest of the boys. But it would have hurt their feelin's since I got the prettiest girl. Beadie Blevins held onto my arm.

"Good-by, boys," I said. "I'll be seein' you when the Old

Line Special takes us back to White Rock."

I took off with Beadie through the crowd. A crowd was still goin' wild and hollerin' for Willard. We heard that a lot of the Bellstrases would come with guns to stop the hangin'. But, an army of Gullets were there with guns. The Gullets said the hangin' would go on. Preacher Hix went to Willard's cell and tried to get him to make peace with his Lord before sunrise. Willard started cussin' the Gullets and sayin' if he met them in hell, as he surely would, they'd fight it out to a finish. Willard's children were around the jail winders a-screamin' and a-prayin'. Bertha Bellstrase was there a-screamin' till you could a-heard her across the mountain. I was the happiest young man in the world. I was with my Beadie. Since daylight had come, I knew Beadie was the prettiest girl at the hangin'.

I saw Sheriff Pennix put the cap over Willard's face and the handcuffs on his hands. Sheriff Pennix had a couple of deputies with him. They carried long rifles over their shoulders and pistols buckled on them. I saw the Bellstrases there, too, with pistols and rifles. They were mad men with dark, beardy faces. I thought surely there'd be war. Maybe the crowd looked too big for the Bellstrases. We'd a had one of the awfulest times there ever was after havin' the train to bring people in from every place and then not have a hangin'. It wouldn't've done. The people intended to see a hangin'. That's what they'd come fer and what they intended to see. But Beadie was with me. She was the nearest thing to Heaven I ever saw.

"Whoopee! Hurrah! Woopee!" The sun was creepin' over the hills now. The sheriff and his two deputies brought Willard out of the jail. Willard was a-kickin' and a-cussin'. He was actin' awful. I saw Pa and Ma by the scaffold. Ma had one of Willard's youngins. Pa was wipin' tears from his eyes. Pa had a chicken heart when an old friend of his was to be hung by the neck. Pa and Ma didn't know me the way I was dressed. I didn't want them to know me until the whole thing was over.

People kept crowdin' closer and Sheriff Pennix and his deputies had to shove them back. They were afraid that it might be one of the Bellstrase boys edgin' up a little too close. The Bellstrases'll fight until they die for one another. But, there were too many people wantin' to see a hangin' and they were agin' the Bellstrases. The Bellstrases didn't have a chance and the sheriff took Willard to the scaffold. Willard scooted and skived-up the grass, cussed, hollered and prayed and his wife and brothers followed him a-screamin'.

"Ah, Buddie, how do you like your nightcap?" some man hollered. He bent over, slapped his thighs with his big hands and laughed and laughed. Preacher Hix tried to say something. He had a Bible in his hand and a page turned. We could just see his lips workin' and that was all. Beadie had me by the arm. I had my eye on Pa and Ma on the other side. Sheriff Pennix led Willard up on the scaffold. Willard was goin' like a blind dog in a meat-house. The sun was comin' up now. All of us were riled until we didn't care what happened.

Sheriff Pennix put the rope around Willard's neck. Fiddle McCarty tied the knot. Fiddle had tied the knots at many a hangin'. He never failed to make the knot hold. "Ready," Fiddle said.

"Let him make his confession," High Sheriff Pennix said.

"I'd like to slit every damn Gullet's throat among these hills," Willard shouted. "The cowardly bastards! Damn every cowardly son and brother among em! I'll show you that I can die like a man. You've got the wrong man on the scaffold. Men right out there in that crowd that's got graveyards all their own of the men they've killed, yet these bastards come to see me hang by the neck. I can see the sun through this damn veil. Let my breath go! Let my neck break! Let my life end! Just one time to die and I'll soon get it over with! All I got to say is turn the button and let the trap fall."

Screams roared from the crowd.

"Take off that hood!"

"Let the trap door fall!"

"Let's see the damn thing end."

People started crowdin' one another so they could see better. Boys started climbin' up among the sycamore limbs so they could see.

"This is a real hangin'," Beadie said. "It's the best hangin' I ever saw, Honey. I'm glad I come and met you."

"You wouldn't kid me, would you?"

"You know I wouldn't kid you fer the world, Honey!"

And about that time "wow" and the trap door opened and Willard fell danglin' on the end of the rope under the floor of the tall scaffold. He swung around and around, and of all the hollerin' the crowd put up!

"Cut the rope and hang him again," one man standin' near us said. "Grab up somebody and hang 'em."

"Shut your damn trap," a Bellstrase boy said. "We'll let you be the next one we hang."

Bertha fainted and her children took off to the weeds a-screamin'! It was gettin' about milkin' time now and the hangin' was over. The Bellstrases went under the scaffold to claim the body. They waited fer Doc Minton to feel of Willard's ticker to see if he was a corpse or a livin' person.

The first I saw on the train were Big Aaron and Little Edd. They didn't get no girls. They were loaded to the gills on moon-shine whiskey. I sat real close to Beadie Blevins and wished life would be just one long train ride goin' someplace down a long river. Professor Brady sat beside me with some woman.

The Old Line Special went down the grade and the boys whooped it up from their stomachs on the flatcars. All fight-ing one another and shootin' at the trees along the railroad track. It's a thousand wonders ten or fifteen hadn't been killed. They fought all the way to the hangin' and all the way back in the coaches, on top of the box cars and on the flatcars. Boys even played poker goin' back on the flatcars.

"It's got so bad here you just can't have a decent hangin' any more," Beadie said.

"You are right, Honey," I said. "My suit looks like it's never been pressed. My shoes are all skinned and the buttons tramped off'n 'em."

I held Beadie in my arms and loved her all the way back to White Rock.

SPRING VICTORY

"I don't know what to do," Mom said. "We've just enough bread for three more days. We don't have much of anything else to eat with our bread. This is a terrible winter and your father down sick."

Mom sat on a hickory-split-bottomed chair. She put the bottom in the chair last spring. I went to the woods after the sap got up and peeled the green hickory bark from the small hickory sapling. Mom took a case knife and scraped the green from the slats of bark and wove them across the bottom of a chair that Pa wanted to throw away.

"If your father was only well," Mom said and looked at the blazing forestick. "I'll have to think of something. You children run along and play. Leave me alone to think."

Sophie and I crossed the floorless dogtrot between the two big log pens of our house. We called this dogtrot the "entry." We kept our stovewood and firewood stacked in the entry. This was a place where the rain, snow and sleet couldn't touch the wood. It was easy to walk out of the kitchen and carry an arm load of the stovewood for the kitchen stove when Mom was getting a meal. It was easy for me to carry firewood from the big stack in the entry to the fireplace where Mom was looking into the fire and dreaming now.

"There's not any place for us to run and play," Sophie

said. "The only place we have to run and play is in the entry. And through here."

"You are right," I said. "But Mom wants us to get away from her for a little while. Mom is worried."

Sophie stood by the firewood pile. She put her small white hand upon a big oak backlog, that had part of the dead bark slipped from it. Sophie's long blond hair was lifted from her shoulders by a puff of wind. The cold wind brought tears to her eyes. Beyond the entry we saw the pine-tops upon the mountainside sagging with snow. We couldn't see any briar thickets on the high hill slopes. They were snowed under. The garden fence posts barely stuck out of the snow. Four paths led away from our house—one to the barn, one to the smokehouse, one to the well and one to the hollow back of our house where Mom and I hauled wood with our horse. The big logs that Fred pulled with a long chain around them made a path through the deep snow from the dark hollow under the pines to our woodyard.

"This snow has been on the ground since last November," Sophie said. "That was 1917. Now it is January, 1918. You are ten years old and I am thirteen years old."

We stood in the entry by the woodpile and talked until we got cold; then Sophie opened the door and we walked into the room. We hurried to the big bright fire to warm our cold hands. Mom was staring into the fireplace with her eagle-gray eyes. She looked steadily toward the fire. She was holding James on her lap. Mary was sitting in a small rocking chair beside her. Pa turned over in bed and asked for water.

Mom got up from the rocking chair with James in her arms. She walked toward Pa's bed. Mom poured a glass of water from a pitcher that was on a stand at the head of Pa's bed.

"Do you feel any better, Mick?" Mom said.

"Nope, I don't Sal" he said. "I feel weak as water. I'll tell you that flu is bad stuff. I got up too soon and took a back set."

Pa took the glass of water and drank. Mom stood and watched him with James in her arms.

"Is the firewood holding out?" Pa asked as he handed Mom the empty glass.

"Yes, it is," Mom said. "We have plenty of wood."

"How about food for the family and for the livestock?"

"We're getting along all right," Mom said. "Don't worry, Mick. We'll take care of everything. You get well just as soon as you can. You won't get well if you keep on worrying."

"I can't keep from worrying," Pa said. "Here I'm down sick and can't get out of bed. Crops failed us last year and we don't have bread for the children. And I've never seen such snow on the ground. This is a dark winter to me."

"It's a dark winter for all of us," Mom said. "But remember the snow will leave the hills one of these days and the sun will shine on blue violets under last year's leaves."

Mom put the water glass back on the standtable beside the water pitcher. She walked back to her rocking chair. The firelight glowed over the room and tiny shadows flickered on the newspaper-papered walls.

"Son, we are not whipped yet," Mom said to me. "Your Pa is asleep now. I'll tell you what we are going to do."

I walked over beside Mom's chair. Sophie stood beside her too.

"Sophie can do the cooking," Mom said. "Can't you bake

bread and cook potatoes, Sophie?"

"Yes, Mom."

"And you can use an ax well for a boy ten years old," Mom said.

"It's easy for me to chop with my pole-ax."

"Then you take your ax and go to the hills," Mom said, pointing from the front window to the steep snow-covered bluff east of our house. "You can find all kinds of tough-butted white oaks on the bluff over there. Cut them down, trim them and scoot them over the hill. We're going to make baskets out of them."

I kept my pole-ax in the entry by the firewood pile, where it would not be snowed under. As I walked out of the front room I pulled my toboggan cap low over my ears. I wrapped my overalls close around my legs so the snow wouldn't get around my feet. I picked up my pole-ax and walked down the path toward the barn. The cold whistling January wind stung my face. Fred nickered to me as I passed the barn. The creek was frozen over and the snow had covered the ice save for a hole that I had chopped so the cow and horse could get water.

I passed the water hole and the empty hog pen. I started up the steep bluff toward the white-oak trees. The snow came to my waist. I held to bushes and pulled up the hills—breaking a tiny path through the waist-deep snow. Finally, I reached the white-oak grove and stood beneath a shaggy-topped white oak sapling. Last year's dead leaves were still clinging to its boughs. These clusters of dead leaves were weighted with snow. When the sharp bit of my pole-ax hit the frozen white oak wood, a loud ring struck the distant frozen hill across the valley. The sounds came back to my ears. Snow rained on me from the top of the white-oak sapling. I felled the white oak down the bluff toward the barn. I trimmed its branches and cut its top away. I slid the sapling over the bluff toward the barn. I cut twelve white-oak saplings, and trimmed and topped them and slid them over the bluff toward the barn.

It was easier for me to get down the bluff than it had been to climb it. The white-oak saplings had made a path through the deep snow. I followed this broken path toward the barn. I carried the white-oak saplings from the barn to the entry. I carried one at a time on my shoulder; the green, white-oak timber was heavy. After I'd carried them to the entry I went into the house to see what Mom wanted me to do next.

"After you warm yourself," Mom said, "I want you to take a handsaw and saw these white-oak saplings into six-foot lengths. After you saw them into lengths, I want you to split the lengths into four quarters and bring them to me."

By the time that Mom had given me instructions, I was warm enough to go to work again. I sawed the poles into six-foot lengths and split them with my pole-ax. I carried them into our front room and stacked them in a pile of small green fence rails. Mom looked the pile over and picked up one of the cuts and started to work. She used a butcher knife, a drawing knife and a case knife. She split the lengths again and again and ripped long splits from each length. She split one length into coarser split to make ribs for the baskets. Another length she split into basket handles.

"I'm going to make feed baskets," Mom said. "People will always need feed baskets. I'm going to make them in three different sizes. I'm going to make peck baskets. Men will want peck baskets to carry eggs to town on Saturdays. They'll want them to carry salt, sugar and coffee from the store where they have a long way to walk. I'm going to make a half-bushel basket for it will be about the right size to carry corn to the mules, nubbins to the cows and ears of corn to the fattening hogs. And I'm going to make bushel feed baskets."

Sophie got supper that night and I fed Fred and fed and milked Gypsy. I found two more hens under our chicken-roost on the snow. They were frozen stiff as boards. I felt of their craws and I could feel only a few grains of corn. I didn't tell Mom about the chickens. I buried them in the snow. Every day a chicken, guinea or a turkey froze to death. Some days as many as six fowls would freeze to death. I found sparrows frozen to death around the barn. When I put hay down for Gypsy and gave her corn nubbins in a feed box I milked cold milk from her into the bucket. There was an icy stillness in the January night air and millions of bright stars shivered in a cold blue sky.

By the time that Sophie had steaming-hot corn bread baked, and I had done the feeding, the milking and carried in firewood and stovewood for the night, Mom had made two baskets. Sophie had crossed the entry from the kitchen to tell Mom that supper was ready, and I was putting my kindling wood in the corner to start the morning fire when Mom held up a basket to us.

"Look, children," she said. "I'm not quite as good as I used to be when I helped Pa make baskets. I need practice."

"Mom, that's a pretty basket," I said.

"Supper is ready," Sophie said.

We crossed the entry for supper. The starlight from the

winter skies couldn't shine in at our entry. Mom carried a pine torch to light our way to the kitchen. Sophie led James across the entry and Mary held to Mom's skirt. The hot steaming corn bread was sweet to our taste. We had milk and bread and hot boiled potatoes.

"Tomorrow," Mom said, "I want you to saddle Fred and ride to Greenwood with four baskets. I'll have two more made by morning. Sell the peck basket for thirty-five cents. Sell the half-bushel basket for sixty cents. Sell the two bushel baskets for a dollar apiece. That will be two dollars and ninety-five cents if you sell all the baskets."

"I'll do it, Mom, just as soon as I get the feeding done," I said.

I went to bed that night and dreamed of riding Fred to town. I dreamed that my baskets sold. I dreamed that men wanted more baskets and I came home with my pockets filled with money and a load of corn meal, flour, lard and candy on Fred's back—all that he could carry.

I awoke and built a fire in the front room to warm it for Mom. She slept in a bed with Sophie and Mary just across from Pa's bed, in the other corner of the room. I slept upstairs with James. After I'd built the fire in the front room, I crossed the entry with a pine torch. It was yet before daylight on the short winter day. I put a fire in the stove and took my milk bucket and feed basket and started toward the barn. I fed Fred corn in his box and threw down hay from the loft. I forked hay to Gypsy's manger and gave her corn nubbins to eat while I milked her.

When I finished my work, Mom had cooked our breakfast. She made griddle cakes for us and we ate sorghum molasses with hot griddle cakes. After breakfast while Mom was feeding Pa, I put the saddle on Fred and bridled him. I rode to our front door. Mom came out with four baskets. She carried two in each hand.

"Watch old Fred," Mom said. "Do be careful. If the snow balls on his feet, get off his back and find you a sharp-edged rock or a sharp stick and knock the snowballs from his feet. If he falls with you and hurts you, what are we going to do then?"

Mom looked serious when she spoke to me. I wasn't afraid of Fred falling with me. I was glad to get on my way. I wasn't afraid. I wanted to ride Fred to town. It was the first time in my life that I had ever been allowed to ride to town to sell anything.

"You get a sack of meal if you sell a basket," Mom said. "It will cost you fifty cents. If you sell all your baskets, get a sack of flour too. That's a dollar. That will make a dollar and a half. You'll have a dollar and forty-five cents left. Get a quarter's worth of salt, a quarter's worth of sugar and a small bucket of lard. If you have a penny left; bring it home to me, I've got a use for every penny."

I tied the basket handles together and put two baskets on each side of me behind the saddle. I pulled my toboggan cap low over my ears and rode Fred up the hollow toward Greenwood. My feet were warm in my wool socks and brogan shoes. The cold wind hit my face as I rode away in the winter morning mists. Mom stood in the door and watched me out of sight. I rode up the dark hollow where frost filled the air and where the rough sides of the black-oak trees that stood on the rocky bluffs were white with frost and looked like shadowy ghosts. The frozen snow crunched beneath Fred's big feet.

As I rode over the hill toward the town, a man was feeding his cattle.

"Would you like to buy a basket, Mister?" I asked.

"How do you sell them, Sonnie?" he asked.

"Thirty-five cents for the peck baskets," I said. "Sixty cents for the half-bushel basket and a dollar apiece for the bushel baskets."

"I'll take both of the bushel baskets," he said as he pulled his billfold from his pocket and reached me two one-dollar bills. I untied the baskets from the saddle and gave them to him. Two dollars in my pocket and two baskets to sell. The next log shack I passed, I climbed down from my saddle and knocked at the door. A man came to the door.

"Do you want to buy a basket, Mister?" I asked.

"Sonnie, it's cold weather to sell baskets, isn't it?" he said. "You're out awfully early too. What time did you start this morning?"

"Daylight."

As we talked, the man stepped out into the yard and looked at my baskets. He asked me the price and I told him.

"I'll take both your baskets," he said. "These are well-made baskets and I need feed baskets. I'll take a couple of bushel baskets if you'll make them for me."

"I'll bring 'em to you in two days from now," I said, "if I live and Mom lives."

"Does your mother make these baskets?"

"Yes."

"She certainly put them together well," he said. "I've made baskets and I know a basket."

I said good-by to the tall beardy-faced man. I felt good to take Pa's place and go to town. I felt like I was helping run the place. I got off Fred's back twice and knocked the balls of snow from his feet with a stick. I rode to town and got my meal and flour. I put a sack of flour in one end of a coffee sack and a sack of meal in the other and balanced it across Fred's broad back-tied the coffee sack to a ring in my saddle. I carried the sugar, salt and lard in another sack in front of my saddle. Slowly, I went over the hill home.

When I rode back home, Mom came out the front door to meet me. I showed her my meal, flour, sugar, salt and lard. Mom's face brightened with a smile. She stood beside the horse and held the bridle reins when I climbed from the saddle a little stiff with cold.

"And here's twenty-five cents left," I said as I pulled my mitten from my right hand and pulled a quarter from my pocket.

"We'll make it," Mom said. "The winter is dark now but after a while spring will come. Violets are budding under the dead leaves beneath the snow right now!"

When I went to the woods to haul wood for the fireplace and the kitchen stove, Mom put on Pa's clothes and went with me. Pa's boots fit tightly on Mom's legs. Mom's long slender body fit well in Pa's corduroy pants. His coat was not too broad for Mom's shoulders.

I tied Fred to a tree by his bridle rein. Then Mom and I took the double-bitted ax and the crosscut saw down to a tall dead oak. I cut a notch part of the way into the dead tree the way I wanted it to fall. Mom took the ax and finished chopping the notch. We got down on our knees together and pulled the long crosscut saw through the hard dead oak tree. After we sawed awhile, we heard a crack and the tree bent earthward and hit the snow-covered hill below with a slash. The snow dashed in a white powdery cloud high into the air. I took the ax and trimmed the knots from the tree while Mom led Fred up to the tree, hooked the snaking chain around the log and fastened the trace chains to the singletree.

"He's ready," Mom said.

I climbed on Fred's back and reined him with the bridle reins down the path. Clouds of snow blew from under Fred's feet as he moved the big dead log toward the woodyard. Mom followed with the ax in her ungloved hand and the crosscut saw across her shoulder. When Fred got to the woodyard, he stopped. I got off his back—unhitched the traces and took him to the barn. I came back to the woodyard. All afternoon Mom got down on her knees in the snow on one side of the log and I got down on the other side of the big dead log. We dragged the crosscut saw across the bone-dry seasoned oak log. We cut stovewood lengths and firewood lengths until we finished the log. Then we split the wood lengths with our axes. I used my pole-ax on the stovewood lengths for the cookstove. Mom used the double-bitted ax and split the longer firewood lengths. After we split the lengths into finer wood, I carried it and stacked it in the entry where it was safe from rain, sleet and snow.

"When your Pa gets well again," Mom said, "I won't have so much work to do. He always took care of the wood getting.

Mom would sit up on the long winter evenings when the wind blew around the house and weave baskets. Sophie would

231

often help her with the white-oak splits after she had washed the supper dishes. Sophie would take the case knife and smooth the splinters from the splits. I would take the drawing knife and rip off long splits from the white-oak sapling lengths. It was fun for us to do this around the winter fire while we laughed and talked and parched corn in a skillet. Mary parched the corn while Sophie and I helped Mom. Pa lay in bed—his face pale on the white pillow in the dim flicker of the pine torch above our mantel and the leaping blazes from the forestick. Sometimes Pa talked to us about spring and when he would be plowing again. He told us he'd never plant the swamps in the hollow again and have the crawdads to cut down the young corn soon as it sprouted from the furrow. One day when Mom worked steadily all day and Sophie and I helped her in the evening, she made twelve baskets.

"It's one of the biggest day's work I've ever done in my life," Mom said. "If I could make twelve baskets every day, your Pa wouldn't have to worry about spring and plowing."

"Mom wanted me to be careful about the horse falling," I thought. "She told me to keep the snow knocked from his feet so it wouldn't ball and throw him when I rode him to Greenwood—Mom doesn't know what she would do without me—well, she'd better watch about making twelve baskets in one day. What would we do if Mom would get sick?"

As I walked toward the barn over the frozen snow, I had these thoughts about my mother.

Every weekday, I took baskets to Greenwood. I sold them almost any place I stopped. When I sold all my baskets one day, I learned to take orders for the next day. There was a ready sale for the baskets my mother made. And I learned to be a good salesman for a boy of ten. After I'd go to Greenwood in the morning and sell baskets and bring back the things Mom told me to get, I'd climb the bluff above the hog pen and cut the bushy-topped white-oak saplings and slide them over the bluff to the barn. Then I'd carry them to the entry and saw them into lengths with a handsaw, split them into quarters and carry them into the house for Mom.

When our feed ran out, Mom sent me to Broughton's to see about feed.

"I think John Broughton's got corn and I know he's got fodder to sell," Mom said. "You get the saddle on Fred and ride out there and see. Don't pay over twenty cents a shock for fodder. Offer him fifteen cents at first and if he won't take that, then offer him twenty cents. We have to have feed for Fred and Gypsy. Offer him ninety cents a barrel for corn and don't give him over a dollar a barrel."

When I rode away to Broughton's to see about feed, I left Mom at home making baskets. I rode down the hollow and turned up the left fork of Ragweed Hollow. The snow was nearly to Fred's neck in places. I found my way to Broughton's barn where Mr. Broughton was feeding his cows.

"I'll take fifteen cents a shock for thirty shocks of fodder," Mr. Broughton said. "That's all I have to sell. That ought to winter your horse and cow until grass gets here this spring. I won't take ninety cents a barrel for my corn. I'll take a dollar a barrel for it and put it in your corncrib. I can let you have ten barrels of corn."

"All right, Mr. Broughton," I said. "I'll pay you for the corn and fodder right now if you'll promise me you'll deliver the fodder while you're bringing the corn."

Mr. Broughton's eyes looked big when I told him I'd pay him now. I know he wondered where I got the money. He knew Pa was sick, for he had been around home a couple of times to see him and talked to him far into the night. I paid Mr. Broughton a ten-dollar bill, four one-dollar bills, and I gave him a half-dollar, and then I rode toward home. The next day we had feed in our barn to last until the hills got green again.

"How's the feed holding out?" Pa asked.

"Mick, we've got plenty of feed."

"That feed's lasting the longest of any feed yet."

"We've got enough to last until the pastures get green."

Pa would curve his thin lips in a smile. He would lie on the bed and ask questions about the horse, cow and the chickens.

Often when I walked along the creek I found rabbits, dead-frozen hard as an icicle. I found dead quails. I found dead possums. Maybe they had starved to death for something to eat. I found still life wherever I went. The weather had been so cold and all life had shrunk to the bone, perished for food or had frozen to death.

The snow didn't show any signs of melting. All we did at home was get wood, feed the horse and cow, cook, eat, sleep and make baskets. I took four, six, eight and often ten baskets away each day to Greenwood. People called me the "Basket Boy." I brought back meal, flour, lard and groceries. Every day I brought back a piece of dry goods for Mom. She'd write down on paper what she wanted and I'd bring it back. Each day I brought back some money to Mom. I never spent all

The snow didn't show any sign of melting.

that I got for the baskets. Mom planned the spending so I'd bring the money home.

"A body needs a little money about the house," Mom said. "We never know what time we might need it. I've got to keep a little ahead to buy medicine for your Pa. He's liable to get worse any time. It's hard to tell. He's had a long lingering spell this winter and his face is awful white. His jawbones look like they'll come through the skin any minute, his face is so thin."

As the winter days dragged on toward spring and the great sheets of snow remained on the steep hill slopes, Mom did not go to the wood yard and help me cut wood like she had. I cut the wood with my pole-ax. Mom sat in her chair before the fire and wove baskets. She seldom got up for anything. Pa talked more to Mom now that he had ever talked. She propped him up in bed with his pillow behind his back and he watched her weave baskets. He talked to her about when the snow would leave and the ground, dark with melted snow, would show water, leaping like fish in the sunlight, running down over the hills.

"Go to Greenwood and get the doctor," Mom said one day. "Get on Fred and hurry to town!"

"Is Pa worse?" I asked.

"Don't ask questions but hurry," Mom said.

I rode Fred over the snow fast as I could go. I got Doctor Morris out of bed. He rode his horse and we raced back over the snow in the winter moonlight and starlight. When we got to the house, I saw a light from the front window. Sophie met me at the front door and told me that we'd have to sit by a fire in the kitchen stove. Doctor Morris went into the house.

It was some time before daylight when I heard a baby cry.

"I hear a baby crying, Sophie," I said.

"Yes, didn't you know?"

"But I never would have thought that."

"Come in the front room, you children," Doctor Morris said as he looked in at the kitchen door. "You will be very happy when you see the big fine brother I have brought you."

Sophie and I ran into the room to see our brother. We had a lamp in our front room now. I could understand why Mom had me to buy it. I could understand about the cloth she had me to get. I thought of these things as I looked at Mom lying on the bed with the quilts turned down enough for us to see our brother. We stood beside the bed watching the quilts shake when he kicked. And he cried like he was mad at everybody. There was a smile on Mom's lips.

It was March and the sun had shone brightly for three days. The snow melted and the snow-water ran in tiny streams down the small drains on the steep bluffs.

When Pop saw the dark hills again he sat up in bed. There was more color in his face now. Each day he looked at the hills and talked to Mom. Soon as Mom got up from the bed, Pa was up walking about. Color was coming back rapidly to his face. Flesh was coming back to his skeleton body. Sophie did the cooking and I did the feeding. I got the wood. Mom had paid all of our bills and she had a little money left after she paid Doctor Morris.

"All our debts are paid, Mick," Mom said. "The hard winter is over. Violets are in bloom and pasture grass is coming back to the pastures."

Mom stood in the late March wind with our tiny brother

wrapped in a blanket in her arms. She kicked the dead leaves away with the toe of her shoe from a clump of blooming violets. I walked ahead of Pa and cut stalks and sprouts with a grubbing hoe. Pa rested between the handles of the plow and looked at Mom standing at the edge of the field with the early buds of spring about her.

THE FREEING OF JASON WHITEAPPLE

"It's a funny thing that Jailer Bert Saddler wants to see me," Pa said. "He sent word by Press Chatman for me to come tonight. That's where we're goin'. I want you to go along and keep me company over this lonesome ridge. Hoot owls hollerin', nighthawks screamin' and foxes barkin' makes a body feel kinda lonesome on this ridge at night by hisself."

When Pa spoke these words he held his ungloved hands up to his mouth and blew his hot breath on his knuckles. Then he whetted his hands together to get them warm. I could see Pa's white breath go out like little patches of vapor into the steel-blue October night. Millions of white stars swarmed on the blue sky over our heads. An October wind whipped lonely through the leafless black-oak tops above our heads and rustled a few clusters of tough-butted white-oak leaves that clung to their swaying branches.

"It puzzles me that Jailer Bert wanted to see me at night," Pa continued. "He's got somethin' up his sleeve."

I could hardly hear the words Pa spoke for two owls hooting to each other from one ridgetop to the other. A fox barked on the path before us and we heard him scamper away over the dead leaves on the ground. We heard him bark like a hound pup as he climbed the rocky bluff on the other side of the hollow. A nighthawk screamed above our heads as we left the bony ridgetop and started down the long crooked path toward Linton. Pa hurried down the path. I kept at his heels. I kept my hands in my pockets to keep them warm. I watched my white breath thin and fade on the steel-blue October wind.

"Shan, we'll soon be there," Pa said. "See the lights from the town!"

The town lights were before us. We stood upon the hill above the town in the Linton Graveyard and looked at the lights below us. "This is the reason Pa wanted me to come along," I thought. "He is afraid to pass through this grave-yard at night by himself. Many of the men buried here fought with Pa when they were boys together. Pa is afraid they'll return to haunt him."

We walked down among the white tombstones that stuck up above the brown October earth like a hound dog's clean white teeth. We hurried down the backstreet and crossed the railroad tracks. Then we went up the alley to the jailhouse.

"Here we are, Shan," Pa said as he looked up at the rusty-red brick building with big iron bars across the windows. The jail was lit up and we could see through the windows. We could see men sitting on their bunks playing cards. We could hear them laugh. We could hear them curse each other and call each other tough names.

Pa walked up the concrete steps to the big door and pushed a button. The door opened and a young man stood there.

"Something for you?"

"Jailer Bert sent for me," Pa answered and blew his breath on his folded hands.

"Your name, please?

240

"Mick Powderjay."

The young man closed the door and went away. In a few minutes the door opened again and Jailer Bert Saddler stood before us.

"Mick, I'm glad to see you," he said. "You got here all right. Is that your boy with you?"

"Yes, Jailer Bert, he's my boy," Pa said as he shook Jailer Bert's big soft hand.

"I thought he was," Jailer Bert laughed. "Mick, he's the spittin' image of you, only he's goin' to make a bigger man."

Jailer Bert Saddler was a big man beside of Pa. He wore a blue overall jumper and a big black umbrella hat. His pant legs fit as tightly around his legs as bark fits a frozen black-oak tree. His blinky eyes were pale blue as melted snow-water running over frozen ground. His thin lips were curved in a smile like a quarter-moon as he talked to Pa.

"Yes sir-ee, Mick Powderjay, you're a stand-by in election times," Jailer Bert said. "Glad to have a man like you in our Party. You hepped put me right here in this jailhouse. And you're a man that anybody can trust. That's why I sent for you tonight. Come back in this little room. I want to talk to you."

"Will it be all right for my boy to go along?" Pa asked.

"Oh, shore, shore," he laughed. "Bring 'im right along. I just don't want him to say anything about what we talk about."

"You won't haf to worry about that," Pa said. "He's all right."

I followed Pa and Pa followed Jailer Bert into a small room in the jailhouse.

"This is the room I keep to talk business with my friends,

Mick," Jailer Bert said. "This jailhouse is full and runnin' over. Winter's settin' in and I'm gettin' my family back."

"How many do you have Jailer Bert?" Pa asked.

"Eighty-six," Jailer Bert said. "Got four comin' tomorrow. This jail was built for only sixty, you know. Even got one in the bull pen. He's a regular customer and I can put him any place. He'd as soon sleep on the floor as in a bed."

"The hell you have," Pa said. His face was red as a turkey snout after he'd come from the cold October wind on the ridgetop and got warm before a fire in the jailhouse.

"Mick," Jailer Bert whispered in a rough whisper, "you remember Jason Whiteapple, don't you?"

"Yuh, I remember 'im," Pa spoke quickly. "He's that big man. He's a powerful man in our Party. He's the road builder."

"You have 'im," Jailer Bert said. "He's the man. Now I just want to tell you about 'im."

"Yuh, I know 'im," Pa said. "He come nigh as a pea goin' to the Pen over shootin' Ham Frazier. Stood right in his own door and turned a double-barreled shotgun loose at 'im when Ham come to arrest 'im. Come nigh as a pea puttin' Ham under the wild honeysuckle."

"Yep, he did, Mick," Jailer Bert said, his pale blue eyes shining in the jailhouse lights like a hound dog's eyes shine after dark. "It's too bad. Both men are wheel hosses in our Party. Fined Jason $5oo and give 'im six months in jail. He can't pay a dollar of his fine. He has to lay it all out in jail at a dollar a day. He'll be here nearly two years. He's got a wife and nineteen youngins at home and I think he'd better be at home with 'em. And to tell you the truth, Mick, if I's to tell you somethin' you wouldn't believe me. You know that boy that let you in at the door a while ago is a Trusty at the jail. He heps me with the work. He carries four and five times as much grub to Jason as he does to anybody in this jailhouse. It will break me up to feed 'im. Last Sunday for dinner Jason et four stewed hens all but the wings. He won't eat chicken wings. That's all he won't eat. I want to get 'im out'n the jail."

"My God," Pa said, "did he eat four stewed hens at one meal?"

"He did, Mick, besides the other grub he et," Jailer Bert said. "I'm not lyin' to you. You know if he wasn't sich a damned big eater I'd like to keep Jason here with me in jail. I get a dollar a day for keepin' a man. It takes as much to feed Jason as it does five men. Now, you see where my profit's goin'. It will pay me to get 'im out and get five men in his place. I'll tell you, Mick, what I want you to do. Don't get me wrong. Let's get Jason back to his family. Let's see the men of our Party and take up money to pay his fine. You know it ain't in my power to turn Jason out'n jail. If I could've turned 'im out, I'd a turned 'im out atter he et his first meal here. But that part of the Law ain't in my power. I'll tell you, I'll put in $200 myself on his fine. Then I'll make money, Mick, for I like old Jason. But my God, he'll break me up if I haf to keep 'im."

"I'm a poor man, Jailer Bert, but I'm in ten dollars on his fine," Pa said.

"That's just it, Mick," Jailer Bert said. "I think all the boys will throw in from ten to five bucks apiece and we'll soon get enough to pay 'im out. I want you to get on a mule tomorrow and go over the county and collect what you can."

"I'll be glad to do it," Pa said. "I'd like to see old Jason,

Jailer Bert, if he ain't gone to bed yet."

"He won't be gone to bed," Jailer Bert said.

Jailer Bert Saddler got up and led the way. We followed him to a big iron door. He took a key from his key ring opened the door and went inside. There was one cell after another all around the big square room. There was one window for each cell. In the middle of the room was a big room with bunks side by side. Old men with mustaches and beardy faces were in bunks fast asleep. Young men were sitting at tables playing cards. Middle-aged men were on bunks trying to go to sleep and cussing the young men for playing cards. Men were smoking pipes, cigars and cigarettes. Men were chewing tobacco and spitting in spittoons. If they didn't hit them, they spit on the floor. When Pa saw all this his eyes got big. When Pa saw the initial-carved walls, he looked curious. He couldn't read the dirty things written on the walls for Pa can't read. He could tell about the dirty pictures drawn all over the walls.

"Jesus Christ," Pa said. "Jailer Bert, this is a hell o' a place."

"Mick, I know you think I ain't worth a damn as a jailer," Bert said, "but I keep my Trusties washin' these walls and cleanin' atter these men. It don't do no good. They just do it over again. They are tough men—a lot o' 'em are purty good fellars. It's a job to keep 'em from fightin'. That's what I worry about most. Last week, they had a free-for-all and one fellar had to be sent from here to the hospital. I had to have Doc Wilburn with five that we kept in the jail. Doc Wilburn pulled a sliver from one's jawbone that looked like a piece of kindlin' wood."

"I'll be damned," Pa said. "Don't you carry a pistol around

this place?"

"No, I don't carry no pistol, Mick," he said. "The boys like to come and stay with me. Hell, I feed 'em good and they like it. It's money for me and a place for them to stay. A lot o' 'em don't have no homes. Their homes are where their hats are."

"Talk about a home," one of the men said that was sitting at a card table. "My home is with old Jailer Bert. He's the best jailer that ever carried a jailhouse key. Long as Bert is jailer, this jailhouse will be my home. And by God, he'll be jailer a long time if people in this county vote like I do."

"Pal, you took the words out'n my mouth," another beardy man said at the same card table. "Old Bert's what I call a man. I'd rather to stay with 'im as to have a home of my own. Get three good meals a day and a fire to sit by and a good bed to sleep on. By God, who'd ast fer a better life?"

The men laughed and threw their cards on the table. When they talked they didn't look at Jailer Bert. They watched to see that the others didn't cheat. They had matches on the table for money, and every few minutes they'd shift the match stems among the four men sitting at the table.

"Boys, I'm glad you like your home," Bert laughed. "I do my best to give you three good meals a day, keep you a good fire and give you good beds to sleep on."

"Boy, this place is somethin'," Pa said as he looked at the vulgar pictures drawn on the wall. "How could a man's mind get that filthy?"

Pa's face got red as he looked at the pictures.

"I've been onery in my young days, but I've never seen anythin' like this. Bert, I wouldn't want a boy of mine to come to this jail. He'd be a heck of a lot onerier when he got out than when he come here. A jail like this can't do a man any good."

"It isn't supposed to do 'em any good, Mick," Bert said. "You can't larn an old dog new tricks is the way I look at it. That's why I never put a man on bread and water. I don't give a damn how tough he gets. I feed 'im."

"Well, I want to see Jason Whiteapple; then I'll be ready to get out'n here," Pa said.

"Who called my name?" a hoarse voice asked from around behind Pa. "It sounds good to hear somebody callin' my name."

"Jason Whiteapple," Pa said. "How are you, Jason?"

"Can't complain, Mick," Jason said. He stood in the door of his cell and shook Pa's hand. "It's good to see you, Mick! Glad you've come to see this old jailbird—the first time I's ever inside of a jail in my life. Mick, I'll be here a long time. Come into my house."

Pa followed Jason into his cell. I followed Pa and Jailer Bert stood on the outside.

"This cell's supposed to be big enough for two men," Jason said. "But I told Jailer Bert that I didn't want nobody stayin' with me. It's a no-account bunch of sorry men in here, Mick. I ain't got no more business in this damned jail than a snowball has in hell. If Ham Frazier had minded his own business so I wouldn't a had to shoot 'im, I wouldn't be here today. I'm glad he lived so I wouldn't haf to spend the balance of my days behind the bars."

"You shouldn't've been," said a voice across the hall. "Why not spend your days behind bars? What's it matter where you spend your days just so you spend 'em?"

"Pay that fellar no minds," Jason said. "He's over there in

246

the bull pen. He's used to jail. It's the only place he's ever been."

"What's this you got here, Jason?" Pa asked as he went over and examined a big mound of yellow clay dirt with streaks of black loam here and there and patches of wood moss stuck here and there.

"That's the county, Mick," Jason said. He got up from the side of his dirt bunk and walked over to the mound. "See the rivers runnin' across it. Here's the Rainy River and here's the Times River."

"I see," Pa said examining the white strips of strings that Jason had put across the mound for rivers. "Looks like you got every curve in 'em."

"I have," Jason said. "See, look at these dark pieces of strings. There are roads that have been completed in this county—roads that I have hepped to build. Now the little piece of sea-grass strings are roads that need to be built. I've got them along the big curves in the roads that have been built—these are places that need to be straightened. The green wood moss is the patches of timber in this county."

When Jason spoke to Pa his keen black eyes looked at the mound. His long red chin stuck out like a limb on a tree. His fence-post arms were folded across his barrel chest. He was a short man; he wasn't fat but he would weigh three hundred and ninety pounds. "Jailer Bert talked about 'im eatin' four stewed hens," I thought. "That's all right for he's big as four small men." And then I wondered how he could tear the meat from the bones when he didn't have a tooth in his head. I had heard Pa talk about what a powerful man Jason was; that when he went to kill a beef, he didn't shoot it, knock it in the head with a hammer or cut its throat and let it bleed to death; he killed it with his fist. When I saw him, I could understand this now. And then I thought, "Maybe the reason Jailer Bert wants to get 'im out is, he's afraid of 'im."

"Jason, how did you get all this dirt in here?"

"I made Bert bring it in to me," Jason said, his black eyes dancing deep in their sockets as he spoke. "I made him get me the twine and the wood moss too. Hell, I can't stay in this jail hole a couple of years and do nothin' but play cards."

"How can you work in all of this noise?"

"When I get to work plannin' roads for this county," Jason said, "all the noise this jailhouse full of men can make, just don't bother me. My mind is on the roads. I'll tell you, Mick, I'm a road builder. My enemies haf to hand that to me. I ain't got no education but when it comes to roads I've got hoss sense. I ain't braggin' but I've had the engineers to ast me my opinion on the roads in this county. I know this county; I know it's dirt—yes, deep, deep deep, down—and I can tell 'em if a road will stand 'r if it'll wash away. I ain't got but one thing to ast of the people when I kick the bucket and leave this world—"

"What's that, Jason?" Pa asked.

"I want somebody to put on my tombstone, Mick, somethin' like this," he said. "Here Jason Whiteapple sleeps. He's out of reach of his enemies. He done one thing in his lifetime which is a damn sight more than a lot of men have done before they left this world. Jason Whiteapple was a road builder. He built the roads in this county in his day. He took them from the creeks and the mudholes and put them on a higher level."

"What's this other mound of dirt you got over here?" Pa asked.

"It's my farm, Mick," Jason said. "I sit right on the edge of this dirty little bed and run my farm. I've drawed a good picture of my farm here. See the Rainey River bottoms! See the black loam and the yellow clay. See the wooded bluffs! My boys come to see me and I show them what to do. I can show 'em better'n I can tell 'em."

From Jason's door I saw Jailer Bert walk around among the prisoners, pat them on the back, laugh and talk with them.

"You belong to our Party, and you're a good man, Jason," Pa said. "I'm goin' to see if we can't get you out'n this durn place and back to your family."

"You'll never do it," Jason said. His face got redder when he spoke. "My enemies put me here. They are goin' to keep me here. It was all over a road, you know. I put the road where it ought to be and a lot of fellars got sore. They tried that gun stuff before on me. I had to shoot first. And when I shot I shot to kill. We had to fight it out one way 'r the other. I'm in jail today over it. Here's the county and here's my farm. I work awhile on my farm and plan things; but I spend most of my time workin' on the county roads while these lazy jailbirds around me are drawin' dirty pictures on the walls, playin' cards, tellin' dirty jokes, cussin' to beat the devil 'r havin' a free-for-all fight that Jailer Bert and all his Trusties can't stop. I stand in my door and not a one of that crowd comes in here. I'd knock the first one cold as a beef that tried to come in here. This is my home and by God I'll pertect it long as I'm in here."

249

"Why pertect it, Jason?" the man asked that was sprawled on the bull-pen floor. "Ain't no ust to do that. I could live anywhere. I could eat grass. I could go months and never shave. It don't bother me. I just don't worry about anythin'. I am happy for I've learned to live. I ust to work. It was a sin if a man didn't work. Now it's a sin if he sweats and I ain't got a job. So, I don't commit a sin by workin'. I just stay with Jailer Bert. This is my home. This bull pen is my part of the house. The other fellars think I'm crazy. They are crazy for they don't know how to live. They couldn't eat grass and sleep beside the river and let their whiskers grow. No. But I can. I tell you life has taught me how to live. Why worry about the county's roads bein' lifted from the creeks and mudholes and put on a higher level? To hell with the county roads and to hell with what goes on your head stone in the marble orchard. Why do you want a stone at all? You air vain to want one, Jason Whiteapple. Why waste your time worryin' about your farm, your wife and your nineteen children? The children'll get along and your wife'll find another man if you don't get out'n here pretty soon."

"Don't pay 'em no minds, Mick," Jason said. "I've heard that sorta talk until I'm sick of it. He goes on like that all day. Atter my wife has had nineteen youngins, if she wants another man she can have 'im."

I looked at the big bearded man lying sprawled on the hard floor of the bull pen. His pants were patched and his beard was long. He was a man with broad shoulders and big arms and hands. He didn't have shoes on his feet. He was barefooted. I stood and looked at him with my hands on the iron bars of the bull pen. I looked through a crack at him like he was a wild animal that would jump at me any minute. Pa and Jason talked. Jailer Bert Saddler made his rounds among the prisoners. I looked at this big strange-looking man in the bull pen. I watched him until Pa walked out of Jason's cell and Jason stood in the door and watched Pa leave. Jason Whiteapple was so broad across the shoulders he had to turn sideways to get out of his door. When Jailer Bert saw Pa leaving, he walked over and got with us. We went out together.

The next day Pa saddled a mule and rode away. Pa was gone three days. He went over the county. He collected money from the men in our Party to pay Jason's fine.

"Jason Whiteapple will go free," said Pa when he rode the mule back home. "I've got what it takes to set 'im free. It's right in my overall pocket. Just a few little pieces of paper, that's called money. I can't forget what that damned man said in the bull pen."

The next morning Pa saddled the mule and rode to town. When Pa rode back from town that day he said, "Old Jason is a free man. He kicked the two mounds of dirt all over his jailhouse cell when he was told that he was free. He was tickled that the men of his Party paid his fine. He said to his friends gathered around the jail when he walked down the steps, 'Night will never get too dark, the days will never be too short or too long or too cold for me to get out and work the ends of my fingernails and toenails off for my Party. Look what you men have done for me. You've got me out'n a place where I didn't belong'."

Autumn went into winter and winter passed slowly toward spring. It was late in February when Pa walked across the ridge to town one day. When he come home that night Pa's face looked sad. "Shan, I've got somethin' to tell you," Pa said. "Tim Blevins told me at the hoss-tradin' grounds today that Jason Whiteapple was dead.

"He said since he'd been kept six months in the jailhouse that he wasn't the man he ust to be. Said his ticker wasn't nigh right. And before the weather got warm, Jason planned to kill a beef. Said he tried to get Jason to shoot it but Jason just cut drive with his fist and killed the beef. Jason's ticker thumped a few times and he was gone.

"And Shan," Pa whispered, "when he kicked the bucket, they found two love letters he was carryin' in his inside coat pocket that some man in the penitentiary wrote his wife while he was up there in jail. What do you know about that? I think about what that fellow in the bull pen said. It just keeps goin' through my head."

I thought about what Jason wanted to put on his tombstone and who would put it there. I wondered if the men in his Party would put a stone to his head and one to his feet and have words chiseled on the stone that he was safe from his enemies and that he'd done a lot more than a lot of fellars had for he'd built the county's roads, that he'd lifted them from the mudholes and the creeks to higher levels. Then I thought about the big man with the broad shoulders, the beardy face and bare feet on the bull-pen floor that told Jason he didn't know how to live, said a road and farms didn't matter—that he could sleep by the river and eat grass.

The words he said sounded crazy, but they were words one couldn't forget.

Dawn of Remembered Spring

"Be careful, Shan," Mom said. "I'm afraid if you wade that creek that a water moccasin will bite you."

"All right, Mom."

"You know what happened to Roy Deer last Sunday!"

"Yes, Mom!"

"He's nigh at the point of death," she said. "I'm going over there now to see him. His leg's swelled hard as a rock and it's turned black as black-oak bark. They're not looking for Roy to live until midnight tonight."

"All water moccasins ought to be killed, hadn't they, Mom?"

"Yes, they're pizen things, but you can't kill them," Mom said. "They're in all these creeks around here. There's so many of them we can't kill 'em all."

Mom stood at the foot log that crossed the creek in front of our house. Her white apron was starched stiff; I heard it rustle when Mom put her hand in the little pocket in the right upper corner to get tobacco crumbs for her pipe. Mom wore her slat bonnet that shaded her suntanned face—a bonnet with strings that came under her chin and tied in a bowknot.

"I feel uneasy," Mom said as she filled her long-stemmed clay-stone pipe with bright burley crumbs, tamped them down with her index finger, and struck a match on the rough bark of an apple tree that grew on the creek bank by the footlog.

"Don't feel uneasy about me," I said.

"But I do," Mom said. "Your Pa out groundhog huntin' and I'll be away at Deers'—nobody at home but you, and so many pizen snakes around this house."

Mom blew a cloud of blue smoke from her pipe. She walked across the footlog—her long clean dress sweeping the weed stubble where Pa had mown the weeds along the path with a scythe so we could leave the house without getting our legs wet by the dew-covered weeds.

When Mom walked out of sight around the turn of the pasture hill and the trail of smoke that she left behind her had disappeared into the light blue April air, I crossed the garden fence at the wild-plum thicket.

Everybody gone, I thought. I am left alone. I'll do as I please. A water moccasin bit Roy Deer but a water moccasin will never bite me. I'll get me a club from this wild-plum thicket and I'll wade up the creek killing water moccasins.

There was a dead wild-plum sprout standing among the thicket of living sprouts. It was about the size of a tobacco stick. I stepped out of my path into the wild-plum thicket. Barefooted, I walked among the wild-plum thorns. I uprooted the dead wild-plum sprout. There was a bulge on it where roots had once been—now the roots had rotted in the earth. It was like a maul with this big bulge on the end of it. It would be good to hit water moccasins with.

The mules played in the pasture. It was Sunday—their day of rest. And the mules knew it. This was Sunday and it was my day of rest. It was my one day of freedom, too, when Mom and Pa were gone and I was left alone. I would like to be a man now, I thought, I'd love to plow the mules, run a farm, and kill snakes. A water moccasin bit Roy Deer but one would never bite me.

The bright sunlight of April played over the green Kentucky hills. Sunlight fell onto the creek of blue water that twisted like a crawling snake around the high bluffs and between the high rocks. In many places dwarf willows, horseweeds, ironweeds, and wild grapevines shut away the sunlight and the creek waters stood in quiet cool puddles. These little puddles under the shade of weeds, vines, and willows were the places where the water moccasins lived.

I rolled my overall legs above my knees so I wouldn't wet them and Mom wouldn't know I'd been wading the creek. I started wading up the creek toward the head of the hollow. I carried my wild-plum club across my shoulder with both hands gripped tightly around the small end of it. I was ready to maul the first water moccasin I saw.

"One of you old water moccasins bit Roy Deer," I said bravely, clinching my grip tighter around my club, "but you won't bite me."

As I waded the cool creek waters, my bare feet touched gravel on the creek bottom. When I touched a wet watersoaked stick on the bottom of the creek bed, I'd think it was a snake and I'd jump. I'd wade into banks of quicksand. I'd sink into the sand above my knees. It was hard to pull my legs out of this quicksand and when I pulled them out they'd be covered with thin quicky mud that the next puddle of water would wash away.

"A water moccasin," I said to myself. I was scared to look at him. He was wrapped around a willow that was bent over the creek. He was sleeping in the sun. I slipped toward him quietly, step by step, with my club drawn over my shoulder. Soon as I got close enough to reach him, I came over my shoulder with the club. I hit the water moccasin a powerful blow that mashed its head flat against the willow. It fell dead into the water. I picked it up by the tail and threw it upon the bank.

"One gone," I said to myself.

The water was warm around my feet and legs. The sharp-edged gravels hurt the bottoms of my feet but the soft sand soothed them. Butterflies swarmed over my head and around me alighting on the wild pink phlox that grew in clusters along the creek bank. Wild honeybees, bumblebees, and butterflies worked on the elder blossoms, the shoemake blossoms and the beet-red finger-long blossoms of the ironweed and the whitish pink-colored smartweed blossoms. Birds sang among the willows and flew up and down the creek with four-winged snakefeeders in their bills.

This is what I like to do, I thought. I love to kill snakes. I'm not afraid of snakes. I laughed to think how afraid of snakes Mom was—how she struck a potato-digger tine through a big rusty-golden copperhead's skin just enough to pin him to the earth and hold him so he couldn't get under our floor. He fought the potato-digger handle until Pa came home from work and killed him. Where he'd thrown poison over the ground it killed the weeds and weeds didn't grow on this spot again for four years.

Once when Mom was making my bed upstairs, she heard a noise of something running behind the paper that was pasted over the cracks between the logs—the paper split and a house snake six feet long fell onto the floor with a mouse in his mouth. Mom killed him with a bed slat. She called me once to bring her a goose-neck hoe upstairs quickly. I ran upstairs and killed two cowsnakes restin' on the wall plate. And Pa killed twenty-eight copperheads out of a two-acre oat field in the hollow above the house one spring season.

"Snakes—snakes," Mom used to say, "are goin' to run us out'n this Hollow."

"It's because these woods haven't been burnt out in years," Pa'd always answer. "Back when I's a boy the old people burnt the woods out every spring to kill the snakes. Got so anymore there isn't enough good timber for a board tree and people have had to quit burning up the good timber. Snakes are about to take the woods again."

I thought about the snakes Pa had killed in the cornfield and the tobacco patch and how nearly copperheads had come to biting me and how I'd always seen the snake in time to cut his head off with a hoe or get out of his way. I thought of the times I had heard a rattlesnake's warning and how I'd run when I hadn't seen the snake. As I thought these thoughts, plop, a big water moccasin fell from the creek bank into a puddle of water.

"I'll get you," I said. "You can't fool me! You can't stand muddy water."

I stirred the water until it was muddy with my wild-plum club. I waited for the water moccasin to stick his head above the water. Where wild ferns dipped down from the bank's edge and touched the water, I saw the snake's head rise slowly above the water—watchin' me with his lidless eyes. I swung sidewise with my club like batting at a ball. I couldn't swing over my shoulder, for there were willow limbs above my head.

I surely got him, I thought. I waited to see. Soon, something like milk spread over the water. "I got 'im." I raked in the water with my club and lifted from the bottom of the creek bed a water moccasin long as my club. It was longer than I was tall. I threw him upon the bank and moved slowly up the creek—looking on every drift, stump, log, and sunny spot. I looked for a snake's head along the edges of the creek bank where ferns dipped over and touched the water.

I waded up the creek all day killing water moccasins. If one was asleep on the bank, I slipped upon him quietly as a cat. I mauled him with the big end of my wild-plum club. I killed him in his sleep. He never knew what struck him. If a brush caught the end of my club and caused me to miss and let the snake get into a puddle of water, I muddied the water and waited for him to stick his head above the water. When he stuck his head above the water, I got him. Not one water moccasin got away from me. It was four o'clock when I stepped from the creek onto the bank. I'd killed fifty-three water moccasins.

Water moccasins are not half as dangerous as turtles, I thought. A water moccasin can't bite you under the water for he gets his mouth full of water. A turtle can bite you under water and when one bites you he won't let loose until it thunders, unless you cut his head off. I'd been afraid of turtles all day because I didn't have a knife in my pocket to cut one's head off if it grabbed my foot and held it.

When I left the creek, I was afraid of the snakes I'd killed. I didn't throw my club away. I gripped the club until my hands hurt. I looked below my path, above my path, and in front of me. When I saw a stick on the ground, I thought it was a snake. I eased up to it quietly as a cat trying to catch a bird. I was ready to hit it with my club.

What will Mom think when I tell her I've killed fifty-three water moccasins? I thought. A water moccasin bit Roy Deer but one's not going to bite me. I paid the snakes back for biting him. It was good enough for them. Roy wasn't bothering the water moccasin that bit him. He was crossing the creek at the footlog and it jumped from the grass and bit him.

Shadows lengthened from the tall trees. The hollow was deep and the creek flowed softly in the cool recesses of evening shadows. There was one patch of sunlight. It was upon the steep broomsedge-covered bluff above the path.

"Snakes," I cried, "snakes a-fightin' and they're not water moccasins! They're copperheads!"

They were wrapped around each other. Their lidless eyes looked into each other's eyes. Their hard lips touched each other's lips. They did not move. They did not pay any attention to me. They looked at one another.

I'll kill 'em, I thought, if they don't kill one another in this fight.

I stood in the path with my club ready. I had heard snakes fought each other but I'd never seen them fight.

"What're you lookin' at, Shan?" Uncle Alf Skinner asked. He walked up the path with a cane in his hand.

"Snakes a-fightin'."

"Snakes a-fightin'."

"Yes."

"I never saw it in my life."

"I'll kill 'em both if they don't finish the fight," I said. "I'll club 'em to death."

"Snakes a-fightin', Shan," he shouted, "you are too young to know! It's snakes in love! Don't kill 'em—just keep your eye on 'em until I bring Martha over here! She's never seen snakes in love!"

Uncle Alf ran around the turn of the hill. He brought Aunt Martha back with him. She was carrying a basket of greens on her arm and the case knife that she'd been cutting greens with in her hand.

"See 'em, Martha," Uncle Alf said. "Look up there in that broomsedge!"

"I'll declare," she said. "I've lived all my life and I never saw this. I've wondered about snakes!"

She stood with a smile on her wrinkled lips. Uncle Alf stood with a wide smile on his deep-lined face. I looked at them and wondered why they looked at these copperheads and smiled. Uncle Alf looked at Aunt Martha. They smiled at each other.

"Shan! Shan!" I heard Mom calling.

"I'm here," I shouted.

"Where've you been?" she asked as she turned around the bend of the hill with a switch in her hand.

"Be quiet, Sal," Uncle Alf said. "Come here and look for yourself!"

"What is it?" Mom asked.

"Snakes in love," Uncle Alf said.

Mom was mad. "Shan, I feel like limbing you," she said. "I've hunted every place for you! Where've you been?"

"Killin' snakes," I answered.

"Roy Deer is dead," she said. "That's how dangerous it is to fool with snakes."

"I paid the snakes back for him," I said. "I've killed fifty-three water moccasins!"

"Look, Sal!"

"Yes, Alf, I see," Mom said.

Mom threw her switch on the ground. Her eyes were wide apart. The frowns left her face.

"It's the first time I ever saw snakes in love," Aunt Martha said to Mom.

"It's the first time I ever saw anything like this," Mom said. "Shan, you go tell your Pa to come and look at this."

I was glad to do anything for Mom. I was afraid of her switch. When I brought Pa back to the sunny bank where the copperheads were loving, Art and Sadie Baker were there and Tom and Ethel Riggs—and there were a lot of strangers there.

They were looking at the copperheads wrapped around each other with their eyes looking into each other's eyes and their hard lips touching each other's lips.

"You hurry to the house, Shan," Pa said, "and cut your

stove wood for tonight."

"I'd like to kill these copperheads," I said.

"Why?" Pa asked.

"Fightin'," I said.

Uncle Alf and Aunt Martha laughed as I walked down the path carrying my club. It was something—didn't know what—all the crowd watching the snakes were smiling. Their faces were made over new. The snakes had done something to them. Their wrinkled faces were as bright as the spring sunlight on the bluff; their eyes were shiny as the creek was in the noonday sunlight. And they laughed and talked to one another. I heard their laughter grow fainter as I walked down the path toward the house. Their laughter was louder than the wild honeybees I had heard swarming over the shoemaker alderberry, and wild phlox blossoms along the creek.

NEST EGG

"Shan I don't want to tell you the second time to break that hen from sittin' on a nest egg," Mom said. "I don't have enough hens to spare to let one sit on a nest egg."

"Why don't you put more eggs under her, Mom?" I asked. "I never saw a hen that wants to sit on a nest like she does."

"It's too late in summer," Mom said. "She'd hatch off a gang of little chickens in dog days and they'd die. Now you go take that nest egg from her nest."

"All right, Mom," I said.

The grass was hot beneath my bare feet as I walked across the carpet of wilted crab grass to a patch of pawpaw sprouts. I followed a little path into the pawpaw sprouts where the white agate sun had wilted the pawpaw leaves until they hung in wilted clusters. When I approached the nest, the old Sebright hen raised her wings and clucked. I thought she was tryin' to tell me to stay away. And when I started to put my hand back under her to get the egg, she pecked my arm in three places faster than I could wink my eyes. Each place she pecked me, my arm bled.

I don't blame her for sittin' in this cool place, I thought. I don't blame her for fightin' over the egg. She laid the egg.

Since Mom had asked me to take the nest egg from the nest, I ran my hand under her and got the egg and put it beside the nest. And when she started rollin' it back under her with her long hooked bill, I left the pawpaw patch.

"Did you take the egg out'n that nest?" Mom asked me soon as I reached the house.

"I took it out this time, Mom," I said. "Look at my arm!"

"That hen's a mean old hussy," Mom said.

That week hadn't passed when Mom called her chickens around the corncrib and fed them shelled corn. Since we lived in the woods and our closest neighbor lived a mile away, hawks, hoot owls, and varmints often caught our chickens. Once a week Mom called them to the corncrib to feed and count them.

"Shan, the old Sebright hen's not here," Mom said. Mom knew her chickens since we had such a variety of mixed chickens there were hardly any two with the same color of feathers.

"I guess something's caught 'er," I said.

"With her bright feathers she's a flowerpot for a hoot owl," Mom said.

Twenty-one days had passed when I saw this old Sebright hen goin' up the hill toward the woods with one little chicken. The nest egg had hatched. I didn't tell Mom what I had seen. I'd let her find out for herself. The old Sebright never came to the corncrib when Mom called our chickens to the house to feed and count them. She lived alone in the woods with her one chicken.

August passed and September came. The leaves had started to turn brown on the trees. I was out huntin' for a hen's nest when I heard a hen cackle, and I looked in time to see our old Sebright hen and her one chicken that was growin' tall and well-feathered disappear into the brush. I was glad to know that they were still alive and I wondered when they would come to the house. And this was a secret I kept from Mom and Pa.

It was in early October that Pa had finished cuttin' our late corn. He had come across the ridge and followed the path down the point to our house. When he reached the house, Mom was callin' our chickens to the corncrib to feed and count them.

"Sal, this reminds me of something," Pa said. "It must've been two miles back on the ridge, I either saw a Sebright hen with a young chicken with her or I saw a pheasant and a young one. They flew through the brush like wild quails before I could get close!"

"Did you take that egg from under that old hen that day?" Mom turned around and asked me.

"I did, Mom," I said.

"I don't want you to lie to me," Mom said.

"I'm tellin' you the truth," I said.

"I guess I saw a couple of pheasants," Pa said.

It was in late November, when the worms and bugs had gone into the ground for the winter, that the old Sebright hen came to the corncrib when Mom called the chickens. Hunger had forced her to come down from the high hills with her young rooster. She was very proud of him; though he was nearly as tall as she was, she clucked to him as if he were still a tiny chicken that had just come from the egg. When one of the hens came close to him, she flogged the hen.

Mom looked at Pa and Pa looked at Mom. They didn't say anything at first, but each stood there lookin' at the old hen and young rooster and then they looked at me.

"But, Mom, I did take the egg from her nest," I said.

"Where did you put the egg?" Mom asked.

"Over in the grass beside the nest."

"Didn't you know an old sittin' hen will roll an egg ten feet to get it back in the nest?"

"No," I said.

"There'll be bad luck among our chickens," Pa said.

"We're havin' enough bad luck already," Mom said. "I can't raise chickens as fast as something catches 'em. I missed eight in September and eleven in October. Since the trees lost their leaves so the hoot owls could see the chickens, I've lost seventeen this month."

"We'll lose more now," Pa said. "I'd put that young gentleman in the skillet and fry 'im if he wasn't sich a fine-lookin' young rooster."

"Don't do it, Pa," I said. "She's had a hard time raisin' 'im.

"Pap had this same thing to happen when I was a little boy," Pa said. "Before the year was over he lost every chicken he had with the cholera. They died in piles."

I didn't want to say anything to Pa, but I didn't see why a hen's sittin' on a nest egg and hatchin' it and raisin' her chicken had anything to do with the cholera. I wanted to beg him to keep this young rooster that I called Nest Egg. Pa must've forgot about killin' 'im and fryin' 'im, for November and December came and passed and Nest Egg still ran with his mother.

Nest Egg wasn't six months old when he started crowin'. Now he was much larger than his mother. He was tall and he had big legs and little straight spurs that looked like long locust thorns. His mother still ran with him and clucked to him, but he didn't pay his mother much attention. He would often stand lookin' at the spring sun and never bat his eyes. He had a mean-lookin' eye and a long crooked bill that looked like a chicken hawk's bill. He didn't look like his mother. Pa said that he was a cross between a Sebright and a black game. He had almost every variety of colors. I thought he was a mongrel rooster—a mixture of many breeds.

We had five roosters at our house; all five of them ran Nest Egg. They'd run him and flog him. Once our black game rooster, War Hawk, just missed Nest Egg's hawk-shaped head with his long, straight spur that had killed four of our roosters. But Nest Egg outran War Hawk. He took to the brush cacklin'.

"He won't always be a-runnin' you, Nest Egg," I said while War Hawk boasted to the big flock of hens around 'im.

Durin' the spring months we seldom saw Nest Egg. He kept a safe distance away from the house. He stayed away from the five old roosters who fought him every time he got near one's flock of hens. But once Mom was huntin' a hen's nest in the woods and she saw a chicken hawk swoop low to catch a hen. She saw Nest Egg hit the hawk with all the power he had. Mom said he tore a small wind-puff of feathers from the hawk. Mom told Pa about Nest Egg's fight with the hawk.

"He's a-goin' to make a powerful fightin' rooster," Pa said. "Any rooster that's game enough to hit a hawk has good metal."

And Pa was right in his prediction about Nest Egg. In early June we saw him a-runnin' Big Bill, our gray game rooster. In late July he whipped Red Ranger, our red game rooster. In July he whipped Lightnin', our black Minorca rooster. Three days later, he whipped our "scrub" rooster that was mixed with many breeds of chickens. We called him Mongrel. He had whipped all the roosters but War Hawk.

"If Nest Egg can stay out'n the way of War Hawk's spurs," Pa said, "he'll whip old War Hawk. He's a young rooster that's run over the hills and scratched for a livin' and he's got better wind."

It was in the middle of August when Nest Egg came down to the barn. He tiptoed, flapped his wings, and crowed in the barn lot. This was War Hawk's territory. It was the choice territory War Hawk had taken for his flocks of hens. Not one of our roosters had dared to venture on War Hawk's territory. Maybe Nest Egg had come down from the hills to challenge War Hawk's supremacy. Since he had whipped Big Bill, Red Ranger, Lightnin', and Mongrel he wouldn't be chased by War Hawk. He was a year old now and he felt his youth. He was ready to fight. And when War Hawk heard another rooster crowin' on his territory, he came runnin' with a flock of hens following 'em. He challenged young Nest Egg for a fight.

At first War Hawk and Nest Egg sparred at each other. War Hawk had fought many fights and maybe he was feelin' out his young opponent. They stuck their heads out at each other and pecked; then they came together with all their might and the feathers flew. Nest Egg hit War Hawk so hard that he knocked him backwards.

Again they struck and again, again, again. Each time the feathers flew lazily away with the August wind. Then War Hawk leaped high into the air and spurred at Nest Egg's head. His spur cut a place in Nest Egg's red comb. That seemed to make Nest Egg madder than ever. He rushed in and grabbed War Hawk by the comb and pushed his head against the ground while he flogged him with wings and feet. When Nest Egg's bill-hold gave away, he left a gap in War Hawk's battered comb.

War Hawk was gettin' weaker. But he leaped high into the air and spurred at Nest Egg's head; Nest Egg dodged and the spur missed his head. That must have given Nest Egg an idea, for he leaped high in the air and War Hawk leaped high to meet him. War Hawk caught Nest Egg's spur in his craw, which ripped it open. War Hawk fell on the barn lot where he had seen others fall. As War Hawk lay dyin, Nest Egg stood above him on his tiptoes and crowed. He was the new king of our barn lot.

The story of Nest Egg's victory over War Hawk spread among our neighbors, and many of them asked to bring their roosters to fight Nest Egg.

"He's not the fightin' stock," Pa told them. "He's only a scrub rooster. I don't like to fight chickens, but if it's a pleasure to you, bring your roosters around."

In September he killed Warfield Flaughtery's great Hercules game rooster that had never lost once in fifty-three fights. Hercules had whipped War Hawk. Two weeks later he killed Warfield Flaughtery's young game rooster, Napoleon. In early October he killed Eif Nippert's red game rooster, Red Devil; two days later he spurred Ennis Sneed's gray game rooster, Big Bee Martin, blind in both eyes. Later that month he pecked a hole in a hoot owl's head that had caught one of our hens. Before January he had killed nineteen roosters and one hoot owl.

"He's some rooster," Pa said. "But he's sure to bring us bad luck."

Pa was offered fifty dollars for Nest Egg by a man from a showboat on the Ohio River. He watched Nest Egg kill his twenty-fifth rooster before he offered Pa the money.

"He's bad among my other roosters here," Pa said. "They used to make him live in the woods; now he makes them live in the woods. But I don't want to sell him."

"That's a big price, Mick," Mom said. "You'd better take it."

But Pa wouldn't sell him. Finally, the man from the showboat offered Pa seventy-five dollars. Then he said he wouldn't offer him another dime. He started back toward town, turned around, and came back and offered Pa a hundred-dollar bill, the first hundred-dollar bill that any of us had ever seen.

"I still won't sell 'im," Pa said.

Then the man went away and Mom was mad.

"Hundred dollars is a lot of money, Mick."

"I like that rooster," Pa said. "I'm not a-sellin' 'im."

Anybody would like Nest Egg if he could've seen him strut about the barn lot with fifty hens around him. He had nearly half the flock followin' him. When Nest Egg wanted one of our other roosters' hens, he just said something to her in his language and she followed 'im. And now when Mom called our chickens to the corncrib to feed and count them she found that our flock was gradually growin'. This was the first time since we had had chickens that our flock had increased without our raisin' chickens or buyin' them. Mom couldn't understand how the number had grown. She saw several different-colored hens among our flock.

In February our flock increased seven; in March it increased twelve; in April it increased twenty-seven; in May it had increased thirty-two. In the meantime, Nest Egg had fought seven more fights and had killed six of the roosters; the seventh finally recovered.

In May, Warfield Flaughtery came to our house with his mule and express wagon.

"Mick, have you got some extra hens in your flock? " he asked Pa.

"Think we have, Warfield," Pa said. "How many did you lose?"

"About sixty," he told Pa.

"Would you know your hens?" Pa asked.

"Shore would," he said. "Call your hens to the corncrib."

"You're not right sure the hawks, hoot owls, and varmints didn't take some of them?" Pa asked.

"I'm sure they didn't," he said. "A two-legged varmint got 'em."

"Do you mean I stole your chickens?" Pa said.

"Not exactly," he grunted.

"They must've come to my rooster," Pa said.

"They didn't do that," Warfield said as Pa called the chickens and they came runnin'. "They wouldn't follow that scrub rooster."

Warfield and Pa were mad. Mom heard them talkin' and hurried to the corncrib.

"Then take your hens," Pa said. "Here's a coop. Catch 'em and put 'em in it."

Mom stood by and didn't say anything until Warfield got Nest Egg's mother. Mom made him put her down.

"You're a-takin' hens that I've raised," Mom said.

But Warfield insisted that he wasn't and kept takin' our hens until he had sixty. Then he hauled them away on his express wagon. He must have told others about our havin' his chickens. Jake Hix came and claimed thirty of our hens. And Pa let 'im have 'em. And then Cy Pennix came and wanted fourteen. We knew that Cy didn't even raise chickens and Pa wouldn't let 'im have 'em. Pa and Cy almost had a fight, but Pa told 'im to climb on his express-wagon seat and get outten the hollow fast as his mule could take him. Wiley Blevins, Ott Jervis, and Jot Seagraves came and claimed our chickens. "Who do you think I am," Pa asked them, "a chicken thief?" Pa showed them the way back down the hollow and they told Pa that he would be sorry.

"That rooster's a-bringin' us bad luck," Pa said. "These men live from one to three miles from us. Nest Egg is goin' back into the hills now since worms are scarce here. And he meets with other roosters and their flocks and he steals the hens. God knows I'm not a chicken thief. It's that goodlookin' rooster Nest Egg that the hens all take to. He tolls the hens here."

In June the four neighbors that Pa had chased away had indicted Pa for stealin' their chickens. Pa was branded as a chicken thief, for it was printed in the *Greenwood County News* about his bein' indicted by four men. And before the trial was called in August, Warfield Flaughtery came back with his express wagon and hauled away forty-six more hens; Jake Hix came and claimed seventy. He said all his hens had left, and Mom said our flock had increased more than a hundred. Warfield Flaughtery and Jake Hix had always been good neighbors to us, but Warfield's roosters had always killed our roosters before, and now Nest Egg had killed two of his best games and he was sore at us over it. Pa asked him if he'd been summoned for a witness in the trial, and he told Pa that he and Jake both had.

Pa was tried on the indictment made by Cy Pennix. The courthouse was filled with people to see how the trial ended since there'd been much chicken stealin' in our county. We proved that Cy Pennix didn't even have any chickens—that he had just claimed our chickens but did not get them. And Pa came clear. Then Wiley Blevin's indictment was next to be tried. And when Wiley said that he would swear to his chickens' feathers, Judge Whittlecomb threw the case out of court. Since Warfield Flaughtery and Jake Hix had claimed and had taken their hens, saying they knew them by the colors, they got scared at the decision made by Judge Whittlecomb and they hauled the chickens they had taken from us back before sunset.

There were chickens every place.

"That Nest Egg's a wonder," Pa said. "Our flock has doubled and he's killed fifty-one roosters. He's just a little past two years old.

But boys threatened me when I went to the store. They threatened me because Nest Egg had killed their roosters. And neighborhood men threatened Pa over our rooster. Once Pa got a letter that didn't have a name signed to it and in it was a threat to burn our barn. He got another letter and the man said he was a little man, that he would meet Pa sometime in the dark. He said a bullet would sink into a chicken thief in the dark same as it would in the daytime.

"I didn't know as little a thing as a rooster could get people riled like that," Pa said. "I didn't know a rooster could turn a whole community of people against a man."

Cy Pennix shook his fist at Pa and dared him to step across the line fence onto his land. And Warfield Flaughtery wouldn't speak to Pa. Tim Flaughtery hit me with a rock and ran. And often Pa would get up in the night and put on his clothes and walk over to our barn. He was afraid somebody would slip in to burn it.

"I feel something's a-goin' to happen soon," Pa told me one day in September. "This can't go on. Our flock is increasin' day by day. Look at the chickens about this place!"

There were chickens every place. Even our old roosters had increased their flocks with hens that Nest Egg had tolled to our house—hens that could not join Nest Egg's ever increasin' flock. When we gathered eggs, two of us took bushel baskets. We found hens' nests under the ferns, under the rock-cliffs, under the smokehouse corncrib, in hollow logs and stumps, and once I found a hen's nest with twenty-two eggs in it on top of our kitchen behind the flue. An egg rolled off and smashed on Pa's hat is how come us to find the nest. We had to haul eggs to town four times a week now.

One early October mornin' when Mom called our chickens to the corncrib to feed them, Nest Egg didn't come steppin' proudly on his tiptoes. And that mornin' he hadn't awakened Pa at four o'clock by his six lusty crows. I missed my first day of school to help Pa hunt for Nest Egg. We looked around the barn. We scoured the steep hill slopes, lookin' under each greenbriar cluster and in each sprout thicket. We looked every place in Nest Egg's territory and were about to give up the hunt when we walked under the white-oak chicken roost between the barn and house. We found Nest Egg sprawled on the ground beneath the roost with several hens gathered around him cacklin'. A tiny screech owl was sittin' on Nest Egg's back, peckin' a small hole in his head.

"Think of that," Pa said. "A rooster game and powerful as Nest Egg would be killed by a damned little screech owl no bigger than my fist. A hundred-dollar rooster killed in his prime by a worthless screech owl."

Pa reached down and grabbed the owl by the head and wrung its neck. "I can't stand to see it take another bite from Nest Egg's head," he said.

I stood over Nest Egg and cried.

"No ust to cry, Shan," Pa said. "Nest Egg's dead. That damned owl fouled 'im. It flew into the chicken roost and lit on his back when he was asleep. It pecked his head until it finished 'im."

"But I haf to cry," I said, watchin' Pa take his bandanna from his pocket to wipe the tears from his eyes.

FROG-TROUNCIN' CONTEST

We had't finished choppin' the sour-wood sprouts from our new-ground corn when Uncle Andy dropped his big sproutin' hoe and crossed my cornbalk to Young Andy's row. He stood lookin' at Young Andy a minute. Then he said, "Andy, you'll make one of the greatest frog trouncers ever to come from these parts. I've been a-watchin' ye ever since we've been choppin' in this corn. Ye air built fer a frog trouncer. Fer twenty-five years I've been the champion trouncer of Ennis County. This year ye can take my place."

Uncle Andy is a-braggin' on Young Andy because he's his namesake, I thought. He wants to make a great frog trouncer out'n him because he's got too old and stiff to trounce frogs. He wants the champion still to be Andy Blevins. And then I thought, I can cut more sprouts from the corn and cut them cleaner than Young Andy.

Young Andy laid his lightweight shop hoe across a cornbalk where the new-ground loam was hot enough to fry an egg as Uncle Andy felt of the muscles in his short thick arms. "Ye've got th' muscles thar," Uncle Andy said. "Muscles might nigh hard as mine. Nigh hard as rocks. Ye can take my place this year. I'll larn ye th' secrets."

I looked at Young Andy's hair. It was red as Uncle Andy's whiskers. Uncle Andy's hairless sun-tanned head was the color of a ripe October pumpkin and tanned brownish-red as a frostbitten persimmon. Since Uncle Andy didn't have hair on his head, he let hair grow on his face until it was bushy and red as a ripe sawbriar cluster.

I don't have hair the color of Young Andy and Uncle Andy, I thought. That's another reason why Uncle Andy's not interested in me. My hair's the color of a ripe chestnut burr and the hair on my head is about as coarse. I stood leanin' on my hoe handle watchin' Uncle Andy examine Young Andy. He was havin' 'im to draw his arms back to see how much muscles he had in his arms. And then he looked at his shoulders and the calves of his legs.

"Ye air a young man built just like I was when I was made the champion frog trouncer of Ennis County," Uncle Andy said, wipin' sweat from his red beard. "I'll be proud of ye, Young Andy, this September."

Young Andy grinned just like he was already the champion. He looked at me as if to say: "What can you do, Jake? You're not the well-made man that I am. You'll never make a frog-trouncer." He didn't exactly say these words to me but I could tell by the way he looked that he thought them. I didn't say anything to Young Andy but thoughts were a-runnin' through my head too. I may not have arms as big as yours, Young Andy, I thought. I may not have shoulders as broad and legs like yours with big bulgin' calves of muscles, but I take the lower row and keep well ahead of you. And if Uncle Andy can make a frog trouncer out'n you, I'll do my best to beat you in September.

As I chopped the smelly sour-wood sprouts, I thought about how much better Uncle Andy was to Young Andy than he was to me. I found myself workin' faster and faster until I was rakin' the sprouts down on Uncle Andy.

"What's come over ye, Jake?" Uncle Andy asked me as he stopped under the July sun and leaned on his hoe handle. "I've never seen ye work like this before."

"Not anything's come over me," I said.

"Then I must be a-slowin' down," Uncle Andy said.

I looked back to see where Young Andy was. He was in the middle of the new ground and we were nearly to the end.

"If Young Andy can't trounce frogs any better than he can chop sprouts, he'll never make a champion," I said.

Uncle Andy didn't answer me. He wiped sweat from his eyes and started cuttin' sprouts fast as he could to keep his row ahead of me. But it was all he could do. I didn't haf to work as hard as he did. Once I thought I'd tell him that because he was the champion frog trouncer of Ennis County for twenty-five years didn't make him the champion sprout cutter. But he was my uncle and he was a lot older than I was and I didn't tell him. Uncle Andy would never let me take the bottom row. All afternoon I crowded him until streams of sweat ran from his beard. Young Andy, with all of his bulgin' muscles, and his barrel chest, followed us through the field.

Next day Uncle Andy sent me to a field in the head of the creek to chop crab grass from the corn by myself. He and Young Andy worked together in the new ground. I knew why he did it. I was too tough for him and Young Andy. I don't have the right color of hair, I thought, and I don't have the right name, the barrel chest, big shoulders, and the bulgin' muscles in my legs and arms, but I'll be in the Dysard Grove on September Frog-Trouncin' Day.

Then I thought about the yearlin' bulls Uncle Andy won every year for twenty-five years. "I allus git my beef free," Uncle Andy would brag to Pa and all the other men that had entered the contest. "I let the other fellers take home the turkey gobblers and the roosters." As I worked and thought of the way I had been treated, I'd strike sparks of fire from my hoe when it hit a rock. And I didn't keep account of the hills of corn I cut down. I worked like I thought I'd be trouncin' frogs in September, the day when I'd get to trounce against my first cousin, Young Andy Blevins.

When I quit the crab-grass cornfield the sun was down. I thought I'd come by the new ground to see how Young Andy had got along. I didn't hear their hoes swishin' the sprouts before I reached the field. I hurried up the steep slope to see if they had finished the field. It wasn't nigh finished. Then I wondered what they had been doin'. I stood listenin' for their voices. I heard 'em on the other hill across the hollow.

"That's the way to do hit," I heard Uncle Andy say.

They're a-practicin' for the big frog trouncin', I thought. I'll see what they're doin'.

The last part of the way, I crawled on my belly like I was slippin' up on a crow to shoot 'im from a tree top. I crawled over and under briars, sprouts and weeds until I could watch Uncle Andy and Young Andy. Sure enough he was a-trainin' Young Andy to trounce. They had a basket of toad frogs and a trouncer. I watched Young Andy swing his mallet and I had to laugh for I knew I could do better. Uncle Andy would show 'm how to stand and how to swing to get more power with his mallet.

"Do ye reckon Jake'll ever make a trouncer, Uncle Andy?" Young Andy asked.

"He don't have the muscles, son," Uncle Andy said. "He hasn't got what it takes to make a champion."

"But he'll try for the bull," Young Andy said.

"He won't even git a rooster," Uncle Andy said; then he laughed a big horselaugh and slapped his knees with his big hands. "Hit takes a Blevins to make a champion. And hit takes me to train a champion. I could still be th' champion but I want to step aside and let a younger man have it."

I watched Young Andy train until the sun went down. Then I crawled back on my belly to the road and I ran for home. When I reached home, I told Pa about what Uncle Andy and Young Andy were doin'.

"Never mind, son," Pa said. "I never made a champion trouncer. I tried as hard as any man all my young days but I never got as much as a rooster. I tried to get a yearlin' bull. But I know how this trouncin' is done and I'll help ye all I can. Maybe, if Young Andy can git the bull, ye can git the turkey gobbler or the rooster!"

"But I don't want a second or third place," I said. "I want first place."

"That's the way to feel, Son," Pa said. "My people air just as tough as yer Ma's people. And I hope ye can git the bull. I'll hep ye all I can. I'll make yer trouncin' mallet. Leave that to me. I know how to make one."

I got so mad at Uncle Andy that I quit workin' in the corn for 'im. I went to work for Pa's brother, Uncle Kim Hornbuckle. I wouldn't work any longer for Uncle Andy when he made me do all the work while he took Young Andy out in a secret place to train 'im to trounce. But they weren't the only ones a-trainin'—nearly every man in Ennis County had been a frog-trouncer in his younger days, and now these men were a-trainin' their sons or their nephews to trounce. Each man wanted his son to be the champion trouncer and walk from the grove with the yearlin' bull. It was a sort of a disgrace to come away with a turkey and it was a disgrace to come away with a squawkin' rooster under your arm. But you were a hero if you went away leadin' the bull.

In late July everybody had quit his cornfields and about all the work a man did was wormin' and suckerin' his terbacker. Uncle Andy didn't raise terbacker and all he did was to train Young Andy to trounce. You'd think that men were a-cuttin' timber everyplace if you'd stand on a hilltop and listen to the mallets.

Pa cut a tough-butted white oak and sawed the toughest part from the butt end for my mallet. He bored into the middle with an inch auger and filled it with buckshot to make it heavier. Then he whittled a glut of white oak and drove into the auger hole to hold the buckshot. He sawed the glut off smooth with the end of the mallet.

"Son, if ye can swing this mallet, ye'll win the Frog-Trouncin'," Pa. said. "There'll not be another mallet like this. Practice with hit until ye can swing it overhanded and let hit come down square on yer trouncer. And as ye swing down, jump up and put all yer weight on the handle. This handle'll hold ye; hit's made of yaller locust."

All through August I practiced trouncin'. Sometimes, Pa would go with me and show me what he knew about trouncin'. But most of the time, I went alone. I practiced swingin' my hammer as Pa had told me. I got so I could swing it easy as I could swing a seven-pound ax. And once, when I was out gatherin' me a basket of toad-frogs, Amos Johnson slipped up on the hill with a rifle.

"Lay that toad-frog down, Jake Hornbuckle," he said. "Put hit down right where ye picked it up. Dump all the frogs ye have in that basket out on the ground and don't ye ever pick up another toad-frog on my farm!"

"But frogs are a-gettin' scarce over on our farm, Mr. Johnson," I said. "I'm learnin' to trounce and I need 'em!"

"That's just hit," Amos Johnson said, "I'm a religious man, but I could shoot a man betwixt the eyes free as I ever et a bit of grub 'r prayed a prayer. Hit's the meanest thing I ever heard of—this trouncin' o' th' poor little frogs. They ketch the flies, bugs and worms and what air the farmers in Ennis County a-goin' to do if young men keep up this crazy trouncin'? Thar won't be a toad-frog left in Ennis County."

I laid the frog down and poured the toads from my basket. I got off Amos Johnson's farm soon as I could.

"Old Andy Blevins has kilt more frogs than any man that's ever lived," I heard Amos Johnson say as I hurried toward home. "If I ever get to the Kentucky Legislature, I'll make a law agin' hit."

But I managed to find frogs on Pa's farm so I could practice trouncin' until September. And durin' the early days of September, I just practiced swingin' my mallet down on the trouncer. I could hardly wait for the last day in September.

Pa went with me. He carried my mallet. Just on ahead of us, we saw Uncle Andy with Young Andy and most all the Blevinses. They looked like a small army of boys, young men and old men, and there were many women among them. There were young couples—boys with their arms around girls, and the girls, not to be outdone since they too were Blevinses, had their arms around the boys. And when we reached the Dysard Grove, we found it filled with people. Many had walked to the grove; many had ridden mules or horses. I'd never seen as many people at the Frog Trouncin' in my life. Pa said he'd never seen so many at a political rally, Children's Day, footwashin' or a Baptist Association.

When we walked into the grove, we saw several boys lookin' at the turkey gobbler. He was in a crate and the boys would whistle to make him gobble and strut. Very few were around the crate that held the rooster. But men shoved each other to get close to the yearlin' bull.

"Hit's the best bull I've seen here in twenty-five years," Uncle Andy said. Then he bent over and whispered something in Young Andy's ear. I thought I heard 'im say, "Son, that bull will be yourn. Jist trounce as I've larned ye."

While the old men, young men and boys stood around the tree admirin' the bull, big Sam Akers stood in a wagon-bed and yelled for the crowd to keep quiet while he read the names of the men who would enter the Frog-Trouncin'. When he read Young Andy Blevins' name, Uncle Andy slapped Young Andy on the shoulder and all the men looked at Young Andy. And when Sam read my name from the list, Young Andy looked at me and said, "Jake, I'm a-goin' to take the bull; I hope ye git the rooster."

"Many a man has trounced twenty years and never got a rooster," I said. Then Young Andy looked at Uncle Andy and laughed.

"Now the Frog Trouncin' is ready to start," Sam Akers said. "Come to the trouncer when I call yer name. Ye git three tries. If ye don't send the frog above the tree-tops in one of yer tries, ye're disqualified. Three judges will make the decisions."

The frog trouncer was a heavy plank balanced on a wooden horse like a teeter-totter. On one end the toad frog was placed and was tied there, with a white thread, so it couldn't jump. The man trouncin' the frog, hit the other end of the trouncer with his mallet and it sent the frog toward the sky and when the frog fell to the ground it was dead as four o'clock. One had to hit the trouncer exactly right to send the frog straight to the air; if he didn't hit it right the frog would go sidewise.

"Who are the judges, Pa?" I asked.

"Flem Spry, Harvey Tuttle and Willie Whittlecomb," Pa said. "See 'em a-sittin' on the hill."

"I see 'em," I said.

"They're all right," Pa said. "Same jedges we had last year. All can see good."

They were sittin' side by side on a log upon the hillside where they could see the frog if the trouncer sent 'im above the tree-tops. There was a clearin' around the trouncer so the frogs would have a chance to trounce toward the sky without hittin' the tree limbs.

"Bill Adams," Sam Akers called.

Then Sam took a frog and threaded 'im to the trouncer. Maybe Bill was scared. He was shakin' mightily and when he hit the trouncer everybody watched for the frog. It didn't go halfway to the tops of the trees around the trouncer. Everybody laughed and took swigs from their jugs.

"Two more tries," Sam said as he threaded another frog and everybody crowded close to the frog trouncer.

Bill swung his mallet over his shoulder with a twist and hit the trouncer on one corner. The frog sailed like a quail just over the tops of the lot of heads and hit a tree.

"One more trial," Sam said, takin' another frog from one of the big willow-baskets and threadin' it to the trouncer.

Bill braced his feet and struck at the trouncer. The frog didn't quite reach the tree-tops.

"Ye'll haf to try again next year," Sam said.

"See, I told ye a lot o' 'em couldn't even qualify," Uncle Andy told Young Andy.

"Young Andy Blevins," Sam Akers called

"Show 'em, Young Andy," Uncle Andy said, slappin' Young Andy on his broad shoulder.

Soon as Sam had the frog threaded, Young Andy was ready. He came over with a wallop that sent the frog, far above the tree-tops as straight toward the sky as it could go.

"Qualified," Flem Spry yelled.

"Who is that boy?" Harvey Tuttle asked.

"Young Andy Blevins," Uncle Andy yelled. "He'll be yer next champion. I can see 'im a-leadin' the bull away!'"

"You've got another nephew to trounce yet and his name is Hornbuckle, not Blevins," I told Uncle Andy. "He's the one that raked the sprouts down on you and Young Andy in the new ground."

"Stay with 'em, Hornbuckle," a beardy-faced man yelled from the crowd as he lifted his jug to his lips. "Don't let a Blevins git the bull every year. Hit isn't fair!"

Bill Cates qualified on the third trounce. Henry Crum, Bill

Dugan and Willie Fultz failed to qualify. Dorsey Gardner qualified on the second trounce.

"Jake Hornbuckle," Sam Akers yelled.

While he threaded the frog, Pa whispered to me, "Don't do yer best. Just send the frog above the tree-tops."

"All right, Pa," I said.

On my first trounce, I swung my heavy mallet over but didn't bear on the handle as I brought it down.

"Qualified," Flem Spry yelled.

"Hit's the second-best trounce," Willie Whittlecomb said. "Only Young Andy Blevins' trounce has it bested."

"Ye may git the turkey gobbler, Jake," Uncle Andy said.

Then Uncle Andy laughed. But Young Andy didn't laugh. He looked surprised when he saw me hit the trouncer with so much ease.

After the sixty men had tried out only eighteen had sent the frogs above the tree-tops. Now we had to fight for first, second and third places. We were ready for round two.

Young Andy trounced his frog far above the tree tops the first lick.

"Hain't seen a frog go outten sight yet," Flem Spry yelled.

"Ye'll see one go outten sight in round three," Uncle Andy said.

Well, everybody cheered, yelled, cussed and carried on so, you couldn't hear your mallet hit the trouncer. We had used two willow baskets of frogs and was ready to start on the third one when we started round three. Ten men were dropped in round two by the judges because they couldn't send the frogs ten feet above the tree tops. Eight men were in the finish; Young Andy was leadin' and I was second.

"Now fer the last trounce," Sam Akers said, opening the fourth basket of frogs. "Do yer level best this time."

Soon as Sam had threaded the frog, Young Andy walked out to the trouncer. He braced his feet, swung a few times in practice and then he came over with a wallop that sent the frog high into the air.

"Not outten sight," Flem Spry said. "I can still see hit."

"I can see hit too," Harvey Tuttle said.

"Boys, I can't see hit," Willie Whittlecomb said.

Then it was my time to trounce. I walked out, didn't swing in practice but I came over with my heavy mallet with all I had.

"Outten sight," Flem Spry said.

"Where did ye send that frog?" Harvey Tuttle said.

"Never did see hit," Willie Whittlecomb said.

And the whole crowd cheered but Uncle Andy and Young Andy. Men and boys swigged from their jugs in my honor. Everybody tried to rush closest to the trouncer.

We had finished the last round and Flem Spry announced: "Jake Hornbuckle is first, Young Andy Blevins is second and Dorsey Gardner is third."

"Ye didn't pick the right nephew, Andy," Bill Wheeler said.

And while the crowd roared and Pa started after the bull, men grabbed me and carried me on their shoulders from the grove because I'd beaten the first Blevins in twenty-five years. And as they carried me a few circles under the grove before they took me to the road, I saw Young Andy and Uncle Andy leavin' the grove together and Young Andy a-carryin' his turkey gobbler under his arm while small boys followed them hissin' to make the turkey gobbler gobble.